Leigh Hunt

Men, Women and Books

Vol. 1

Leigh Hunt

Men, Women and Books
Vol. 1

ISBN/EAN: 9783337366889

Printed in Europe, USA, Canada, Australia, Japan

Cover: Foto ©Andreas Hilbeck / pixelio.de

More available books at **www.hansebooks.com**

MEN, WOMEN, AND BOOKS;

A SELECTION OF

SKETCHES, ESSAYS, AND CRITICAL MEMOIRS,

FROM HIS

UNCOLLECTED PROSE WRITINGS.

BY

LEIGH HUNT.

IN TWO VOLUMES.
VOL. I.

NEW YORK:
HARPER & BROTHERS, PUBLISHERS,
FRANKLIN SQUARE.
1873.

PREFACE.

For the power to make the greater part of this selection from his prose writings, the Author has to thank the proprietors of the *Edinburgh and Westminster Reviews*, of the *New Monthly Magazine*, of *Tait*, and *Ainsworth*, and the *Monthly Chronicle*. The courtesy which he experienced from all these gentlemen, and the instant cordiality of those with whom he was best acquainted, merit his warmest acknowledgments.

He has little to add, except that he has taken the opportunity of making a few corrections; and that he hopes the sincerity with which he writes everything, grave or gay, will procure him the usual indulgence for the defects that remain.

The title of the book, though a peculiar, is not a forced one. The reader will see that "Women," upon their own grounds, form an essential portion of its contents; and the word suggested itself as soon as the book was thought of. The name of the heroine might almost as well have been omitted, when the

critic was giving an account of the history of "Angelica and Medoro."

Should anything else in the impulsive portions of
those essays, which were written when he was young,
appear a little out of the pale of recognized manners,
in point of style and animal spirits, the new reader
will be good enough to understand, what old ones
have long been aware of, and grown kind to,—namely,
that the writer comes of a tropical race ; and that
what might have been affectation in a colder blood,
was only enthusiasm in a warm one. He is not conscious, however, of having suffered anything to remain, to which a reasonable critic could object. He
has pruned a few passages, in order that he might
not seem to take undue advantage of an extempore or
anonymous allowance ; and in later years, particularly
when seated on the critical bench, he has been pleased.
and perhaps profited, in conforming himself to the
customs of "the court." But had he attempted to
alter the general spirit of his writings, he would have
belied the love of truth that is in him, and even shown
himself ungrateful to public warrant.

With regard to the engraved portrait of himself,
from the masterly sketch of Mr. Severn, his publishers will allow him to say, that it makes its appearance
only in compliance with their urgent wishes. The
period of life at which it was taken, corresponds with
that of the greater part of the volume. A work of a
staider nature is in preparation, a contemporary por-

trait in which will duly present the Author as the battered senior which he is. Meantime, if the collection of articles now published shall be found to contain a less amount of gravity or reflection than may have been looked for from a man of his years, he hopes that the comparatively youthful face at the beginning of it may help to excuse the deficiency.

Not that he has abated a jot of those cheerful and hopeful opinions, in the diffusion of which he has now been occupied for nearly thirty years of a life passed in combined struggle and studiousness: for if there is anything which consoles him for those short-comings either in life or writings, which most men of any decent powers of reflection are bound to discover in themselves as they grow old, and of which he has acquired an abundant perception, it is the consciousness, not merely of having been consistent in opinion (which might have been bigotry), or of having lived to see his political opinions triumph (which was good luck), or even of having outlived misconstruction and enmity (though the goodwill of generous enemies is inexpressibly dear to him), but of having done his best to recommend that belief in good, that cheerfulness in endeavor, that discernment of universal beauty, that brotherly consideration for mistake and circumstance, and that repose on the happy destiny of the whole human race, which appear to him not only the healthiest and most animating principles of action, but the only truly religious homage to Him that made us all.

Let adversity be allowed the comfort of these reflections , and may all who allow them, experience
the writer's cheerfulness, with none of the troubles
that have rendered it almost his only possession.

KENSINGTON,

May 1st, 1847.

CONTENTS.

———✳———

V.

A MAN INTRODUCED TO HIS ANCESTORS.

VI.

A NOVEL PARTY.

VII.

BEDS AND BEDROOMS.

VIII.

THE WORLD OF BOOKS.

IX.

JACK ABBOTT'S BREAKFAST.

MEN, WOMEN, AND BOOKS.

FICTION AND MATTER OF FACT.

"There are more things in heaven and earth, Horatio,
Than are dreamt of in your philosophy."

SHAKSPEARE.

Sympathies of these two supposed incompatible things.—Mistake of Newton. —Poets not liable to such mistakes.—False alarm about Science becoming the ruin of Poetry.—Imagination not to be limited by second causes. —Apologue on the Press.

A PASSION for these two things is supposed to be incompatible. It is certainly not; and the supposition is founded on an ignorance of the nature of the human mind, and the very sympathies of the two strangers. Mathematical truth is not the only truth in the world. An unpoetical logician is not the only philosopher. Locke had no taste for fiction; he thought Blackmore as great a genius as Homer; but this was a conclusion he could never have come to, if he had known his premises. Newton considered poetry as on a par with "ingenious nonsense;" which was an error as great as if he had ranked himself with Tom D'Urfey, or made the apex of a triangle equal to the base of it.

Newton has had good for evil returned him by "a greater than himself;" for the eye of imagination sees farther than the glasses of astronomy. I should say that the poets had praised their scorner too much, illustrious as he is, if it were not delightful to see that there is at least one faculty in the world which knows how to do justice to all the rest. Of all the universal privileges of poetry, this is one of the most peculiar. and marks her for what she is. The mathematician, the schoolman, the wit, the statesman, and the soldier, may all be blind to the merits of poetry, and of one another; but the poet, by the privilege which he possesses of recognizing every species of truth, is aware of the merits of mathematics, of learning, of wit, of politics, and of generalship. He is great in his own art, and he is great in his appreciation of that of others. And this is most remarkable in proportion as he is a *poetical* poet—a high lover of fiction. Milton brought the visible and invisible together " on the top of Fiesole," to pay homage to Galileo; and the Tuscan deserved it, for he had an insight into the world of imagination. I cannot but fancy the shade of Newton blushing to reflect that, among the many things which he professed to *know not*, poetry was omitted, of which he knew nothing. Great as he was, he indeed saw nothing in the face of nature but its lines and colors; not the lines and colors of passion and sentiment included, but only squares and their distances, and the anatomy of the rainbow. He thought the earth a glorious planet; he knew it better than any one else. in its connection with other planets; and yet half the beauty of them all, that which sympathy bestows and imagination colors, was to him a blank. He took space to be the sensorium of the Deity, (so noble a fancy could be struck out of the involuntary encounter between his intense sense of a mystery and the imagination he despised!) and yet this very fancy was but an escape from the horror of a vacuum, and a substitution of the mere consciousness of existence for the thoughts and images with which a poet would have accompanied it. He imagined the form of the house, and the presence of the builder; but the life and the variety, the paintings, the imagery, and the music—the loves and the joys, the whole riches of the place, the whole riches in the distance, the creations heaped upon creation, and the particular as well as aggregate consciousness of all this in the great mind of whose presence he was conscious—to all this his want of imagination rendered him insensible. The *Fairy Queen* was to him a trifle; the dreams of Shakspeare " ingenious nonsense." But courts were something, and so were the fashions there. When the name of the Deity was mentioned, he took off his hat!*

There are two worlds; the world that we can measure with line and rule, and the world that we feel with our hearts and imaginations. To be sensible of the truth of only one of these, is to know truth but by halves. Milton said, that he " dared be known to think Spenser a better teacher than Scotus or Aquinas ;" he

* Sir Isaac Newton rejected the doctrine of the Trinity, because he could not reconcile it to his arithmetic. The " French Prophets," not being cognizable by the mathematics, were very near having him for a proselyte. His strength and his weakness were hardly equal in this distinction : but one of them, at least, serves to show how more than conventional his understanding was inclined to be, when taken out of its only faculty; and I do not presume to think that any criticism of mine can be thought even invidious against it. I do not deny the sun, because I deny that the sun has a right to deny the universe. I am writing upon Matter of Fact now myself, and Matter of Fact will have me say what I do.

1*

did not say than Plato or Pythagoras, who understood
the two spheres within our reach. Both of these, and
Milton himself, were as great lovers of physical and
political truth as any men ; but they knew that it was
not all ; they felt much beyond, and they made experi-
ments upon more. It is doubted by the critics, whether Chaucer's delight in the handling of fictions, or in
the detection and scrutiny of a piece of truth, was the
greater. Chaucer was a conscientious Reformer, which
is a man who has a passion for truth ; and so was
Milton. So in his way was Ariosto himself, and indeed
most great poets ; part of the very perfection of their
art, which is veri-similitude, being closely connected
with their sense of truth in all things. But it is not
necessary to be great, in order to possess a reasonable
variety of perception. That nobody may despair of
being able to indulge the two passions together, I can
answer for them by my own experience. I can pass,
with as much pleasure as ever, from the reading of one
of Hume's Essays to that of the Arabian Nights, and
vice versa; and I think, the longer I live, the closer,
if possible, will the union grow.* The roads are found
to approach nearer, in proportion as we advance upon
either ; and they both terminate in the same prospect.

I am far from meaning that there is nothing real in
either road. The path of matter of fact is as solid as
ever ; but they who do not see the reality of the other,
keep but a blind and prone beating upon their own

---

* It has done so. This Essay was written in the year 1821; and
within the last few years I have had the pleasure of reading (besides
poets) three different histories of Philosophy, histories of Rome and
England, some of the philosophy of Hume himself, much of Abraham
Tucker's, all the novels of Fielding and Smollett (including Gil Blas,)
Mr. Lane's Arabian Nights, Don Quixote, a heap of English Memoirs,
and the whole of the romances of Mrs. Radcliffe.

surface. To drop the metaphor, matter of fact is our perception of the grosser and more external shapes of truth; fiction represents the residuum and the mystery. To love matter of fact is to have a lively sense of the visible and immediate; to love fiction is to have as lively a sense of the possible and the remote. Now these two senses, if they exist at all, are of necessity as real, the one as the other. The only proof of either is in our perception. To a blind man, the most visible colors no more exist, than the hues of a fairy tale to a man destitute of fancy. To a man of fancy, who sheds tears over a tale, the chair in which he sits has no truer existence in its way, than the story that moves him. His being touched is his proof in both instances.

But, says the mechanical understanding, modern discoveries have acquainted us with the cause of lightning and thunder, of the nature of optical delusions, and fifty other apparent wonders; and therefore there is no more to be feigned about them. Fancy has done with them, at least with their causes; and witches and will-o'-the-wisps being abolished, poetry is at a stand. The strong glass of science has put an end to the assumptions of fiction.

This is a favorite remark with a pretty numerous set of writers; and it is a very desperate one. It looks like reasoning; and by a singular exercise of the very faculty which it asserts the death of, many persons take the look of an argument for the proof of it. Certainly, no observation can militate more strongly against existing matter of fact; and this is the reason why it is made. The mechanical writers of verse find that it is no longer so easy to be taken for poets, because fancy and imagination are more than usually in request: so they would have their revenge, by asserting, that poetry is no longer to be written.

When an understanding of this description is told, that thunder is caused by a collision of clouds, and that lightning is a well-known result of electricity, there may be an end, if he pleases, of his poetry with him. He may, if he thinks fit, or if he cannot help it, no longer see anything in the lightning but the escape of a subtile fluid, or hear anything more noble in the thunder than the crack of a bladder of water. Much good may his ignorance do him. But it is not so with understandings of a loftier or a more popular kind. The wonder of children, and the lofty speculations of the wise, meet alike on a point, higher than he can attain to, and look over the threshold of the world. Mechanical knowledge is a great and a glorious tool in the hands of man, and will change the globe. But it will still leave untouched the invisible sphere above and about us; still leave us all the great and all the gentle objects of poetry,—the heavens and the human heart, the regions of genii and fairies, the fanciful or passionate images that come to us from the seas, and from the flowers, and all that we behold.

It is, in fact, remarkable, that the growth of science, and the reappearance of a more poetical kind of poetry, have accompanied one another. Whatever may be the difference of opinion as to the extent to which our modern poets have carried their success, their inclinations cannot be doubted. How is it, that poetical impulse has taken this turn in a generation pronounced to be so mechanical? Whence has arisen among us this exceeding fondness for the fictions of the East, for solitary and fanciful reveries, for the wild taste of the Germans, (themselves more scientific and

wild than ever,) and even for a new and more primi-
tive use of the old Pagan mythology, so long and so
mechanically abused by the Chloes and Venuses of the
French? Politics may be thought a very unlikely
cause for poetry, and it is so with mere politicians;
yet politics, pushed farther than common, have been
the cause of the new and greater impetus given to the
sympathies of imagination; for the more we know of
any one ground of knowledge, the farther we see into
the general domains of intellect, if we are not mere
slaves of the soil. A little philosophy, says Bacon,
takes men away from religion; a greater brings them
round to it. This is the case with the reasoning
faculty and poetry. We reason to a certain point,
and are content with the discoveries of second causes.
We reason farther, and find ourselves in the same airy
depths as of old. The imagination recognizes its
ancient field, and begins ranging about at will, doubly
bent upon liberty, because of the trammels with which
it has been threatened.

Take the following Apologue.—During a wonderful period of the world, the kings of the earth leagued
themselves together to destroy all opposition; to root
out, if they could, the very thoughts of mankind. In-
quisition was made for blood. The ears of the grov-
elling lay in wait for every murmur. On a sudden,
during this great hour of danger, there arose in a
hundred parts of the world, a cry, to which the cry
of the Blatant Beast was a whisper. It proceeded
from the wonderful multiplication of an extraordinary
creature, which had already turned the cheeks of the
tyrants pallid. It groaned and it grew loud : it spoke
with a hundred tongues; it grew fervidly on the ear,
like the noise of millions of wheels. And the sound

of millions of wheels was in it, together with other
marvellous and awful noises.   There was the sharpen-
ing of swords, the braying of trumpets, the neighing
of war-horses, the laughter of solemn voices, the rush-
ing by of lights, the movement of impatient feet, a
tread as if the world were coming.   And ever and
anon there were pauses with " a still small voice,"
which made a trembling in the night time.   But still
the glowing sound of the wheels renewed itself;
gathering early towards the morning.   And when you
came up to one of these creatures, you saw, with fear
and reverence, its mighty conformation, being like
wheels indeed, and a great vapor.   And ever and
anon the vapor boiled, and the wheels went rolling,
and the creature threw out of its mouth visible words,
that fell into the air by millions, and spoke to the uttermost parts of the earth.   And the nations (for it was
a loving though a fearful creature,) fed upon its words
like the air they breathed : and the monarchs paused,
for they knew their masters.

   This is Printing by Steam.—It will be said that it is
an allegory, and that all allegories are but fictions,
and flat ones.   I am far from producing it as a specimen
of the poetical power now in existence.   Allegory itself is out of fashion, though it was a favorite exercise
of our old poets, when the public were familiar with
shows and spectacles.   But allegory is the readiest
shape into which imagination can turn a thing mechanical ; and in the one before us is contained the mechanical truth and the spiritual truth of that very matter of fact thing called a Printing Press : each of them
as true as the other, or neither could take place.   A
business of screws and iron wheels is, or appears to be,
a very commonplace matter : but not so the will of

the hand that sets them in motion; not so the operations of the mind that directs them what to utter. We
are satisfied respecting the one by science; but what
is it that renders us sensible of the wonders of the
other, and their connection with the great mysteries
of nature? Thought—Fancy—*Imagination.* What
signifies to her the talk about electricity, and suction,
and gravitation, and alembics, and fifty other mechanical operations of the marvellous? This is but the
bone and muscle of wonder. Soul, and not body, is
her pursuit; the first cause, not the second; the whole
effect, not a part of it; the will, the invention, the
marvel itself. As long as this lies hidden, she still
fancies what agents for it she pleases. The science
of atmospherical phenomena hinders not her angels
from "playing in the plighted clouds." The analysis
of a bottle of salt water does not prevent her from
" taking the wings of the morning, and remaining in the
uttermost parts of the sea." You must prove to her
first, that you understand the simple elements, when
decomposed; the reason that brings them together;
the power that puts them in action; the relations which
they have to a thousand things besides ourselves and
our wants; the necessity of all this perpetual motion;
the understanding that looks out of the eye; love, joy,
sorrow, death and life, the future, the universe, the
whole invisible abyss. Till you know all this, and can
plant the dry sticks of your reason, as trophies of possession, in every quarter of space, how shall you oust
her from her dominion?

THE INSIDE OF AN OMNIBUS.

Elevation of society by this species of vehicle.—Metamorphosis of Dr. Johnson into an Omnibus.—His dialogue thereon with Boswell.—Various passengers in Omnibuses.—Intense intimacy with the face of the man opposite you.—Boys and young ladies.—Old gentlemen unable to pull up the glass.—Young gentlemen embarrassed with eating an orange.—Exhibition of characters and tempers.—Ladies obliged to sit on gentlemen's laps.—Last passengers at night.

ENOUGH has been said, in this quick and graphic age, respecting coachmen and cabmen, and conductors, and horses, and all the exterior phenomena of things vehicular; but we are not aware that an "article" has yet been devoted to the subject before us.

Come, then, our old friend Truth! do what thou canst for us. If thou dost not, we know, that with all our trying, we can do nothing for ourselves. Men will have nothing to do with our representations, though we paint for them the prettiest girl in the world,—unlike!

By the invention of the Omnibus, all the world keeps its coach!—And with what cheapness! And to how much social advantage! No " plague with servants ;" —no expense for liveries ;—no coack-makers' and horse-doctors' bills ;—no keeping one's fellow-creatures waiting for us in the cold night-time and rain, while the dance is going down the room, or another hour is spent in bidding good-bye, and lingering over the comfortable fire. We have no occasion to think

of it at all till we want it; and then it either comes to
one's door, or you go forth, and in a few minutes see it
hulling up the street,—the man-of-war among coaches
—the whale's back in the metropolitan flood,—while
the driver is beheld sitting, super-eminent, like the
guide of the elephant on his neck.

We cannot say much for the beauty of the omnibus;
but there is a certain might of utility in its very bulk,
which supersedes the necessity of beauty, as in the
case of the whale itself, or in the idea that we enter-
tain of Dr. Johnson, who shouldered porters as he
went, and "laughed like a rhinoceros." Virgil meta-
morphosed ships into sea-nymphs. The Doctor, by a
process not more violent, might be supposed trans-
formed into a vehicle for his favorite London streets;
and, if so, he would undoubtedly have anticipated the
date of the present invention, and become an omnibus.
His mouth seems to utter the word.

BOSWELL (*in Elysium*). "Sir, if you were living
now, and were to be turned into a coach, what sort of
coach would you become?"

JOHNSON (*rolling about, and laughing with bland
contempt*). "Sir, in parliamentary language, you are
'frivolous and vexatious;' but the frivolity surmounts
the vexatiousness."

BOSWELL (*tenderly*). "Nay, sir, but to oblige an
humble, and, I hope, not altogether undeserving friend."

JOHNSON. "Sir, where reply is obvious, interroga-
tion is disgusting. Nay, sir, (*seeing the tears in Boswell's eyes*), I would not be harsh or uncomplying;
but do you not see the case at once? I should formerly have chosen to be a bishop's carriage perhaps,
or a chancellor's, or any respectable lord's."

BOSWELL (*smiling*). "Except a lord mayor's."

JOHNSON (*angrily*). "And why, sir, should I not have been a lord mayor's? What have I done, that it should be doubted whether I would countenance the dignity of integrity and the universality of commerce?"

BOSWELL (*in confusion*). "Sir, I beg pardon; but to confess the truth, I was thinking of Mr. Wilkes."

JOHNSON. "And why, sir, think of Mr. Wilkes, when the smaller idea should be merged into the greater? when the great office itself is concerned, and not the pettiness of an exception? Besides, sir, Wilkes, though a rascal and a Whig, was a gentleman in *manners*, as well as birth (*looking sternly at Boswell*). He would not have made such a remark.—To be sure (*relenting a little, and looking arch*) he got drunk sometimes."

BOSWELL (*interrupting*). "Dear sir!—"

JOHNSON. "Neither was he scrupulous in his admiration of beauty."

BOSWELL. "Dearest sir!—"

JOHNSON. "Though whatsoever the frenzy of his inebriation, or the vagrancy of his nocturnal revels, he would hardly have mistaken an oyster-woman for a Hebe. Well, well, sir, let us be mutually considerate. Let us be decent. To cut this matter short, sir, I should be an *omnibus*."

BOSWELL (*with grateful earnestness*). "May I presume, dear sir, to inquire the reason?"

JOHNSON. "Sir, I should not be a cart. That would be low. Neither should I aspire to be the triumphant chariot of an Alexander, or the funeral car of a Napoleon. Posthumous knowledge has corrected those sympathies with ambition. A gig is pert; a curricle coxcombical; and the steam-carriage is too violent, perturbed, and migratory. Sir, the omnibus for me. It suits with my past state and my present; with the humanities I have retained, and with those which I have acquired. Sir, it even makes me beg pardon for what I have said of Wilkes. *Mors omnibus communis.* Like death, it is common to all, and gathers them into its friendly bosom. It is decent, deliberate, and unpretending; no respecter of persons; a king has been known to ride in it;* and opposite the king may have sat a republican weaver."

BOSWELL. "But you would choose, sir, to be a London omnibus, rather than a Parisian one, or even a Litchfield?"

JOHNSON (*with bland indulgence*). "Surely, sir; and to go up the Strand and Fleet-street, and occasionally to stop at the Mitre. And, sir, I would not be driven by everybody, though I can now tolerate everybody. I would have a humane and respectable driver; an elderly man, sir;—and my windows should be taken care of, that the people might not catch cold."

Here Boswell, begging a thousand pardons, with shrugged shoulders, lifted eyebrows, and hands spread out in deprecation of offence, bursts, nevertheless, into an uncontrollable fit of laughter, at the idea of the solemn and illustrious Johnson converted into an omnibus. And the Doctor, though a little angry at first, recollects his Elysian experiences, and at length contributes to a roar worthy of the inextinguishable laughter of the gods in Homer.

JOHNSON (*subsiding into a human measure of joviality*). "Sir, it was ludicrous enough, if you consider it as a man; but if you consider it as a child, or as a divine person, (to speak in the language of our new

* So it has been said of Louis Philippe, during his "citizen-king" days.

friend, Plato), the subject will be invested with the mild
gravity of an impartial universality. I see, however,
that it will take many more draughts of Lethe, before
you, Boswell, can get the fumes of the old tavern wine
out of your head: so let us consult your capabilities,
and return to human measures of discourse; let us have
reason once more, sir;—sir (for I see you wish me to
say it), let us be good mortal jolly dogs, and have
t'other bottle."

Vanish the ever pleasant shades of Johnson and Boswell, and enter the omnibus in its own proper person.—
If a morning omnibus, it is full of clerks and merchants;
if a noon, of chance fares; if a night, of returning citizens and fathers of families; if a midnight, of play-
goers, and gentlemen lax with stiff glasses of brandy-
and-water.

Being one of the chance fares, we enter an omnibus
which has yet no other inside passenger; and having
no book with us, we make intense acquaintance with
two objects: the one being the heel of an outside passenger's boot, who is sitting on the coach-top; and the
other, that universally studied bit of literature, which
is inscribed at the further end of every such vehicle,
and which purports, that it is under the royal and
charming jurisdiction of the young lady now reigning
over us,

V.   R.

by whom it is permitted to carry "*twelve inside passengers,* AND NO MORE:—thus showing extreme consideration on her Majesty's part, and that she will not
have the sides of her loving subjects squeezed together
like figs.

Enter a precise personage, probably a Methodist,

certainly " well off," who seats himself right in the midway of his side of the Omnibus; that is to say, at equal
distances between the two extremities; because it is
the spot in which you least feel the inconvenience of
the motion. He is a man who seldom makes a remark,
or takes notice of what is going forward, unless a payment is to be resisted, or the entrance of a passenger
beyond the lawful number. Now and then he hems,
and adjusts a glove; or wipes a little dust off one of
the cuffs of his coat.

In leaps a youngster, and seats himself close at the
door, in order to be ready to leap out again.

Item, a maid-servant, flustered with the fear of being
too late, and reddening furthermore betwixt awkward-
ness, and the resentment of it, at not being quite sure
where to seat herself. A jerk of the Omnibus pitches
her against the precisian, and makes both her and the
youngster laugh.

Enter a young lady, in colors and big ear-rings,
and excessively flounced and ringleted, and seats herself opposite the maid-servant, who beholds her with
admiration, but secretly thinks herself handsomer, and
what a pity it is she was not a lady herself, to become
the ringlets and flounces better.

Enter two more young ladies, in white, who pass to
the other end in order to be out of the way of the knees
and boots of those who quit. They whisper and giggle
much, and are quizzing the young lady in the reds and
ringlets; who, for her part (though she knows it, and
could squeeze all their bonnets together for rage), looks
as firm and unconcerned as a statue.

Enter a dandy, too handsome to be quizzed; and
then a man with a bundle, who is agreeably surprised

with the gentlemanly toleration of the dandy and un-
aware of the secret disgust of the Methodist.

Item, an old gentleman; then, a very fat man; then,
two fat elderly women, one of whom is very angry at
the incommodious presence of her counterparts, while
the other, full of good humor, is comforted by it. The
youngster has in the meantime gone to sit on the coach-
top, in order to make room; and we set off to the
place of our destination.

What an intense intimacy we get with the face,
neckcloth, waistcoat, and watch-chain of the man who
sits opposite us! Who is he? What is his name?
Is his care a great care,—an affliction? Is his look
of cheerfulness real? At length he looks at ourselves,
asking himself, no doubt, similar questions; and, as it
is less pleasant to be scrutinized than to scrutinize, we
now set him the example of turning the eyes another
way. How unpleasant it must be to the very fat man
to be so gazed at! Think, if he sat as close to us in
a private room, in a chair! How he would get up,
and walk away! But here, sit he must, and have his
portrait taken by our memories. We sigh for his
plethora, with a breath almost as piteous as his wheez-
ing. And he has a sensible face withal, and has, perhaps, acquired a painful amount of intellectual as well
as physical knowledge, from the melancholy that has
succeeded to his joviality. Fat men always appear
to be "good fellows," unless there is some manifest
proof to the contrary; so we wish, for his sake, that
everybody in this world could do just as he pleased,
and die of a very dropsy of delight.

Exeunt our fat friend, and the more ill-humored of
the two fat women; and enter, in their places, two
young mothers,—one with a good-humored child, a

female; the other with a great, handsome, red-cheeked wilful boy, all flounce and hat and feathers, and red legs, who is eating a bun, and who seems resolved that the other child, who does nothing but look at it, shall not partake a morsel. His mother, who " snubs" him one instant, and lets him have his way the next, has been a spoiled child herself, and is doing her best to learn to repent the sorrow she caused her own mother, by the time she is a dozen years older. The elderly gentleman compliments the boy on his likeness to his mamma, who laughs and says he is " very polite." As to the young gentleman, he fancies he is asked for a piece of his bun, and falls a kicking; and the young lady in the ringlets tosses her head.

Exit the Methodist, and enter an affable man; who, having protested it is very cold, and lamented a stoppage, and vented the original remark that you gain nothing by an omnibus in point of time, subsides into an elegant silence; but he is fastened upon by the man with the bundle, who, encouraged by his apparent good-nature, tells him, in an under tone, some anecdotes relative to his own experience of omnibuses; which the affable gentleman endures with a variety of assenting exclamations, intended quite as much to stop as to encourage, not one of which succeeds; such as " Ah"—" Oh"—" Indeed"—" Precisely"—" I dare say"—" I see"—" Really?"—" Very likely;"—jerking the top of his stick occasionally against his mouth as he speaks, and nobody pitying him.

Meantime the good-humored fat woman having expressed a wish to have a window closed which the ill-humored one had taken upon her to open, and the two young ladies in the corner giving their assent, but none of the three being able to pull it up, the elderly

gentleman, in an ardor of gallantry, anxious to show
his pleasing combination of strength and tenderness,
exclaims, " Permit *me* ;" and jumping up, cannot do it
at all.   The window cruelly sticks fast.   It only
brings up all the blood into his face with the mingled
shame and incompetence of the endeavor.   He is a
conscientious kind of incapable, however, is the elderly
gentleman ; so he calls in the conductor, who does it
in an instant.   " He knows the trick," says the elderly
gentleman.   " It's only a little bit new," says the conductor ; who hates to be called in.

Exeunt elderly and the maid-servant, and enter an
unreflecting young gentleman who has bought an
orange, and must needs eat it immediately.   He accordingly begins by peeling it, and is first made aware
of the delicacy of his position by the gigglement of the
two young ladies, and his doubt where he shall throw
the peel.   He is " in for it," however, and must proceed ; so being unable to divide the orange into its
segments, he ventures upon a great liquid bite, which
resounds through the omnibus, and covers the whole
of the lower part of his face with pip and drip.   The
young lady with the ringlets is right before him.   The
two other young ladies stuff their handkerchiefs into
their mouths, and he, into his own mouth, the whole
of the rest of the fruit, " sloshy" and too big, with desperation in his heart, and the tears in his eyes.   Never
will he eat an orange again in an omnibus.   He
doubts whether he shall even venture upon one at all
in the presence of his friends, the Miss Wilkinsons.

Enter, at various times, an irascible gentleman, who
is constantly threatening to go out ; a long-legged
dragoon, at whose advent the young ladies are smit
with sudden gravity and apparent objection ; a young

sailor, with a face innocent of everything but a pride
in his slops, who says his mother does not like his
going to sea; a gentleman with a book, which we
long to ask him to let us look at; a man with a dog,
which embitters the feet and ankles of a sharp-visaged
old lady, and completes her horror by getting on the
empty seat next her, and looking out of the window;
divers bankers' clerks and tradesmen, who think of
nothing but the bills in their pockets; two estranged
friends, *ignoring* each other; a pompous fellow, who
suddenly looks modest and bewitched, having detected
a baronet in the corner; a botanist with his tin *her-
barium;* a young married couple, assuming a right
to be fond in public; another from the country, who
exalt all the rest of the passengers in self-opinion by
betraying the amazing fact, that they have never before seen Piccadilly; a footman, intensely clean in his
habiliments, and very respectful, for his hat subdues
him, as well as the strange feeling of sitting inside;
four boys going to school, very pudding-faced, and
not knowing how to behave (one pulls a string and
top halfway out of his pocket, and all reply to questions in monosyllables;) a person with a constant
smile on his face, having just cheated another in a
bargain; close to him a very melancholy person,
going to see a daughter on her death-bed, and not
hearing a single one of the cheater's happy remarks;
a French lady, looking at once amiable and wordly,—
hard, as it were, in the midst of her softness, or soft in
the midst of her hardness,—which you will,—probably
an actress, or a teacher; two immense-whiskered
Italians, uttering their delicious language with a pre-
cision which shows that they are singers; a man in a
smock-frock, who, by his sitting on the edge of the

seat, and perpetually watching his time to go out,
seems to make a constant apology for his presence ;
ditto, a man with some huge mysterious accompaniment of mechanism, or implement of trade, too big to
be lawfully carried inside ; a pedant or a fop, ostenta-
tious of some ancient or foreign language, or talking
of a lord ; all sorts of people talking of the weather,
and the harvest, and the Queen, and the last bit of
news ; in short, every description of age, rank, temper,
occupation, appearance, life, character, and behavior,
from the thorough gentleman who quietly gives himself a lift out of the rain, secure in his easy unaffected
manner, and his accommodating good-breeding, down
to the blackguard who attempts to thrust his opinion
down the throat of his neighbor, or keeps his leg thrust
out across the doorway, or lets his umbrella drip
against a sick child.

Tempers are exhibited most at night, because people by that time have dined and drunk, and finished
their labors, and because the act of going home serves
to bring out the domestic habit.   You do not then, indeed, so often see the happy fatigue, delighted with the
sudden opportunity of rest ; nor the anxious look, as if
it feared its journey's end ; nor the bustling one, eager
to get there.   The seats are most commonly reckoned
upon, and more allowance is made for delays ; though
some passengers make a point of always being in a
state of indignation and ill-treatment, and express an
impatience to get home, as if their house were a paradise (which is assuredly what it is not, to those who
expect them there).   But at night tongues are loosened,
wills and pleasures more freely expressed, and faces
rendered less bashful by the comparative darkness.   It
is then that the " jovial old boy" lets out the secret of

his having dined somewhere, perhaps at some Company's feast in Goldsmiths' or Stationers' Hall; and it is with difficulty he hinders himself from singing. Then the arbitrary or the purse-proud are wrathful if they are not driven up to the identical inch of curbstone fronting their door. Then the incontinent nature, heedless of anything but its own satisfaction, snores in its corner; then politicians are loud; and gay fellows gallant, especially if they are old and ugly; and lovers, who seem unconscious of one another's presence, are intensely the reverse. Then also the pickpocket is luckiest at his circumventions; and the lady, about to pay her fare, suddenly misses her reticule. Chiefly now also, sixpences, nay purses, are missed in the straw, and lights are brought to look for it, and the conductor is in an agonizing perplexity whether to pronounce the loser an impudent cheat, or to love him for being an innocent and a ninny. Finally, now is the time when selfishness and generosity are most exhibited. It rains, and the coach is full; a lady applies for admittance; a gentleman offers to go outside; and, according to the natures of the various passengers, he is despised or respected accordingly. It rains *horribly :* a " young woman" applies for admittance ; the coach is overstocked already ; a crapulous fellow who has been allowed to come in by special favor, protests against the exercise of the like charity to a female, (*we have seen it !*) and is secretly detested by the least generous; a similar gentleman to the above, offers to take the applicant on his knee, if she has no objection; and she enters accordingly, and sits. Is she pretty? Is she ugly? Above all, is she good-humored? A question of some concern, even to the least interested of knee-givers. On the other hand, is

the gentleman young or old, pleasant or disagreeable ;
a real gentleman, or only a formal "old frump," who
has hardly a right to be civil ?   At length the parties
get a look at one another, the gentleman first, the young
woman suddenly from under her bonnet.   Ought she
to have looked at all ?   And what is the particular re-
trospective expression which she instinctively chooses
out of many, when she has looked ?   It is a nice question, varying according to circumstances.   "Making
room" for a fair interloper is no such dilemma as that ;
though we may be allowed to think, that the pleasure
is greatly enhanced by the pleasantness of the countenance.   It is astonishing how much grace is put, even
into the tip of an elbow, by the turn of an eye.

There is a reflection which all omnibus passengers
are agreed upon, and which every one of them perhaps
has made, without exception, in the course of their intellectual reciprocities ; which is, that omnibuses are
" very convenient ;"—" an astonishing accommodation
to the public ;"—not quick,—save little time, (as aforesaid),—and the conductors are very tiresome ; but a
most useful invention, and wonderfully cheap.   There
are also certain things which almost all omnibus passengers *do ;* such as help ladies to and fro ; gradually
get nearer to the door whenever a vacant seat occurs,
so as to force the new comer further up than he likes ;
and all people stumble, forward or sideways, when
they first come in, and the coach sets off before they
are seated.   Among the pleasures, are seeing the
highly satisfied faces of persons suddenly relieved from
a long walk ; being able to read a book ; and, occasionally, observing one of a congenial sort in the hands
of a fellow passenger.   Among the evils, are dirty
boots and wetting umbrellas ; broken panes of glass

in bad weather, afflicting the napes of the necks of invalids : and fellows who endeavor to convenience themselves at everybody's expense, by taking up as much room as possible, and who pretend to alter their oblique position when remonstrated with, without really doing it. Item, cramps in the leg, when thrusting it excessively backwards underneath the seat, in making way for a new comer,—the patient thrusting it forth again with an agonized vivacity, that sets the man opposite him laughing. Item, cruel treading, upon corns, the whole being of the old lady or gentleman seeming to be mashed into the burning foot, and the sufferer looking in an ecstacy of tormented doubt whether to be decently quiet or murderously vociferous,—the inflicter, meanwhile, thinking it sufficient to say "Very sorry," in an indifferent tone of voice, and taking his seat, with an air of luxurious complacency. Among the pleasures also, particularly in going home at night, must not be forgotten the having the omnibus finally to yourself, re-adjusting yourself in a corner betwixt slumbering and waking, and throwing up your feet on the seat opposite ; though as the will becomes piqued in proportion to its luxuries, you always regret that the seats are not wider, and that you cannot treat your hat, on cold nights, as freely as if it were a night-cap.

The last lingerers on these occasions (with the exception of play-goers), are apt to be staid suburb-dwelling citizens,—sitters with hands crossed upon their walking-sticks,—men of parcels and eatables, breakers of last baskets of oranges, chuckling over their bargains. There's one in the corner sleeping,—the last of the dwellers in Paddington. To deposit him at his door is the sole remaining task of the conductor.

He wakes up; hands forth a bag of apples,—a tongue, a bonnet, and four pairs of ladies' shoes. A most considerate spouse and "Papa" is he, and a most worthy and flourishing hosier. Venerable is his lax throat in his bit of white neckcloth (he has never taken to black); but jovially also he shakes his wrinkles, if you talk of the stationer's widow, or the last city feast.

"Don't drop them ladies' shoes, Tom," says he, chuckling; "they'll be worn out before their time."

"Wery expensive, I believe, sir, them 'ere kind o' shoes," says Tom.

"Very;—oh, sadly. And no better than paper. But men well to do in the world, can't live as cheap as poor ones."

Tom thinks this a very odd proposition; but it does not disconcert him. Nothing disconcerts a conductor, except a passenger without a sixpence.

"True, sir," says Tom; "it's a hard case to be forced to spend one's money; but then you know—I beg pardon" (with a tone of modest deference and secret contempt,) "it's much harder, as they say, where there's none to spend."

"Hah! Ha, ha! Why, yes, eh?" returns the old gentleman, again chuckling; "so there's your sixpence, Tom, and good-night."

"Good-night, sir." And up jumps Tom on the coach-box, where he amuses the driver with an account of the dirt which the hosier has got from the coach-wheel without his knowing it; and off they go to a far less good supper, but, it must be added, a much better sleep, than the rich old citizen.

THE DAY OF THE DISASTERS OF CARFINGTON BLUNDELL, ESQUIRE.

Description of a penurious independent gentleman, fond of invitations and the great.—He takes his way to a " dining out."—His calamities on the road.—And on his return.

CARFINGTON BLUNDELL, Esquire, aged six-and-thirty, but apparently a dozen years older, was a spare, well-dressed, sickly-looking, dry sort of leisurely individual, of respectable birth, very small income, and no abilities. He was the younger son of the younger son of a younger brother; and not being able to marry a fortune, (which once, they say, nearly made him die for love), and steering clear, with a provoking philosophy, of the corkscrew curls and pretty staircase perplexities of the young ladies of lodging-houses, contrived to live in London upon the rent of half a dozen cottages in Berkshire.

Having, in fact, no imagination, Carfington Blundell, Esquire, had no sympathies, except with the wants and wishes of that interesting personage, Carfington Blundell, Esquire—of whom he always bore about with him as lively an image in his brain as it was possible for it to possess, and with whom, when other people were of the least consequence to his inclinations, he was astonished that the whole world did not hasten to sympathize. On every other occasion, the only thing which he had to do with his fellow-

creatures, all and every of them, was, he thought, to
leave them alone;—an excellent principle, as far as
concerns their own wish to be so left, but not quite so
much so in the reverse instances; such, for example,
as when they have fallen into ditches, or want to be
paid their bills, or have a turn for delicate attentions,
or under any other circumstances which induce people
to suppose that you might as well do to them as you
would be done by.   Mr. Blundell, it is true, was a
regular payer of his bills ; and though, agreeably to
that absorption of himself in the one interesting idea
above mentioned, he was not famous for paying delicate attentions, except where he took a fancy to having
them paid to himself; yet, provided the morning was
not very cold or muddy, and he had a stick with him
for the individual to lay hold of, and could reckon upon
using it without soiling his shoes, or straining his
muscles, the probability is, that he might have helped
a man out of a ditch.   As people, however, are not in
the habit of falling into ditches, especially about
Regent-street, and as it was not easy to conjecture in
what other instances Mr. Blundell might have deemed
it fitting to evince a sense of the existence of anything
but his own coat and waistcoat, muffins, mutton cutlet,
and bed, certain it is, that the sympathies of others
were anything but lively towards himself; and they
would have been less so, if the only other intense idea
which he had in his head, to wit, that of his birth and
connections (which he pretty freely overrated), had
not instinctively led him to hit upon the precise class
of acquaintances, to whom his insipidity could have
been welcome.

These acquaintances, with whom he dined fre-
quently (and breakfasted too), were rich men, of a

grade a good deal lower than himself; and to such of
these as had not "unexpectedly left town," he gave a
sort of a quiet, particular, just-enough kind of a lodging-house dinner once a year, the shoe-black in gloves
assisting the deputy under-waiter from the tavern.
The friends out of town he paid with regrets at their
"lamented absence;" and the whole of them he would
have thought amply recompensed, even without his
giving into this fond notion of the necessity of a dinner
on his part, by the fact of his eating their good things,
and talking of his fifth cousin the Marquis; a personage, by the way, who never heard of him. He did,
indeed, once contrive to pick up the Marquis's glove
at the opera, and to intimate at the same time that his
name was Blundell; upon which the noble lord, staring somewhat, but good-humoredly smiling withal,
said, "Much obliged to you, Mr. Bungle." As to his
positive insipidity over the hock and pine-apples of his
friends, Mr. Blundell never dreamt of such a thing;
and if he happened to sit next to any wit, or other lion
of the day, who seemed of consequence enough to
compete with the merits of his presence, he thought it
amply set off by his taste in having had such ancestors,
and indeed in simply being that identical Mr. Blundell,
who, in having no merits at all, was gifted by the kind
providence of nature with a proportionate sense of his
enjoying a superabundance of them.

To complete the idea of him in the reader's mind,
his manners were gentlemanly, except that they be-
trayed now and then too nice a sense of his habiliments. His hat he always held in the best way
adapted to keep it in shape; and a footman coming
once too softly into a room where he was waiting
during a call, detected him in the act of dusting his

2*

boots with an extra colored handkerchief, which he always carried about with him for that purpose. He calculated, that with allowance for changes in the weather, it saved him a good four months' coach-hire.

Such was the accomplished individual, who, in the month of May, in the year of our Lord one thousand eight hundred and twenty-seven, and in a "fashionable dress of the first water" (as Sir Phelim called it), issued forth from his lodgings near St. James's, drawing the air through his teeth with an elegant indifference, coughing slightly at intervals out of emotion, and, to say the truth, as happy as coat and hat, hunger, a dinner-party, and a fine day could make him. Had the weather been in the smallest degree rainy, or the mansion for which he was bound at any distance, the spectators were to understand that he would have come in his own carriage, or at least that he intended to call a coach; but as the day was so very fine, and he kept looking at every door that he passed, as though each were the one he was about to knock at, the conclusion to be drawn was, that having but a little way to go, and possessing a high taste for superiority to appearances, it was his pleasure to go on foot. Vulgar wealth might be always making out its case. Dukes and he could afford to dispense with pretension.

The day was beautiful, the sky blue, the air a zephyr, the ground in that perfect state for walking (a day or two before dust), when there is a sort of dry moisture in the earth, and people in the country prefer the road to the path. The house at which our hero was going to dine, was midway between the west end and the north-east; and he had just got half-way, and was in a very quiet street, when in the "measureless content" of his anticipations, he thought he would indulge his eyesight with one or two of those personal ornaments, the presence of which, on leaving the house, he always ascertained with sundry pattings of his waistcoat and coat pockets. Having, therefore, again assured himself that he had duly got his two pocket-handkerchiefs, his ring, his shirt-pin, his snuff-box, his watch, and his purse *under* his watch, he first took off a glove that he might behold the ring: and then, with the ungloved hand, he took out the snuff-box, in order that he might as delicately contemplate the snuff-box.

Now the snuff-box was an ancient but costly snuff-box, once the possession of his grandmother, who had it from her uncle, whose arms, flaming in *or* and *gules*, were upon the lid ; and inside the lid was a most ingeniously-contrived portrait of the uncle's lady, in a shepherdess's hat and powdered toupee, looking, or to be supposed to be looking, into an actual bit of looking-glass.

Carfington Blundell, Esquire, in a transport of ease, hope, and ancestral elegance, and with that expression of countenance, the insipidity of which is bound to be in proportion to the inward rapture, took a pinch out of this hereditary amenity, and was in the act of giving a glance at his grand-aunt before he closed the lid, when a strange, respectably-dressed person, who seemed to be going somewhere in a great hurry, suddenly dashed against him ; and, uttering the words, "With pleasure," dipped his fingers into the box, and sent it, as Carfington thought, half-way across the street.

Intense was the indignation, but at the same time highly considerate the movement, of Mr. Blundell ; who seeing the "impertinent beast" turn a corner, and

hearing the sound of empty metal dancing over the
street, naturally judged it better to secure the box,
than derange his propriety further by an idle pursuit.
Contenting himself, therefore, with sending an ejaculation after the vagabond to the purpose just quoted, and
fixing his eye upon the affecting movable now stationary, he delicately stepped off the pavement towards it,
with inward congratulation upon its not being muddy,
when imagine his dismay and petrifaction, on lifting
up, not the identical box, but one of the commonest
order! To be brief, it was of pewter; and upon
the lid of it, with after-dinner fork, was scratched a
question, which, in the immediate state of Mr. Blundell's sensations, almost appeared to have a supernatu-
ral meaning; to wit: " How's your mother?"

Had it been possible for a man of the delicacy of
Mr. Blundell's life and proportions to give chase to a
thief, or had he felt it of the least use to raise a hue
and cry in a gentlemanly tone of voice—or, indeed, in
any voice not incompatible with his character—doubtless he would have done so with inconceivable swift-
ness; but, as it was, he stood as if thunderstruck; and,
in an instant, there were a dozen persons about him,
all saying—" What is it?" " Which?" " Who?"

Mr. Blundell, in his first emotions, hardly knew
" what it was" himself: the " which" did not puzzle
him quite so much, as often as he looked upon the
snuff-box; but the " who" he was totally at a loss to
conjecture; and so were his condolers.

" What—was it that chap as run agin you," said
one, " jist as I was coming in at t'other end of the
street? Lord love you! you might as well run arter
last year. He's a mile off by this time."

" If the gentleman 'll give me a shilling," said a boy, " *I'll* run arter him."

"Get out, you young dog," said the first speaker ; "d'ye think the gentleman's a fool ?"

" It is a circumstance," said Mr. Blundell, grateful for this question, and attempting a breathless smile, " which—might have—surprised—anybody."

" What *sort* of a man was it ?" emphatically inquired a judicious-looking person, jerking his face into Mr. Blundell's, and then bending his ear close to his, as though he were deaf.

" I—declare," said Mr. Blundell, " that I can—hardly say, the thing was so very unexpected ; but—from the glimpse I had of him, I should—really say—he looked like a gentleman—(here Mr. Blundell lifted up his eyebrows,)—not indeed a *perfect* gentleman."

" I dare say not, sir," returned the judicious-looking person.

" *What is* all this ?" inquired a loud individual, elbowing his way through.

" A gentleman been robbed," said the boy, " by another gentleman."

" Another gentleman ?"

" Yes ; not a *perfect* gentleman, he says ; but highly respectable."

Here, to the equal surprise and grief of the sufferer, the crowd laughed and began joking with one another. None but the judicious-looking, deaf individual seemed to keep his countenance.

" Well," quoth the loud man, " here's a policeman coming at the end of the street ; the gentleman had better apply to him."

" Yes, sir," said the deaf friend, " that's your resource, and God bless you with it !" So saying, he

grasped Mr. Blundell's hand with a familiarity more
sympathizing than respectful; and treading at the same
time upon his toes in the most horrible manner, begged
his pardon and went away.

Mr. Blundell stooped down, partly to rub his toes,
and partly to hide his confusion, and the policeman
came up. The matter was explained to the policeman, all the while he was hearing the sufferer, by a
dozen voices, and the question was put, " What sort of
a man was it?"

" Here's a gentleman," said Mr. Blundell, " who saw
him."

The policeman looked about for the witness, but
nobody answered; and it was discovered, that all
the first speakers had vanished,—loud man, boy, and
all.

" Have you lost anything else, sir?" inquired the policeman.

" Bless me!" said Mr. Blundell, turning very red,
and feeling his pockets, " I really—positively I do fear
—that——"

" You can remember, sir, what you had with you
when you came out?"

" *One* handkerchief," continued Mr. Blundell, " has
certainly gone; and ——"

" Your watch is safe," returned the policeman, " for
it is hanging out of your waistcoat. Very lucky you
fastened it. Have you got your purse, sir?"

" The purse was under the watch," breathed Mr.
Blundell; " therefore I have no doubt that—but I regret to say—that I do not—feel my *ring*."

A laugh, and cries of " too bad."

" A man shook your hand, sir," said the policeman;
" did you not feel it then?"

"I did not, indeed," replied Mr. Blundell; "I felt nothing but the severity of the squeeze."

"And you had a brooch, I perceive."

The brooch was gone too.

"Why don't you run arter him," cried a very little boy in an extremely high and loud voice, which set the crowd in a roar.

The policeman, as speedily as he could, dispersed the crowd, and accompanied Mr. Blundell part of his way; whither the latter knew not, for he walked along as if he had taken too much wine. Indeed, he already doubted whether he should proceed to recruit himself at his friend's table, or avoid the shame of telling his story, and return home. The policeman helped to allay his confusion a little by condolence, by promises of search, and accounts of daring robberies practised upon the most knowing; and our hero, in the gratitude of his heart, would have given him his card; but he now found that his pocket-book was gone! His companion rubbed his face to conceal a smile, and received with great respect, an oral communication of the address. Mr. Blundell, to show that his spirit as a gentleman was not subdued, told him there was half-a-crown for him on his calling.

Alone, and meditative, and astonished, and, as it were, half undone, Mr. Blundell continued his journey towards the dinner, having made up his mind, that as his watch-chain was still apparent, and had the watch attached to it, and as the disorder of his nerves, if not quite got rid of, might easily be referred to delicacy of health, he would refresh his spirits with some of that excellent port, which always made him feel twice the man he was.

Nor was this judicious conclusion prevented, but

rather irritated and enforced, by one of those sudden showers, which in this fickle climate are apt to come pouring down in the midst of the finest weather, especially upon the heels of April. This, to be sure, was a tremendous one; though, by diverting our hero's chagrin, and putting him upon his mettle, it only made him gather up his determination, and look extremely counter-active and frowning. Would to Heaven his nerves had been as braced up as his face! The gutters were suddenly a torrent; the pavement a dancing wash; the wind a whirlwind; the women all turned into distressed Venuses de Medici. Everybody got up in door-ways, or called a coach.

Unfortunately no coach was to be had. The hacks went by, insolently taking no notice. Mr. Blundell's determination was put to a nonplus. The very door-ways in the street where he was, being of that modern, *skimping*, inhospitable, penny-saving, done-by-contract order, so unlike the good old projecting ones with pediments and ample thresholds, denied security even to his thin and shrinking person. His pumps were speedily as wet through as if they had been made of paper; and what rendered this ruin of his hopes the more provoking, was, that the sunshine suddenly burst forth again, as powerful as the rain which had interrupted it. A coach, however, he now thought, would be forthcoming; and it would at least take him home again; while the rain, and "the previous inability to get one," would furnish a good excuse for returning.

But no coach was to be had so speedily, and meantime his feet were wet, and there was danger of cold. "As I *am* wet," thought Mr. Blundell, sighing, "a little motion, at all events, is best. It would be better, considering I am so, not to stop at all, nor perhaps get into a coach ; but then how am I to get home in these shoes, and this highly evening dress? I shall be a sight. I shall have those cursed little boys after me. Perhaps I shall again be hustled."

Bewildered with contending emotions of shame, grief, disappointment, anger, nay hunger, and the sympathy between his present pumps and departed elegancies, our hero picked his way as delicately as he could along the curb-stones ; and turning a corner, had the pleasure of seeing a hackney-coach slowly moving in the distance, and the man holding forth his whip to the pedestrians, evidently disengaged. The back of it, to be sure, was towards him, and the street long, and narrow, and very muddy. But no matter. An object's an object ;—a little more mud could not signify : our light-footed sufferer began running.

Now runners, unfortunately, are not always prepared for corners ; especially when their anxiety has an object right before it, and the haste is in proportion. Mr. Blundell, almost before he was aware of it, found himself in the middle of a flock of sheep. There was a hackney-coach also in the way ; the dog was yelping, and leaping hither and thither ; and the drover, in a very loud state of mind, hooting, whistling, swearing, and tossing up his arms.

Mr. Blundell, it is certain, could not have got into a position less congenial to his self-possession, or more calculated to commit his graces in the eyes of the unpropitiated. And the sheep, instead of sympathizing with him, as in their own distress they might (poetically) be supposed to do, positively seemed in the league to distress his stockings, and not at all to consider even his higher garment. They ran against him ; they bolted at him ; they leaped at him ; or if they seemed

to avoid him, it was only to brush him with muddier
sides, and to let in upon his weakend forces the frightful earnestness of the dog, and the inconsiderate, if not
somewhat suspicious, circumambiences of the coachman's whip.

Mr. Blundell suddenly disappeared.

He fell down, and the sheep began jumping over
him ! The spectators, I am sorry to say, were in an
ecstacy.

You know, observant reader, the way in which
sheep carry themselves on abrupt and saltatory occasions ; how they follow one another with a sort of
spurious and involuntary energy ; what a pretended
air of determination they have ; how they really have
it, as far as example induces, and fear propels them ;
with what a heavy kind of lightness they take the
leap ; how brittle in the legs, lumpish in the body, and
insignificant in the face ; how they seem to quiver
with apprehension, while they are bold in act ; and
with what a provoking and massy springiness they
brush by you, if you happen to be in the way, as
though they wouldn't avoid the terrors of your presence, if possible,—or rather, as if they would avoid it
with all their hearts, but insulted you out of a desperation of inability. *Baas* intermix their pensive objec-
tions with the hurry, and a sound of feet as of water.
Then, ever and anon, come the fiercer leaps, the con-
glomerating circuits, the dorsal visitations, the yelps
and tongue-lollings of the dog, lean and earnest minister of compulsion ; and loud, and dominant over all
exult the no less yelping orders of the drover,—indefi-
nite, it is true, but expressive,—rustical cogencies of
oo and *ou*, the intelligible jargon of the Corydon or
Thyrsis of Chalk-Ditch, who cometh, final and hu

mane, with a bit of candle in his hat, a spike at the
end of his stick, and a hoarseness full of pastoral catarrh
and juniper.

Thrice (as the poets say) did Carfington Blundell,
Esquire, raise his unhappy head out of the *mêlée*, hat-
less and muddied ; thrice did the spectators shout ; and
thrice did he sink back from the shouts and the sheep,
in calamitous acquiescence.

" Lie still, you fool !" said the hackney-coachman,
" and they 'll jump easy."

" JUMP EASY !" Heavens ! how strange are the
vicissitudes of human affairs. To think of Mr. Blundell only but yesterday, or this evening rather,—nay,
not an hour ago,—his day fine, his hopes immense, his
whole life lapped up, as it were, in cotton and lavender,
his success elegant, his evening about to be spent in a
room full of admirers ; and now, his very prosperity
is to consist in lying still in the mud, and letting sheep
jump over him!

Then to be called a " fool :"—" Lie still, *you fool.*"

Mr. Blundell could not stand it any longer (as the
Irishman said) ; so he rose up just in time to secure a
kick from the last sheep, and emerged amidst a roar
of congratulation.

He got as quickly as possible into a shop, which
luckily communicated with a back street ; and, as
things generally mend when they reach their worst
(such at least was the consolatory reflection which
our hero's excess of suffering was glad to seize hold
of), a hackney-coach was standing close to him, empty,
and disengaged. It has just let a gentleman down
next door.

Our hero breathed a great breath, returned his
handkerchief into his pocket (which had been made a

sop of to no purpose), and uttering the word "*accident*," and giving rapid orders where to drive to, was hastening to hide himself from fate and the little boys within the vehicle, when, to his intense amazement, the coachman stopped him.

"Hollo!" quoth the Jarveion mystery; "what are you arter?"

"Going to get in," said Blundell.

"I'm bless'd if you do," said the coachman.

"How, fellow! Not get in?" cried Mr. Blundell, irritated that so mean an obstacle should present itself to his great wants. "What's your coach for, sir, if it isn't to accommodate gentlemen;—to accommodate *any*body, I may say?"

Now it happened, that the coachman, besides having had his eye caught by another fare, was a very irritable coachman, given to repenting or being out of temper all day, for the drinking he solaced himself with over night; and he didn't choose to be called "fellow," especially by an individual with a sort of dancing-master appearance, with his hat jammed in, his silk stockings untimely, and his whole very equivocal man all over mud. So jerking him aside with his elbow, and then turning about, with the steps behind him, and facing the unhappy Blundell, he thus, with a terrible slowness of articulation, bespoke him, the countenances of both getting redder as he spoke:—

"And do you think now,—Master ' Fellow,' or Fiddler, or Mudlark,—or whatsoever else you call yourself,—that I'm going to have the new seats and lining o' *my* coach dirtied so as not to be fit to be seen, by such a TRUMPERY BEAST, as *you* are?"

"It is for light sorrows to speak," saith the philosopher; "great ones are struck dumb." Mr. Blundell was struck dumb; dumber than ever he had conceived it possible for a gentleman to be struck. It is little to say that he felt as if heaven and earth had come together. There was *no* heaven and earth; nothing but space and silence. Mr. Blundell's world was annihilated.

Alas! it was restored to him by a shout from the "cursed little boys." Mr Blundell mechanically turned away, and began retracing his steps homeward, half conscious, and all a spectacle; the little boys following and preceding him, just leaving a hollow space for his advances, and looking back, as they jogged, in his face. He turned into a shop, and begged to be allowed to wait a little in the back parlor. He was humanely accommodated with soap and water, and a cloth; and partly out of shame at returning through the gazes of the shopman, he stayed there long enough to get rid of his tormentors. No great-coat, however, was to be had; no shoes that fitted; no stockings; and though he was no longer in his worst and wettest condition, he could not gather up courage enough to send for another coach. In the very idea of a coachman he beheld something that upturned all his previous existence:—a visitation—a Gorgon—a hypochondria. "Don't talk to me like a death's head," said Falstaff to Doll Tearsheet, when she reminded him of his age. Mr. Blundell would have said, "Don't talk to me like a hackney-coachman." The death's head and cross-bones were superseded in his imagination by an old hat, wisp of hay, and arms akimbo.

Our hero had washed his hands and face, had set his beaver to rights, had effaced (as he thought) the worst part of his stains, and succeeded in exchanging his boot-pocket-handkerchief for a cleaner one: with

which, alternately concealing his face as if he had a
toothache, or holding it carelessly before his habiliments, he was fain, now that the day was declining, to
see if he could not pick his way home again, not quite
intolerably. It was a delicate emergency: but experience having somewhat rallied his forces, and gifted
him with that sudden world of reflection which is produced by adversity, he bethought himself, not only that
he must yield, like all other great men, to necessity,
but that he was a personage fitted for nice and ulti-
mate contrivances. He was of opinion, that although
the passengers, if they chose to look at him, could not
but be aware that he had sustained a mischance common to the meanest, yet, in consideration of his air and
manners, perhaps they would not choose to look at him
very much; or if they did, their surprise would be
divided between pity for his mishap, and admiration
of his superiority to it.

Certainly the passengers who met him did look a
good deal. He could not but see it, though he saw as
little as he could help. How those who came behind
him looked, it would have been a needless cruelty to
himself to ascertain; so he never turned his head. No
little boys thought it worth their while to follow his
steps, which was a great comfort; though whenever
any observers of that class met him, strange and most
disrespectful were their grins and ejaculations. " Here's
a Guy !" was the most innocent of their salutes. A
drunken sailor startled him with asking how the land
lay about " Tower Ditch ?" And an old Irishwoman,
in explanation of his appearance to the wondering eyes
of her companions, defined him to be one that was so
fond of " crame o' the valley," that he must needs be
" roudling in it."

Had "cabs" been then, Mr. Blundell would unquestionably have made a compromise with his horror of
charioteers, and on the strength of the mitigated de-
facements of his presence, have risked a summons to
the whip. As it was, he averted his look from every
hackney-coach, and congratulated himself as he began
nearing home—home, sweet even to the most insipid
of the Blundells, and never so sweet as now, though
the first thoughts of returning to it had been accompanied with agonies of mortification. " In a few minutes," thought he, " I shall be *seen* no more for the day
(O strange felicity for a dandy!); in a few minutes I
shall be in other clothes, other shoes, and another train
of feelings—not the happiest of men, perhaps, retro-
spectively, but how blest in the instant and by comparison! In a few minutes all will be silence, security,
dryness. I shall be in my arm-chair, in my slippers—
shall have a fire; and I will have a mutton-cutlet, hot—
and refresh myself with a bottle of the wine my friend
Mimpin sent me."

Alas! what are the hopes of man, even when he
concludes that things *must* alter for the better, seeing
that they are at their worst? How is he to be quite
sure, even after he has been under sheep in a gutter
that things *have* been at their worst?—that his cup of
calamity, full as it seemed, is not to be succeeded by,
or wonderfully expanded into, a still larger cup, with a
remaining draught of bitterness, amazing, not to have
been thought of, making the sick throat shudder, and
the heart convulse?

Scarcely had the sweet images of the mutton-cutlet
and wine risen in prospect upon the tired soul of our
hero, than he approached the corner of the street round
which he was to turn into his own; and scarcely had

he experienced that inward transport, that chuckle of
the heart, with which tired homesters are in the habit
of turning those corners.—in short, scarcely had his
entire person manifested itself *round* the corner, and
his eyes lifted themselves up to behold the side of the
blessed threshold, than he heard, or rather was saluted
and drowned with a roar of voices the most huge, the
most unexpected, the most terrific, the most weighty,
the most world-like, the most grave yet merry, the
most intensely stupefying, that it would have been possible for Sancho himself to conceive, after all his experience with Don Quixote.

It now struck Mr. Blundell that, with a half-consci-
ous, half-unconscious eye, he had seen people running
towards the point which he had just attained, and
others looking out of their windows; but as they did
not look at *him*, and every one passed him without
attention, how was he to dream of what was going
forward; much more, that it had any relation to himself? Frightful discovery! which he was destined
speedily to make, though not on the instant.

The crowd (for almost the whole street was one
dense population) seemed in an agony of delight.
They roared, they shrieked, they screamed, they
writhed, they bent themselves double, they threw about
their arms, they seemed as if they would have gone
into fits. Mr. Blundell's bewilderment was so complete, that he walked soberly along, steadied by the
very amazement; and as he advanced, they at once,
as in a dream, appeared to him both to make way for
him, and to advance towards him; to make way in the
particular, but advance in the mass; to admit him with
respect, and overwhelm him with familiarity.

" In the name of Heaven!" thought he, "*what can*

it all be? It is impossible the crowd can have any connection with me in the *first* instance. I cou'd not have *brought* them here; and my appearance, though unpleasant, and perhaps somewhat ludicrous, cannot account for such a perfect mass and conspiracy of astonishment. *What is it?*"

And all the way he advanced, did Mr. Blundell's eyes, and manner, and whole person, exhibit a sort of visible echo to this internal question of his—*What is it?*

The house was about three-quarters of the way up the street, which was not a long one; and it stood on the same side on which our unfortunate pedestrian had turned.

As he approached the denser part of the crowd, words began to develop themselves to his ear—" Well, this beats all!" "Well, of all the sights!" "Why, it's the man himself, the very man, poor devil!" "Look at his face!" "What the devil can he have been at?" "Look at the pianoforte man—he's coming up!"

Blundell mechanically pursued his path, mystified to the last depths of astonishment, and scarcely seeing what he saw. Go forward he felt that he must; to turn back was not only useless, but he experienced the very fascination of terror and necessity. He would have proceeded to his lodgings, had Death himself stood in the door-way. Meantime up comes this aforesaid mystery, the pianoforte man.

"Here's a pretty business you've been getting us into," said this amazing stranger.

"What business!" ejaculated Mr. Blundell.

"What business! Why, all this here d——d business—all this blackguard crowd—and my master's ruined pianoforte. A pretty jobation I shall get; and

I should like to know what for, and who's to pay me ?"

"In the name of God !" said our hero, "what is it ?"

"Why, don't you see what it is ?—a *hoax*, and be d——d to it. It's a mercy I wasn't dashed to pieces when these rascals tipped over the pianoforte; and there it lies, with three of its legs smashed and a corner split. I should like to know what I'm to have for the trouble ?"

" And I," said the upholsterer's man.

" And I," said the glass-man.

" And this here coffin," said the undertaker.

There had been a hoax sure enough ; and a tremendous hoax it was. A plentiful space before the door was strewed with hay, boxes, and baskets. There stood the coffin, upright, like a mummy ; and here lay the pianoforte, a dumb and shattered discord.

Mr. Blundell had now arrived at his door, but did not even think of going in ; that is to say, not instantly. He mechanically stopped, as if to say or do something : for something was plainly expected of him ; but what it was he knew not, except that he mechanically put his hand towards his purse, and as mechanically withdrew it.

The crowd all the while seemed to concentrate their forces towards him,—all laughing, murmuring, staring—all eager, and pressing on one another ; yet leaving a clear way for the gentleman, his tradesmen, and his goods.

What was to be done ?

Mr. Blundell drew a sigh from the bottom of his heart, as though it were his last sigh or his last sixpence ; yet he drew forth no sixpence. Extremes met, as usual. The consummation of distress produced calmness and reflection.

"You must plainly perceive, gentlemen," said our hero, "that it could be no fault of mine."

"I don't know that," said the pianoforte man. The crowd laughed at the man's rage, and at once cheered him on, and provoked him against themselves. He seemed as if he did not know which he should run at first,—his involuntary customer, or the "cursed little boys."

"Zounds, sir!" said the man, "you *oughtn't* to have been hoaxed."

"Oh! oh!" said the parliamentary crowd.

"I mean," continued he, "that none but some d——d disagreeable chap, or infernal fool, is ever treated in this here manner."

"Oh! oh!" reiterated the bystanders. "Come, that's better than the last."

"Which is the biggest fool?" exclaimed a boy, in that altitude of voice which is the most sovereign of provocations to grown ears.

The man ran at the boy, first making a gesture to our hero, as much as to say, "I'll be with you again presently." The crowd hustled the man back;—the undertaker had seized the opportunity of repeating that he "hoped his honor would consider his trouble;"—the glass-man and the upholsterer were on each side of him;—and suddenly the heavy shout recommenced, for a new victim had turned the corner,—a stranger to what was taking place,—a man with some sort of milliner's or florist's box. The crowd doated on his face. First, he turned the corner with the usual look of indifferent hurry; then he began to have an inquiring expression, but without the least intimation that the catastrophe applied to himself; then the stare became wider, and a little doubtful; and then he stopped short, as if to reconnoitre—at which the laugh was prodigious. But the new-comer was wise; for he asked what was the matter, of the first person he came up with; and learning how the case stood, had energy enough to compound with one more hearty laugh, in preference to a series of mortifications. He fairly turned back, pursued by a roar; and, oh! how he loved the corner, as he went round it! Every hair at the back of his head had seemed to tingle with consciousness and annoyance. He felt as if he saw with his shoulder-blades;—as if he was face to face at the back of his hat.

At length, the misery and perplexity of Mr. Blundell reached a climax so insurmountable, that he would have taken out his second and (as he thought) remaining pocket-handkerchief, if even that consolation had been left him; for the tears came into his eyes. But it was gone! The handkerchief, however, itself, did not distress him. "Nothing could touch him further." He wiped his eyes with the ends of the fingers of his gloves, and stood mute,—a perplexity to the perplexed,—a pity even to the "little boys."

Now tears are very critical things, and must be cautiously shed, especially in critical ages. In a private way, provided you have locked the door, and lost three children, you may be supposed to shed a few without detriment to your dignity; and in the heroical ages, the magnitude and candor of passion permitted tears openly, the feelings then being supposed to be equally strong in all respects, and a man to have as much right to weep as a woman. But how lucky was it for poor Blundell that no brother dandy saw him!

His tormentors did not know whether to pity or despise him. The pianoforte man, with an oath, was going to move off; but, on looking again at his broken instrument, remained, and urged compensation. The others expressed their sorrow, but repeated that they hoped his honor would consider them; and they repeated it the more, because his tears raised expectations of the money which he would be weak enough to disburse.

Alas! they did not know that the dislike of disbursement, and the total absence of all sympathy with others in our weeping hero (in this as in other respects, very different from the tear-shedding Achilles), was the cause of all which they and he were at this moment enduring; for it was the inability to bring out his money which kept Mr. Blundell lingering outside his lodging, when he might have taken his claimants into it; and it was the jovial irascibility of an acquaintance of his, which, in disgust at his evasion of dinner-givings, and his repeatedly shirking his part of the score at some entertainments at which he pretended to consider himself a guest, had brought this astounding calamity to his door.

Happily for these "last infirmities" of a mind which certainly could not be called "noble," there are hearts so full of natural sympathy, that the very greatest proofs of the want of it will but produce, in certain extremities, a pity which takes the want itself for a claim and a misfortune; and this sympathy now descended to Mr. Blundell's aid, like another goddess from heaven, in a shape not unworthy of it,—to-wit, that of the pretty daughter of his landlord, a little buxom thing, less handsome than good-natured, and with a heart that might have served to cut up into cordial bosoms for half a dozen fine ladies. She had once nursed our hero in sickness, and to say the truth, had not been disinclined to fall in love with him, and be made "a lady," half out of pure pity at his fever, had he given her the slightest encouragement; but she might as well have hoped to find a heart in an empty coat. However, a thoroughly good-nature never entirely loses a sort of gratitude to the object that has called forth so sweet a feeling as that of love, even though it turn out unworthy, or the affections (as in our heroine's case) be transferred elsewhere; and accordingly, in sudden bonnet and shawl, and with a face blushing partly from shame, and partly from anger at the crowd, forth came the vision of pretty, plump little Miss Widgeon (Mrs. Burrowes "as is to be"), and tapping Mr. Blundell on the shoulder, and begging the "other gentlemen" to walk in, said, in a voice not to be resisted, "Hadn't you better settle this matter indoors, Mr. Blundell? I dare say it can be done very easily."

Blundell has gone in, dear reader; the other gentlemen have gone in; the crowd are slowly dislodging; Miss Widgeon, aided partly by the generosity of her nature, partly by the science of lodging-house economy, and partly by the sense and manhood of Mr. William Burrowes, then present, a strapping young citizen from Tower-hill, takes upon herself that ascendency of the moment over Mr. Blundell due to a superior nature, and settles the very illegitimate claims of the goods-and-chattel bringers to the satisfaction of all parties, yea, even of Mr. Blundell himself. The balm of the immediate relief was irresistible, even though he saw a few of his shillings departing.

What he felt next morning, when he woke, this history sayeth not : for we like to leave off, according to the Italian recommendation, with a *bocca dulce*, a sweet mouth; and with whose mouth, even though it was not always grammatical, can the imagination be left in better company than with that of the sweet-hearted and generous little Polly Widgeon ?

A VISIT TO THE ZOOLOGICAL GARDENS.*

The collection there at the time of the visit.—A tiger broke loose.—Mild anthropophagy of the bear.—The elephant the Dr. Johnson of animals. —Giraffes.— Monkeys. — Parrots. — Eagles. — Mysteries of animal thought.—Is it just in human beings to make prisons of this kind?

WE went to the Zoological Gardens the other day for the first time, to see our old friends " the wild beasts" (grim intimates of boyhood), and enjoy their lift in the world from their lodgings in Towers and Exeter Changes, where they had no air, and where an elephant wore boots, because the rats gnawed his feet! The first thing that struck us, next to the beauty of the Gardens, and the pleasant thought that such flowery places were now prepared for creatures whom we lately thrust into mere dens and dust-holes, was the quantity of life and energy they displayed. What motion!—what strength!—what elegance! What prodigious chattering, and brilliant colors in the macaws and paroquets! What fresh, clean, and youthful salience in the *lynx!* What a variety of dogs, all honest fellows, apparently of the true dog kind; and how bounding, how intelligent, how fit to guard our doors and our children, and scamper all over the country! And then the *Persian* greyhound!—how like a *patrician* dog (better even than Landseer's), and made as if expressly to wait upon a Persian prince; its graceful slender-

* In the year 1835.

ness, darkness, and long silken ears, matching his gentlemanly figure, and well-dressed beard!

We have life enough, daily, round about us—amazing,
if we did but think of it; but our indifference is a part
of our health. The blood spins in us too quickly to
let us think too much. This sudden exhibition of life,
in shapes to which we are unaccustomed, reminds us
of the wonderful and ever-renewing vitality of all
things. Those animals look as fresh, and strong, and
beautiful, as if they were born in a new beginning of
the world. Men in cities hardly look as much!—and
horses dragging hackney-coaches are not happy specimens. But the horse in the new carriage is one, if we
considered it. The leaves and flowers in the nursery
gardens exhibit the same untiring renewal of life. The
sunbeam, in the thick of St. Giles's, comes as straight
and young as ever from the godlike orb that looks at
us from a distance of millions of miles, out of the depths
of millions of ages. But the sun is a visitor as good-
natured as it is great, and therefore we do not think too
much even of the sunbeam. This bounding creature
in its cage is not a common sight; so it comes freshly
and wonderfully upon us. What brilliancy in its
eyes! What impetuous vigor in its leap! What fear-
lessness of knocks and blows! And how pleasant to
think it is on the other side of its bars! What a sensation would ensue, if that pretty-coated creature,
which eats a cake so good-naturedly, were suddenly
out of its cage, and the cry were heard—"A tiger
loose!"—"A panther!"—"A lion!" What a rush and
screaming of all the ladies to the gates!—and of gentlemen too! How the human voices, and those of the
paroquets would go shrieking to heaven together!
Fancy the bear suddenly jumping off his pole upon the

cake-shop! A tiger let loose at day-time would not
be so bad as at night. Perhaps he would be most
frightened himself. There was an account of one that
got loose in Piccadilly, and slunk down into a cellar,
where he was quietly taken; but at night, just before
feeding, it might not be so pleasant. Newspapers tell
us of a lion which got out of one of the travelling car-
avans in the country, and, after lurking about the
hedges, tore a laborer that he met, in full daylight.
Nervous people in imaginative states of the biliary
vessels—timid gentlemen taking easy rides—old ladies
too comfortable in their homes and arm-chairs—must
sometimes feel misgivings while making their circuit
of the Regent's Park, after reading news of this de
scription. Fancy yourself coming home from the play
or opera, humming "Deh vieni, non tardar," or "Meet
me by moonlight alone;" and, as you are turning a
corner in Wimpole-street, meeting——a tiger!

What should you *say?* You would find yourself
pouring forth a pretty set of Rabelaesque exclamations:
"Eh—Oh—Oh   Lord!—Hollo!—Help!—Help!—
Murder!—Tigers!—U-u-u-u-u-u!—*My* God!—*Policeman!*"

Enter Policeman.

Policeman.—"Good God!—A gentleman with a
tiger!"   [*Exit Policeman.*

In one of Molière's exquisite extravaganzas between
his acts, is a scene betwixt a man and a bear, who has
caught him in its arms. The man tries every expedient he can think of to make the bear considerate;
and, among others, flatters him in the most excessive
manner, calling him, at last, his Royal Highness. The
bear, however, whom we are to fancy all this while
on its hind legs, looking the man with horrible indiffer-

ence in the face, and dancing him from side to side in its heavy shuffle, is not at all to be diverted from his dining purposes ; and he is about to act accordingly, when hunters come up and take off his attention.   Up springs the man into a tree ; and with the cruelty of mortified vanity (to think of all the base adulation he has been pouring forth) the first words he utters respecting his Royal Highness are " Shoot him."

Not without its drollery, though real, is a story of a bear in one of the northern expeditions.   Two men, a mate and a carpenter, had landed somewhere to cut wood, or look for provisions ; and one of them was stooping down, when he thought some shipmate had followed him, who was getting, boy-like, on his shoulders.   " Be quiet," said he ; " get down."   The unknown did not get down ; and the man, looking up as he stooped, saw the carpenter staring at him in horror.

" Oh, mate !" exclaimed the carpenter, " *it's a bear !*" Think what the man must have felt, when he heard this explanation of the weight on his shoulders.   No tragedy, however, ensued.

Pleasant enough are such stories, so ending.   But of all deaths. that by a wild beast must be one of the most horrible.   There is action, indeed, to diminish the horror ; but frightful must be the unexpectedness—the unnaturalness—the clawing and growling—the hideous and impracticable fellow-creature, looking one in the face, struggling with us, mingling his breath with ours —tearing away scalp or shoulder-blade.

To return, however, to our Gardens.   The next thing that struck us was *the quiet ;* and in connection with this, *the creatures' accommodation of themselves to circumstances,* and the *human-like sort of intercourse into which they get with their visitors.*   With wild beasts we associate the ideas of constant rage and assault. On reflection, we recollect that this is not bound to be the case ; that travellers pass deserts in day-time, and neither hear nor see them ; and that it is at night they are to be looked for in true wild-beast condition, and then only if wild with hunger. It is no very extraordinary matter, therefore, to find them quiet by day, especially when we consider how their wants are attended to : and yet we cannot but think it strange that they should be so put, as they are, into an unnatural condition, under bars and bolts. More of this, however, presently. Let us look at them as making friends with us, receiving our buns and biscuits, and being as close to us (by permission of those same bars) as dogs and cats. This is a very different position of things from the respectful distance kept in the African sands or in the jungle ! We are afraid it breeds contempt in some of the spectators, or at least indifference ; and that people do not always find the pleasure they expected. We could not help admiring one visitor the other day, who hastened from den to den, and from beast to bird, twirling an umbrella, and giving little self-complacent stops at each, no longer than if he were turning over some commonplace book of prints. " Hah !" he seemed to be saying to himself, " this is the panther, is it ? *Hm*—Panther. What says the label here ? 'Hyæna Capensis.' *Hm*—Hyæna—ah ! a thing untamable. 'Grisly Bear.' Hah !—grisly— *hm*. Very like. Boa—'Tiger Boa'—ah !—Boa in a box—*Hm*—Sleeping, I suppose. Very different from seeing him squeeze somebody. *Hm*. Well ! I think it will rain. Terrible thing *that*—spoil my hat." Perhaps, however, we are doing the gentleman injustice, and he was only giving a glance, preparatory to a

longer inspection. When a pleasure is great and multitudinous, one is apt to run it all over hastily in the
first instance ; as in an exhibition of paintings, or with
a parcel of books.

It is curious to find one's self (literally) hand and
glove with a bear ; giving him buns, and watching his
face, like a school-boy's, to see how he likes them. A
reflection rises—"If it were not for those bars, perhaps
he would be eating *me*." Yet how mild they and his
food render him. We scrutinize his countenance and
manners at leisure, and are amused with his apparently
indolent yet active lumpishness, his heavy kind of in-
telligence (which will do nothing more than is necessary), his almost hand-like use of his long, awkward-
looking toes, and the fur which he wears clumsily
about him, like a watchman's great-coat. The darker
bears look, somehow, the more natural ; at least to
those whose imaginations have not grown up amidst
polar narratives. The white bear in these Gardens
has a horrible mixed look of innocence and cruelty.
A Roman tyrant kept a bear as one of his executioners,
and called it "Innocence." We could imagine it to
have had just such a face. From that smooth, unim-
pressible aspect there is no appeal. He has no ill-will
to you ; only he is fond of your flesh, and would eat
you up as meekly as you would sup milk or swallow
a custard. Imagine his arms around you, and your
fate depending upon what you could say to him, like
the man in Molière. You feel that you might as well
talk to a devouring statue, or to the sign of the Bear
in Piccadilly, or to a guillotine, or to the cloak of Nes-
sus, or to your own great-coat (to ask it to be not so
heavy), or to the smooth-faced wife of an ogre, hungry

and deaf, and one that did not understand your language.

Another curious sensation arises from being so tranquil yourself, and slow in your movements, while you are close to creatures so full of emotion and action. And you know not whether to be more pleased or disappointed at seeing some of them look so harmless, and others so small. On calling your recollections together, you may know, as matters of fact, that lynxes and wolves are no bigger; but you have willingly made them otherwise, as they appear to you in the books of your childhood; and it seems an anti-climax to find a wolf no bigger than a dog, and a lynx than a large cat. The lynx in these Gardens is a beautiful, bounding creature. You know him at once by his ears, if not by his eyes; yet he does not strike you like the lynx you have read of. You are obliged to animate your respect for him, by considering him under the title of "cat-o'-mountain:"

> "The owl is abroad, the bat and the toad,
> And so is the cat-o'-mountain."

Alas! poor cat-o'-mountain is not abroad here, in the proper sense; he is "abroad and at home," and yet neither. You see him by daylight, without the proper fire in his eyes. You do not meet him in a mountain pass, but in a poor closet in Mary-le-bone; where he jumps about like a common cat, begging for something to eat. Let him look as he may, he does not look so well as in a book.

We saw no lion. Whether there is any or not, at present, we cannot say. I believe there is. But friends get talking, and one of them moves away, and carries off the rest; and so things are passed by. We did not even see the rhinoceros; or the beaver, which

would not come out (if there) ; or the seal (which we
particularly wished to see, having a respect for seals
and their affections :—there is one species in particular, remarkable for the mobility of its expression,
which we should like to get acquainted with ; but this
is not the one in the Garden catalogue).   The lioness
was asleep, as all well-behaved wild beasts ought to
be at that hour ; and another, or a tigress (we forget
which), pained the beholder by walking incessantly to
and fro, uttering little moans.   She seemed incapable
of the philosophy of her fellow-captives.   The dogs
are an interesting sight, particularly the Persian grey-
hounds already mentioned, and the St. Bernard dogs,
famous for their utility and courage.   But it was a
melancholy thing to see one of these friends of the
traveller barking and bounding incessantly for pieces
of biscuit, and jerked back by the chain round his
neck.   It seemed an ill return for the Alpine services
of his family.

The boa in his box was asleep.   He is handsomely
spotted : but the box formed a sorry contrast in the
imagination with his native woods.   He seemed to be
in terrible want of "air and exercise."   Is not the box
unconscionably small and confined ?   Could not a
snake-safe be contrived, of good handsome dimensions?
There is no reason why a serpent should not be made
as comfortable as possible, even though he would make
no more bones of us that we do of an oyster.

The squirrels are better off, and are great favorites,
being natural crackers of nuts ; but could no trees be
contrived for them to climb, and grass for their feet ?
It is unpleasant to see them so much on the ground.

The elephant would seem to be more comfortably
situated than most.   He has water to bathe in, mud to

stick in, and an area many times bigger than himself
for his circuit.   Very interesting is it to see him throw
bits of mud over himself, and to see, and *hear* him,
suck the water up in his trunk and then discharge it
into his great red throat; in which he also receives,
with sage amenity, the biscuits of the ladies.   Certainly, the more one considers an elephant, the more
he makes good his claim to be considered the Doctor
Johnson of the brute creation.   He is huge, potent,
sapient, susceptible of tender impressions; is a good
fellow; likes as much water as the other did tea; gets
on at a great uncouth rate when he walks; and though
perhaps less irritable and melancholy, can take a witty
revenge ; as witness the famous story of the tailor that
pricked him, and whom he drenched with ditch water.
If he were suddenly gifted with speech, and we asked
him whether he liked his imprisonment, the first words
he would utter would unquestionably be—" Why, no,
sir."   Nor is it to be doubted, when going to dinner,
that he would echo the bland sentiment of our illustrious countryman on a like occasion, " Sir, I like to
dine."   If asked his opinion of his keeper, he would
say, " Why, sir, Hipkins is, upon the whole, 'a good
fellow,'—like myself, sir, (*smiling*),—but not quite so
considerate; he knows I love him, and presumes a
little too much upon my forbearance.   He teazes me
for the amusement of the bystanders.   Sir, Hipkins
takes the display of allowance for the merit of ascendency."

This is what the elephant manifestly thought on the
present occasion; for the keeper set a little dog at
him, less to the amusement of the bystanders than he
fancied ; and the noble beast, after butting the cur out
of the way, and taking care to spare him as he ad-

vanced (for one tread of his foot would have smashed the little pertinacious wretch as flat as a pancake), suddenly made a stop and, in rebuke of both of them, uttered a high indignant scream, much resembling a score of cracked trumpets.

Enter the three lady-like and most curious giraffes, probably called forth by the noise; which they took, however, with great calmness. On inspection, their faces express insipidity and indifference more than anything else—at least the one that we looked at did; but they are interesting from their novelty, and from a singular look of cleanliness, delicacy, and refinement, mixed with a certain *gaucherie*, arising from their long, poking necks, and the disparity of length between their fore and hind legs. They look like young ladies of animals, naturally not ungraceful, but with bad habits. Their necks are not on a line with their fore legs, perpendicular and held up; nor yet arched like horses' necks; but make a feeble-looking, obtuse angle, completely answering to the word " poking." The legs come up so close to the necks, that in front they appear to have no bodies; the back slopes like a hill, producing the singular disparity between the legs; and the whole animal, being slender, light-colored, and very gentle, gives you an idea of delicacy amounting to the fragile. The legs look as if a stick would break them in two, like glass. Add to this, a slow and un-couth lifting of the legs, as they walk, as if stepping over gutters; and the effect is just such as has been described,—the strangest mixture in the world of elegance and uncouthness. The people in charge of them seemed to be constantly currycombing them after a gentle fashion, for extreme cleanliness is neces-sary to their health; and the novelty of the spectacle

is completed by the appearance of M. Thibaut in his
Arab dress and beard,—the Frenchman who brought
them over. The one we spoke of, moving its lips, but
not the expression of its countenance, helped itself to
a mouthful of feathers out of a lady's bonnet, as it
stooped over the rails.

The sight of new creatures like these throws one
upon conjectures as to the reasons why nature calls
them into existence. The conjectures are not very
likely to discover anything; but nature allows their
indulgence. All one can suppose is, that, besides helping to keep down the mutual superfluity of animal or
vegetable life, and enabling the great conditions of
death and reproduction to be fulfilled, their own portion of life is a variety of the pleasurable, which
could exist only under that particular form. We are
to conclude, that if the giraffe, the elephant, the lion,
&c. &c., were not formed in that especial manner,
they could neither perform the purposes required of
them in the general scheme of creation, nor realize
certain amounts of pleasurable sensation peculiar to
each species. Happiness can only be added, or at
least is only added, to the general stock, under that
shape. And thus we can very well imagine new
shapes of happiness called into being; just as others
appear to have been worn out, or done with, as in the
mammoth and other antediluvian creatures. If we can
conceive no end of space, why should we conceive an
end of new creations, whatever our poor little bounds
of historical time might appear to argue to the contrary? What are a few thousands of years? What
would be millions? Not a twinkle in the eye of eternity. To return, however, to our first proposition,—
human beings, brutes, fish, insects, serpents, vegetables,

appear to be all varieties of pleasurable or pleasure-giving vitality, necessary to the harmony and completeness of the music of this state of being; the worst discords of which (by our impulses to that end) seem destined to be done away, leaving only so much contrast as shall add another heavenly orb to the spheres. (Permit at least this dream by the roadside of creation. Who can contemplate its marvellousness and beauty, and not think his best thoughts on the subject)?

We forgot to mention the porcupine. It is very curious, and realizes a dream, yet not the most romantic part of it. The real porcupine is not so good a thing as it is in an old book; for it *doesn't shoot*. Oh, books! you are truly a world by yourselves, and a " real world" too, as the poet has called you, for you make us feel; and what can any reality do more?* Heaven made you, as it did the other world. Books were contemplated by Providence, as well as other matters of fact. In the time of Claudian, the mere sight of this animal seems to have been enough to convince people of its powers of warfare. At least it convinced the poet. The darts were before his eyes; and he took the showman's word for the use which could be made of them; only, it seems, the cunning porcupine was not " lavish of his weapons," nor chose to part with them, unless his life was in danger. He was very cautious, says the poet, how he got in a passion. He contented himself with threats.

> " Additur armis
> Calliditas, parcusque sui timor, iraque nunquam

---

* Books are a real world,
Round which, with tendrils strong as flesh and blood,
Our pastime and our happiness may grow.
WORDSWORTH.
A passage often quoted—it cannot be too often.

Prodiga telorum, caute contenta minari,
Nec nisi servandæ jactus impendere vitæ."

DE HYSTRICE.

The rattling of the prickles described by Claudian
is still to be heard, when the creature is angry; at
least so the naturalists tell us ; and it is added, that
they " occasionally fall off, particularly in autumn ;"
but it has no power of " shooting them at its pur-
suers."*

The dromedary looked very uncomfortable. His
coat was half gone, as if from disease : and he appeared to sit down on the earth for the purpose of
screening as much of his barenness as he could, and
of getting warmth. But there was that invincible
look of patience in the face, which is so affecting, and
which creates so much respect in whatever face it be
found. Animals luckily have no affectation. What
you see in their faces is genuine ; though you may
overrate it, or do the reverse. When the lion looks
angry, nobody believes he is feigning. When the dog
looks affectionate, who doubts him ?

But the monkeys—What a curious interest *they*
create,—half-amusing, half-painful ! The reflection
forced upon one's vanity is inevitable—" They are
very like men." *Oh, quam simillima turpissima bestia
nobis!*

Oh, how like us is that most vile of brutes!

The way in which they receive a nut in their *hands*,
compose themselves with a sort of bustling *nonchalance* to crack it, and then look about for more with
that little, withered, winking, half-human face, is startling. The hand in particular mortifies one, it looks
so very unbrute-like, and yet at the same time is so

* Gore's Translation of Blumenbach, p. 49.

small, so skinny, so like something elvish and unnat
ural. No wonder it has been thought in some coun
tries that monkeys could speak, but avoided it for fear
of being set to work. In their roomy cages here they
look like a set of half-human pigmy school-boys withered into caricatures of a certain class of laborers, but
having neither work nor want,—nothing to do but to
leap out, or sit still, or play with, or plague one another. Classes of two very gallant nations have been
thought like monkeys; and it ought not to mortify
them, any more than the general resemblance to man
should mortify the human species. The mortification
in the latter instance is undoubtedly felt, but it tells
more against the man than the monkey. To the
monkey it is, in fact, "a lift;" and that is the reason
why the man resents it. We wish to stand alone in
the creation, and not to be approached by any other
animal, especially by one so insignificant,—so little
"respectable" on the score of size and power. We
would rather be resembled by lions and tigers. It is
curious to observe, that in British heraldry there are
but three coats of arms which have monkeys for sup-
porters. One is the Duke of Leinster's (owing, it is
said, to a monkey having carried off a Fitzgerald in
a time of danger to the house-top, and safely brought
him back). The others belong to the houses of Digby
and St. John. Lions, tigers, eagles, all sorts of fero-
cious animals, are in abundance. This is natural
enough, considering that this kind of honor originated
in feudal times; but the mind (without losing its just
consideration for circumstances past or present, and
all the strength, as well as weakness, which they include) has yet to learn the proper respect for qualities
unconnected with brute force and power; and it will

do so in good time : it is doing so now, and therefore
one may remark, without too much chance of rebuke,
that as all nations, indeed all individuals, according to
some, have been said to be like different classes of
the lower creation (Englishmen like mastiffs or bull-
dogs, Italians like antelopes, &c.), so it ought not to be
counted the most humiliating of such similitudes, when
certain nations, or particular portions of a nation,
especially of those that for wit and courage rank
among the foremost, are called to mind by expressions
in the faces of a tribe of animals, remarkable not only
for that circumstance, but for their superiority to
others in shrewdness, in vivacity, in mode of life, nay,
in the affections ; for most touching stories have been
told of the attachments of monkeys to one another, and
to the human race too, and particularly of their behavior when their companions or young ones have
been killed.   What ought to mortify us in the likeness
of brutes to men is the anger to which we see them
subject,—the revenge, the greediness, and other low
passions.   But these they have in common with most
animals.   Their shrewdness and their sympathies they
share with few.   And there is a residuum of mystery
in them, as in all things, which should lead us to culti-
vate as much regard for them as we can, thus turning
what is unknown to us to good instead of evil.   It is
impossible to look with much reflection at any animal,
especially one of this apparently half-thinking class,
and not consider that he probably partakes far more
of our own thoughts and feelings than we are aware
of, just as he manifestly partakes of our senses ; nay,
that he may add to this community of being, faculties
or perceptions, which we are unable to conceive.   We
may construe what we see of the manifestation of

animal's feelings into something good or otherwise, as it happens; perhaps our conjectures may be altogether wrong, but we cannot be wrong in making the best of them,—in getting as much pleasure from them as possible, and giving as much advantage to our fellow-creatures. On the present occasion, as we stood watching these strange beings, marvelling at their eatings, their faces, and at the prodigious jumps they took from pillar to post, careless of thumps that seemed as if they would have dislocated their limbs, we observed one of them sitting by another with his arm around his neck, precisely as a school-boy will sit with his friend ; and rapidly grinning at a third, as if to keep him off. The grin consisted of that incessant and ap-parently malignant retraction of the lips over the teeth which look as if it were every instant going to say something, and break forth into threat and abuse. The monkey that was thus kept on, leaped up every now and then towards the parties (who were sitting on a shelf), and gave a smart slap of the hand to the pro-tecting individual, or received one instead. We did not know enough of their habits to judge whether it was play or warfare ; whether the assailant wished to injure the one that seemed protected, or whether the protector wrongly or rightly kept him away, from jealousy or from sport. At length the prohibited in-dividual was allowed quietly to make one of the trio ; and there he sat, nestling himself against the *protegé*, and so remained as long as we saw them. The proba-bility therefore was, that it was all sport and good humor, and that the whole trio were excellent friends.

Nations of a very different sort from Africans have seen such a likeness between men and monkeys, that the Hindoos have a celebrated monkey-general (Han-

uman), who cuts a figure in their mythology and their
plays, and was a friend of the god Rama.*   Young
readers (nor old ones, who have wit or good spirits
enough to remain young) need not be reminded of the
monkey in "Philip Quarll;" nor of him that became
secretary to a sultan in the "Arabian Nights."   After
all, let nobody suppose that it is the intention of these
remarks to push the analogy between the two classes
further than is warrantable, or to lessen the real
amout of the immeasurable distance between them.
But anything that looks like humanity on the part of
the poor little creature need not be undervalued for all
that, or merely because we pay it the involuntary compliment of a mortified jealousy.   And as to its face,
there is unquestionably a look of reflection in it, and
of care too, which ought not to be disrespected.   Its
worst feature is the inefficient nose, arguing, it would
seem, an infirmity of purpose to any strong endeavor
(if such arguments are derivable from such things);
and yet, as if to show her love of comedy, and render
the class a riddle for alternate seriousness and laughter, Nature has produced• a species of ape, ludicrous
for the length of this very feature.†   Nature has made
levity as well as gravity; and really seems inclined,
now and then, to play a bit of farce in her own person,
as the gods did on Mount Olympus with Vulcan—

    "When unextinguished laughter shook the skies."

Fit neighbors for the monkeys are the paroquets—

---

* Wilson's "Select Specimens of the Theatre of the Hindus."   For
an account of a festival in honor of Rama, in which his monkey-friend
is conspicuous, see "Bishop Heber's Journal," chap. xiii. ●

† The *Simia Rostrata*—"long-nosed ape."   "It is *simia*, but not
sima," says Blumenbach, "being remarkable for its long proboscis-like
nose."

themselves, in some respects, a kind of monkey-bird—
with claws which they use like hands, a faculty of im
itation in voice, and something in the voice so like
speech and articulation that one almost fancies the gut-
tural murmuring about to break out into words, and
say something. But what colors!—What blazes of
red and gold, of green, blue, and all sorts of the purest
splendors! How must those reds and blues look, when
thronging and shining amidst the amber tops of their
trees, under a tropical sun! And for whose eyes are
those colors made? Hardly for man's—for man does
not see a hundred-millionth part of them, nor perhaps
would choose to live in a condition for seeing them, at
least not in their true state : unless, indeed, he should
come to like their screaming in the woods, for the same
reason that we like the cawing of rooks. Meantime
they would appear to be made for their own. "Why
not?" asks somebody. True, but we are not accustomed to consider them in that light, or as made for
any other purpose than for some distinction or attrac-
tion of sex. In nothing, however, does Nature seem
to take more delight than in colors; and perhaps (to
guess reverently, not profanely) these gorgeous hues
are intended for the pleasure of some unknown class of
spiritual eyes, upon which no kind of beauty is lost, as
it is too often upon man's. It is impossible to picture
to ones-self the countless beauties of nature, the myriads of paintings, animal, vegetable, and mineral, with
which earth, air, and seas are thronged, and fancy
them all made for no eyes but man's. Neither is it
easy to suppose that other animals have eyes, and yet
look upon these riches of the eyesight with no feeling of admiration analogous to our own. The peacock's expansion of his plumage, and the apparent

pride he takes in it, force us to believe otherwise in his particular case; and yet, with our tendency to put the worst or least handsome construction on what our inferior fellow-creatures do, we attribute to pride, jealousy, and other degrading passions, what may really be attributable to something better; nor may it be *pride* in the peacock, which induces him to display his beauty, but some handsomer joy in the beauty itself. You may call every man who dresses well a coxcomb —but it is possible he is not so. He may do it for the same reason that he dresses his room well with pictures, or loves to see his wife well-dressed. He may be such an admirer of the beautiful in all things, that he cannot omit a sense of it even in his own attire. Raphael is understood to have been an elegant dresser; and it has been conjectured from a sonnet of Shakspeare's (No. 146) that he was one. Yet who could suppose Shakspeare a coxcomb? much less *proud!* He had too much to be proud of in petty eyes, to be so in his own—standing, as he did, a wise and kind atom, but still an atom, in the midst of the overwhelming magnificence of nature and the mysteries of worlds. The same attention to dress is recorded of the grave philosopher, Aristotle; and the story of Plato's carpet, and of the "greater pride" with which Diogenes trampled upon it, is well known. Now, inasmuch as pride is an attribute of narrowness of spirit and want of knowledge, the lower animals may undoubtedly be subject to it,—though still to be proud of a color, and of external beauty, would imply an association of ideas more subtle than we are accustomed to attribute to them; and proud or not, there appears great reason to believe, that conscious of these colors and beauties they are. If so, the eyes of a crowd of paroquets and

macaws, assembled in the place before us, must have
a constant feast. Does their talk mean to say anything
of this? Is it divided between an admiration of one
another, and their dinner? For, assuredly, they do
talk of something or other, from morning till night, like
a roomful of French milliners; and apparently, they
ought to be as fond of colors, and of their own appearance. These lively and brilliant creatures seem the
happiest in the Gardens, next to the ducks and *spar-
rows ;* the latter of whom, by the way, are in exquisite
luck here, having a rich set of neighbors brought them,
without partaking of their imprisonment. It would be
delightful to see them committing their thefts upon
cage and pan, if it were not for the creatures caged.

And the poor eagles and vultures! The very instinct
of this epithet shows what an unnatural state they must
have been brought to. Think of *eagles* being com-
miserated, and called " poor !" It is monstrous to see
any creature in a cage, far more any winged creature,
and, most of all, such as are accustomed to soar through
the vault of heaven, and have the world under their
eye. Look at the eyes of these birds here, these eagles
and vultures! How strangely clouded *now* seems that
grand and stormy depression of the eyelid, drawn with
that sidelong air of tightness, fierceness, and threat, as
if by the brush of some mighty painter. That is an eye
for the clouds and the subject-earth, not for a misera-
ble hen-coop. And see, poor flagging wretches! how
they stand on their perches, each at a little distance
from one another. in poor stationary exhibition, eagles
all of a row !—quiet, impaired, *scrubby ;* almost mo-
tionless! Are these the sovereign creatures described
by the Buffons and Mudies, by the Wilsons of ornithology and poetry, by Spenser, by Homer? Is this

the eagle of Pindar, heaving his moist back in sleep
upon the sceptre of Jove, under the influence of the
music of the gods?*   Is this the bird of the English
poet,

> " Soaring through his wide empire of the air,
> *To weather his broad vans?*"

Wonderful and admirable is the quietness, the philosophy, or whatever you choose to call it, with which
all the creatures in this place, the birds in particular,
submit themselves to their destiny.   They do not howl
and cry, brutes though they be ; they do not endeavor
to tear their chains up, or beat down their dens ; they
find the contest hopeless, and they handsomely and
wisely give it up.   It is true, their wants are attended
to as far as possible, and they have none of the more
intolerable wants of self-love and wounded vanity—
no vindictiveness seemingly, nor the love of pure ob-
stinate opposition, and. of seeing whose will can get
the day.   If they cannot have liberty, they will not
disgrace captivity.   But then what a loss to them is
that of liberty !   It is thought by some, that all which
they care for is their food ; and that, having plenty of

---

* Gray's translation, " Perching on the sceptred hand," &c., is very
fine ; but he has omitted this exquisite epithet of the eagle's sleep, *moist*
(ύγρον), so full of the depth of rest and luxury.   Gilbert West's version
of the passage has merit, but he wanted *gusto* enough to venture on this
epithet.   Cary (thanks to his Dantesque studies !) has not dishonored it.

> " Jove's eagle on the sceptre slumbers,
> Possest by thy enchanting numbers ;
> On either side, his rapid wing
> Drops, entranced, the feather'd king ;
> Black vapor o'er his curved head
> Sealing his eyelids, sweetly shed,
> *Upheaving his moist back he lies,*
> Held down by thrilling harmonics."

CARY'S *Pindar*, p. 62.

this, they must be comfortable. But feeding, though a pleasure of life, is not the end of it; it is only one of its pleasurable supports. Or grant it even to be one of the ends of life, as indeed it may be considered by reason of its being a pleasure, more especially with some animals (not excepting some human ones), still, consider what a far greater portion of existence is passed by all creatures in the exercise of their other faculties, and in some form of *motion;* so much so, that even food would seem not so much an object of the exercise as a means of it—life itself being motion in pulse and thought. Then think of how much of the very spirit of their existence all imprisoned creatures are deprived.

The truth is, that if a man has happened, by the circumstances of his life, to feel and endure much—to enjoy much, and to know what it is to be deprived of enjoyment—and, above all, to know what this very want of liberty is—this confinement for a long time to one spot—the sight of these Gardens ends in making him more melancholy than comfortable. Hating to interfere with other people's pleasures, or to seem to pretend to be wiser or better than our neighbors (especially when speaking, as circumstances sometimes render expedient, in our own name), we did not well know how to get this truth out of our lips, till seeing the interesting article in the "Quarterly Review" on the same subject, and finding the writer confessing that he could never pass by these eagles "without a pang," we felt that we might protest against the *whole business of captivity* with the less hazard of a charge of immodesty and self-opinion.* Let us not be understood

* "But we must bend our steps to the eagle-house, and we confess we never pass it by without a pang. Eagles, laemergyers, condors,

as implying blame against any one. We have the
greatest respect for the persons and motives of gentlemen who compose the Zoological Society, and who
have (as already hinted) given a prodigious lift in the
scale of comfort to creatures hitherto worse dealt with
in shows and menageries.   Their zeal in behalf of the
general interests of knowledge and humanity is, we
have no doubt, fervid; and their plea, in the present
instance, is obvious, and (unless Parliament choose to
answer it) unanswerable. *If they did not take charge
of animals for exhibition, others would, and would do
it badly; and the old system would return.*   There
would be no such handsome prisons for them any
longer as the Marylebone and Surrey gardens. Granted. We are only restoring the principle to its element,
or pushing the abstract defence of the whole system
to its utmost, and trying whether it would stand the
test of a final judgment, if action were free, *and pro-
hibition could be secured.*

And why could it not? Why can we have acts of
Parliament in favor of other extension of good treatment to the brute creation, and not one against their
tormenting imprisonment? At all events, we may ask
meantime, and perhaps not uselessly even for present

creatures of the element, born to soar over Alps and Andes, in helpless,
hopeless imprisonment.   Observe the upper glance of that golden eagle,
—ay, look upon that glorious orb—it shines wooingly: how impossible
is it to annihilate hope!—he spreads his ample wings, springs towards
the fountain of light, strikes the netting, and flaps heavily down:—
' Lasciate ogni speranza, voi ch'entrate.'   We know not what their
worships would say or do to us, if we were to work our wicked will;
but we never see these unfortunates without an indescribable longing to
break their bonds, and let the whole bevy of these

　　　' Souls made of fire and children of the sun '

wander free.'

purposes, whether a great people under a still finer aspect of knowledge and civilization than at present, would think themselves warranted in keeping *any* set of fellow-creatures in a state of endless captivity—their faculties contradicted, their very lives, for the most part, turned into lingering deaths? Every now and then the lions, and other animals in these places, disappear. They die off from some malady or other, either of inactivity, or of some other contradiction to their natures, or from the soil or climate. The "Quarterly Review" thinks that the London clay is pernicious to the collection in Marylebone Gardens. The Surrey collection, though the smaller, is the healthier. But how long do the animals last there? Or is captivity a good thing for them anywhere?

The main arguments in favor of such collections are, that they increase the stock of knowledge, encourage kindly feelings towards the lower creation, and tend to substitute rational for irrational amusements. They who object to them are warned, furthermore, how they render the imagination over-nice and sensitive, or make worse what cannot be helped ; and something is occasionally added respecting the perplexed question of good and evil, and the ordinances of Providence. We have not room to repeat what has been often said in answer to reasonings of this description, which, in truth, are but so many beggings of the question, all of them to be set aside till the first doubts of the manliest and most honest conscientiousness be disposed of. Providence is to be reverenced at all times, and its mysteries to be brought in, humbly, when man comes to the end of his own humble endeavors ; but till then it is not his business to play with the awful edge-tools of a right of providential force, and its mixture of apparent evil. He must do what his conscience tells him, all kindly, and nothing (where he can help it) with a mixture of unkindness; and thus I know not how a conscientious naturalist, setting aside the argument *that others will do worse*, could allow himself, if nations were to come to such a pitch of refinement as above stated, to *do the evil* of imprisoning and withering away the lives of his fellow animals, in order that some problematical *good might come.*

A paragraph in the newspapers the other day, speaking of a lion that died after three years' incarceration (one in four of its whole life), said, that the Zoological Society have "never been able to keep any of the larger carnivora longer than that time; they have lost (it adds) nine lions since January 1832." It is not easy to reconcile this statement with others which tells us of tens and twenties of years passed by lions and other beasts under the like circumstances. Imprisonments of that duration have been known in the Tower and other places—jails far less favorable, one would think, to the lives of the inmates, than these open and flowery spots. The Society's catalogue informs us, that the grisly bear in their possession "was brought to England upwards of twenty years since by the Hudson's Bay Company," and that it remained in the Tower till the accession of his present Majesty. And their harpy eagle was caught in 1822. Long life in a prison, however, is a very different thing from natural life out of it.

At all events, on the principle of doing the very best possible, would it not be desirable, nay, is it not imperative on societies possessed of funds, *to enlarge even the better accommodation they have provided*, to give elephants and giraffes still greater ranges ; and, above all, to supply far better dens to the lions and tigers, &c. ? For dens they still are, of the narrowest description.*

* Since the date of these remarks, the improvements here desired, we understand, have taken place. The main objection, however, remains to be answered.

4*

A MAN INTRODUCED TO HIS ANCESTORS.

Astonishing amount of a man's ancestors at the twentieth remove—The variety of ranks as great as the multitude.—Bodily and mental characteristics inherited.—What it becomes a man to consider as the result.

HAPPENING to read the other evening some observations respecting the geometrical ratio of descent, by which it appears that a man has, *at the twentieth remove, one million forty-eight thousand five hundred and seventy-six ancestors in the lineal degree—grandfathers and grandmothers,*—I dropped into a revery, during which I thought I stood by myself at one end of an immense public place, the other being occupied with a huge motley assembly, whose faces were all turned towards me. I had lost my ordinary sense of individuality, and fancied that my name was Manson.

At this multitudinous gaze, I felt the sort of confusion which is natural to a modest man, and which almost makes us believe that we have been guilty of some crime without knowing it. But what was my astonishment, when a Master of the Ceremonies issued forth, and saluting me by the title of his great-grandson, introduced me to the assembly in the manner and form following :—

May it please your Majesties and his Holiness the Pope:

My Lord Cardinals, may it please your most reverend and illustrious Eminences ;

May it please your graces, my lord Dukes ;

My Lords, and Ladies, and Lady Abbesses ;

Sir Charles, give me leave ; Sir Thomas also, Sir John, Sir Nicholas, Sir William, Sir Owen, Sir Hugh, &c.

Right worshipful the several courts of Aldermen ;

Mesdames, the Married Ladies ;

Mesdames, the Nuns and other Maiden Ladies ;—
Messieurs Manson, Womanson, Jones, Hervey, Smith, Merryweather, Hipkins, Jackson, Johnson, Jephson, Damant, Delavigne, De la Bleterie, Macpherson, Scott, O'Bryan, O'Shaughnessy, O'Halloran, Clutterbuck, Brown, White, Black, Lindygreen, Southey, Pip, Trip, Chedorlaomer (who the devil, thought I, is he ?), Morandi, Moroni, Ventura, Mazarin, D'Orsay, Puckering, Pickering, Haddon, Somerset, Kent, Franklin, Hunter, Le Fevre, Le Roi (more French !), Du Val (a highwayman, by all that's gentlemanly !), Howard, Cavendish, Russell, Argentine, Gustafson, Olafson, Bras-defeu, Sweyn, Hacho and Tycho, Price, Lloyd, Llewellyn, Hanno, Hiram, &c., and all you intermediate gentlemen, reverend and otherwise, with your infinite sons, nephews, uncles, grandfathers, and all kinds of relations ;—

Then, you, sergeants and corporals, and other pretty fellows ;—

You footmen there, and coachmen younger than your wigs ;—

You gipsies, pedlars, criminals, Botany-Bay men, old Romans, informers, and other vagabonds ;

Gentlemen and ladies, one and all ;—

Allow me to introduce to you, your descendant,
Mr. Manson

Mr. Manson, your ANCESTORS.

What a sensation.

I made the most innumerable kind of a bow I could
think of, and was saluted with a noise like that of a
hundred oceans.   Presently I was in the midst of the
uproar, which became like a fair of the human race.

Dreams pay as little attention to ceremony, as the
world of which they are supposed to form a part.
The gentleman usher was the only person who retained a regard for it.   Pope Innocent himself was but
one of the crowd.   I saw him elbowed and laughing
among a parcel of lawyers.   It was the same with the
dukes and the princes.   One of the kings was familiarly addressed by a lord of the bed-chamber, as Tom
Wildman ; and a little French page had a queen much
older than himself by the arm, whom he introduced to
me as his daughter.   I discerned very plainly my immediate ancestors the Mansons, but could not get near
enough to speak to them, by reason of a motley crowd,
who, with all imaginable kindness, seemed as if they
would have torn me to pieces.   " This is my arm,"
said one, " as sure as fate ;" at the same time seizing
me by the wrist.   " The Franklin shoulder," cried
another.   A gay fellow pushing up to me, and giving
me a lively shake, exclaimed, " The family mouth, by
the Lord Harry ! and the eye—there's a bit of my
father in the eye."—" A very little bit, please your hon-
or," said a gipsy, a real gipsy, thrusting in her brown
face : "all the rest's mine, Kitty Lee's, and the eyebrows are Johnny Faw's to a hair."—" The right leg
is my property, however," returned the beau ; " I'll
swear to the calf."—" *Mais*—but—*notta to de autre*

calf," added a ludicrous voice, half gruff and half polite, belonging to a fantastic-looking person, whom I found to be a dancing-master. I did not care for the gipsy; but to owe my left leg to a dancing-master was not quite so pleasant, especially as, like Mr. Brummel's, it happens to be my favorite leg. Besides, I cannot dance. However, the truth must out. My left leg is more of a man's than my right, and yet it certainly originated with Mons. Fauxpas. He came over from France in the train of the Duke of Buckingham. The rest of me went in the same manner. A Catholic priest was rejoiced at the sight of my head of hair, though by no means remarkable but for quantity; but it seems he never expected to see it again since he received the tonsure. A little coquette of quality laid claim to my nose, and a more romantic young lady to my chin. I could not say my soul was my own. I was claimed not only by the Mansons, but by a little timid boy, a bold patriot, a moper, a merry-andrew, a coxcomb, a hermit, a voluptuary, a water-drinker, a Greek of the name of Pythias, a free-thinker, a religionist, a bookworm, a simpleton, a beggar, a philosopher, a triumphant cosmopolite, a trembling father, a hack-author, an old soldier dying with harness on his back.

" Well," said I, looking at this agreeable mixture of claimants, " at any rate my vices are not my own."

" And how many virtues?" cried they in a stern voice.

" Gentlemen," said I, " if you had waited, you would have seen that I could give up one as well as the other; that is to say, as far as either can be given up by a nature that partakes of ye all. I see very plainly, that all which a descendant no better than myself has to do, is neither to boast of his virtues, nor pretend exemption from his vices, nor be overcome with his misfortunes; but solely to regard the great mixture of all as gathered together in his person, and to try what he can do with it for the honor of those who preceded him, and the good of those that come after."

At this I thought the whole enormous assembly put on a very earnest but affectionate face; which was a fine sight. A noble humility was in the looks of the best. Tears, not without dignity, stood in the eyes of the worst.

"It is late for me," added I; "I can do little. But I will tell this vision to the younger and stouter; they perhaps may do more."

"Go and tell it," answered the multitude.—But the noise was so loud, that I awoke, and found my little child crowing in my ear.

A NOVEL PARTY.

—Hic ingentem comitum affluxisse novorum
Invenio admirans numerum.

VIRGIL.

O the pleasure that attends
Such flowings in of novel friends!

Spiritual creations more real than corporeal.—A party composed of the heroes and heroines of novels.—Mr. Moses Primrose, who has resolved not to be cheated, is delighted with some information given him by Mr. Peregrine Pickle.—Conversation of the author with the celebrated Pamela.—Arrivals of the rest of the company.—The party found to consist of four smaller parties.—Characters of them.—Character of Mr. Abraham Adams.—Pamela's distress at her brother's want of breeding.—Settlement together of Lovelace and Clarissa.—Desmond's Waverly asks after the Antiquary's Waverly.—His surprise at the coincidence of the adventure on the sea-shore.—Misunderstanding between Mrs. Slipslop and Mrs. Clinker.—The ladies criticised while putting on their cloaks.

WHEN people speak of the creations of poets and novelists, they are accustomed to think that they are only using a form of speech. We fancy that nothing can be created which is not visible ;—that a being must be as palpable as Dick or Thomas, before we can take him for granted ; and that nobody really exists, who will not die like the rest of us, and be forgotten. But as we have no other certainty of the existence of the grossest bodies, than by their power to resist or act upon us,—as all which Hipkins has to show for his

entity is his power to consume a barrel of oysters, and
the only proof which Tomkins can bring of his not
being a figment is his capacity of receiving a punch
in the stomach,—I beg leave to ask the candid reader,
how he can prove to me that all the heroes and
heroines that have made him hope, fear, admire, hate,
love, shed tears, and laugh till his sides were ready to
burst, in novels and poems, are not in possession of as
perfect credentials of their existence as the fattest of
us ?   Common physical palpability is only a proof of
mortality.   The particles that crowd and club together
to form such obvious compounds as Tomson and Jackson, and to be able to resist death for a little while, are
fretted away by a law of their very resistance ; but
the immortal people in Pope and Fielding, the death-
less generations in Chaucer, in Shakspeare, in Goldsmith, in Sterne, and Le Sage, and Cervantes,—
acquaintances and friends who remain for ever the
same, whom we meet at a thousand turns, and know
as well as we do our own kindred, though we never
set gross corporeal eyes on them,—what is the amount
of the actual effective existence of millions of Jacksons
and Tomkinses compared with theirs?   Are we as
intimate, I wish to know, with our aunt, as we are
with Miss Western ?   Could we not speak to the character of Tom Jones in any court in Christendom ?
Are not scores of clergymen continually passing away
in this transitory world, gone and forgotten, while
Parson Adams remains as stout and hearty as ever ?

But why need I waste my time in asking questions?
I have lately had the pleasure of seeing a whole party
of these immortal acquaintances of ours assembled at
once.   It was on the 15th of February in the present
year..   I was sitting by my fire-side ; and, being in the

humor to have more company than I could procure, I
put on my Wishing-cap, and found myself in a new
little world that hovers about England, like the Flying
Island of Gulliver. The place immediately about me
resembled a common drawing-room at the West end
of the town, and a pretty large evening party were
already assembled, waiting for more arrivals. A
stranger would have taken them for masqueraders.
Some of the gentlemen wore toupees, others only
powder, others their own plain head of hair. Some
had swords by their sides, others none. Here were
beaux in the modern coat and waistcoat, or habiliments
little different. There stood coats stuck out with
buckram, and legs with stockings above the knees.
The appearance of the ladies presented an equal variety. Some wore hoops, others plain petticoats.
The heads of many were built up with prodigious
edifices of hair and ribbon; others had their curls
flowing down their necks; some were in common
shoes, others in a kind of slippered stilts. In short,
not to keep the reader any longer upon trifles, the
company consisted of the immortal though familiar
creatures I speak of, the heroes and heroines of the
wonderful persons who have lived among us, called
Novelists.

Judge of my delight when I found myself among a
set of old acquaintances, whom I had never expected
to see in this manner. Conceive how I felt, when I
discovered that the gentleman and lady I was sitting
next to, were Captain and Mrs. Booth; and that another couple on my left, very brilliant and decorous,
were no less people than Sir Charles and my Lady
Grandison! In the centre were Mr. and Mrs. Roderick Random; Lieutenant Thomas Bowling, of the Royal

Navy; Mr. Morgan, a Welch gentleman; Mr. and
Mrs. Peregrine Pickle; Mr. Fathom, a Methodist—(a
very ill-looking fellow)—Sir George Paradyne, and
Mr. Hermsprong; Mr. Desmond, with his friend
Waverley, (a relation of the more famous Waverley);
a young gentleman whose Christian name was Henry
—(I forget the other, but Mr. Cumberland knows) and
Mr., formerly Serjeant Atkinson, with his wife, who
both sat next to Captain and Mrs. Booth.   There were
also some lords whose names I cannot immediately .
call to mind; a lady of rank, who had once been a
Beggar-girl; and other persons too numerous to mention.   In a corner, very modest and pleasing, sat Lady
Harold, better known as Miss Louisa Mildmay, with
her husband, Sir Robert.   From the mixed nature of
the company, a spectator might have concluded that
these immortal ladies and gentlemen were free from
the ordinary passions of created beings; but I soon
observed that it was otherwise.   I found that some of
the persons already assembled had arrived at this
plebeian hour out of an ostentation of humility; and
that the others, who came later, were influenced by
the usual variety of causes.

The next arrival—(conceive how my heart expanded
at the sight)—consisted of the Rev. Dr. Primrose,
Vicar of Wakefield, with his family, and the Miss
Flamboroughs; the latter red and staring with delight.
The Doctor apologized for not being sooner; but Mrs.
Primrose said she was sure the gentlefolks would excuse him, knowing that people accustomed to good
society were never in a flurry on such occasions.   Her
husband would have made some remark on this; but
seeing that she was prepared to appeal to her " son,
the Squire," who flattered and made her his butt, and

that Sir William Thornhill and both the young married
ladies would be in pain, he forbore. The Vicar made
haste to pay his respects to Sir Charles and Lady
Grandison, who treated him with great distinction, Sir
Charles taking him by the hand, and calling him his
" good and worthy friend." I observed that Mr. Moses
Primrose had acquired something of a collected and
cautious look, as if determined never to be cheated
again. He happened to seat himself next to Peregrine
Pickle, who informed him, to his equal surprise and
delight, that Captain Booth had written a refutation of
Materialism. He added, that the Captain did not
choose at present to be openly talked of as the author,
though he did not mind being complimented upon it in
an obscure and ingenious way. I noticed, after this,
that a game of cross purposes was going on between
Booth and Moses, which often forced a blush from the
Captain's lady. It was with much curiosity I recognized the defect in the latter's nose. I did not find it
at all in the way when I looked at her lips. It appeared to me even to excite a kind of pity, by no
means injurious to the most physical admiration; but I
did not say this to Lady Grandison, who asked my
opinion on the subject. Booth was a fine strapping
fellow, though he had not much in his face. When
Mr. and Mrs. Booby (the famous Pamela) afterwards
came in, he attracted so much attention from the latter,
that upon her asking me, with a sort of pitying smile,
what I thought of him, I ventured to say, in a pun,
that I looked upon him as a very good " Booth for the
Fair ;" upon which, to my astonishment, she blushed as
red as scarlet, and told me that her dear Mr. B. did
not approve of such speeches. My pun was a mere
pun, and meant little ; certainly nothing to the disad-

vantage of the sentimental part of the sex, for whom I thought him by no means a finished companion. But there is no knowing these precise people.

But I anticipate the order of the arrivals. The Primroses were followed by Sir Launcelot Greaves and his lady, Mr. and Mrs. Thomas Jones, Mr. and Miss Western, and my Lady Bellaston. Then came Miss Monimia (I forget her name) who married out of the old Manor House; then Mr. and Mrs. Humphrey Clinker (I believe I should rather say Bramble) with old Matthew himself, and Mrs. Lismahago; and then a whole world of Aunt Selbys, and Grandmamma Selbys, and Miss Howes, and Mr. Harlowes, though I observed neither Clarissa nor Lovelace. I made some inquiries about them afterwards, which the reader shall hear.

Enter Mr. John Buncle, escorting five ladies, whom he had been taking to an evening lecture. Tom Gollogher was behind them, very merry.

Then came my Lord and Lady Orville (Evelina), Mr. and Mrs. Delville (Cecilia), Camilla (I forget her surname) with a large party of Mandleberts, Clarendels, Arlberys, Orkbornes, Marglands, and Dubsters, not omitting the eternal Mrs. Mitten. Mrs. Booby and husband came last, accompanied by my Lady Booby, Mr. Joseph Andrews and bride, and the Rev. Mr. Adams, for whom Mrs. B. made a sort of apology, by informing us that there was no necessity to make any,—Mr. Adams being an honor to the cloth. Fanny seated herself by Sophia Western (that was) with whom I found she was intimate; and a lovelier pair of blooming, unaffected creatures, whose good-nature stood them instead of wit, I never beheld. But I must discuss the beauties of the ladies by-and-by.

An excuse was sent by Mr. Tristram Shandy for his Uncle Tobias, saying that they were confined at home, and unfit for company, which made me very sorry, for I would rather have seen the divine old invalid than any man in the room, not excepting Parson Adams. I suspect he knew nothing of the invitation. Corporal Trim brought the letter; a very honest, pathetic fellow, who dropped a tear. He also gave a kiss, as he went out, to one of the maid-servants. The Rev. Mr. Yorick, friend of the Shandy family, sent his servant La Fleur to wait on us; a brisk, active youth, who naturalized himself among us by adoring the ladies all round. The poor lad manifested his admiration by various grimaces, that forced the Miss Flamboroughs to stuff their handkerchiefs in their mouths. Our other attendants were Strap, Tom Pipes, Partridge, and two or three more, some of them in livery, and others not, as became their respective ranks. The refreshments were under the care of Mrs. Slipslop; but underwent, as they came up, a jealous revision from Mrs. Lismahago, and Mrs. Humphrey Clinker, who, luckily, for her, differed considerably with one another, or none would have been worth eating.

I have omitted to observe that the meeting was of the same nature with assemblies in country towns, where all the inhabitants, of any importance, are in the habit of coming together for the public advantage, and being amiable and censorious. There the Sir Charles Grandison of the place meets the Tom Jones and the Mrs. Humphrey Clinker. There the Lady Bellaston interchanges courtesies and contempt with the Miss Marglands; and all the Dubsters in their new yellow gloves, with all the Delvilles.

Having thus taken care of our probabilities (or verisimilitudes, as the critics call it) to which, in our highest flights, we are much attached, we proceed with our narrative.

We forgot to mention that Mrs. Honor, the famous waiting-maid of Sophia Western, was not present. Nothing could induce her to figure as a servant, where that "infected upstart," as she called her, Mrs. Humphrey Clinker, fidgeted about as a gentlewoman.

The conversation soon became very entertaining, particularly in the hands of the Grandisons and Harlowes, who, though we could perceive they were not so admired by the rest of the company as by one another, interested us in spite of ourselves by the longest, and yet most curious gossip in the world. Sir Charles did not talk so much as the others; indeed he seemed to be a little baffled and thrust off the pinnacle of his superiority in this very mixed society; but he was thought a prodigious fine gentleman by the gravest of us, and was really a good-natured one. His female friends, who were eternally repeating and deprecating their own praises, were pronounced by Hermsprong, as well as Peregrine Pickle, to be the greatest coxcombs under the sun. The latter said something about Pamela and Covent-Garden which we do not choose to repeat. The consciousness of doing their duty, however, mixed as it might be with these vain mistakes, gave a certain tranquillity of character to the faces of some of this party, which Peregrine, and some others about him, might have envied. At the same time, we must do the justice to Peregrine to say, that although (to speak plainly) he had not a little of the blackguard in him, he displayed some generous qualities. We cannot say much for his wit and talents, which are so extolled by the historian; nor even for those of his friend Roderick Random, though he carries some good qualities still further. Roderick's conversation had the vice of coarseness, to the great delight of Squire Western, who said he had more spirit than Tom himself. Tom did not care for a little freedom, but the sort of conversation to which Roderick and his friends were inclined, disgusted him ; and, before women, astonished him. He did not, therefore, very well fall in with this society, though his wit and views of things were, upon the whole, pretty much on a par with theirs. In person and manners he beat them hollow. Sophia nevertheless took very kindly to Emily Gauntlett and Narcissa, two ladies rather insipid.

We observed that the company might be divided into four different sorts. One was Sir Charles Grandison's and party ; another, the Pickles and Joneses ; a third, the Lord Orvilles, Evelinas, and Cecilias, with the young lady from the old Manor House ; and a fourth, the Hermsprongs, Desmonds, and others, including a gentleman we have forgotten to mention, Mr. Hugh Trevor. In this last were some persons whose names we ought to have remembered, for an account of whom we must refer to Mrs. Inchbald. The first of these parties were for carrying all the established conventional virtues to a high pitch of dignity ; so much so, as to be thinking too much of the dignity, while they fancied they were absorbed in the virtue. They were very clever and amusing, and we verily believe could have given an interest to a history of every grain of sand on the sea-shore ; but their garrulity and vanity, united, rendered other conversation a refreshment. The second were a parcel of wild, but not ill-natured young fellows, all very ready to fall in with what the others thought and recommended, and to forget it the next moment, especially as their teachers laid themselves open to ridicule. It must be added, that their very inferiority in some respects gave them a more general taste of humanity, particularly Tom Jones; who was a pleasant, unaffected fellow, and upon the whole perhaps as virtuous, in his way, as could be expected of a sprightly blood educated in the ordinary fashion. The Camillas and Evelinas were extremely entertaining, and told us a number of stories that made us die with laughter. Their fault consisted in talking too much about lords and pawnbrokers. Miss Monimia, too, from the old Manor House, ridiculed vulgarity a little too much to be polite. The most puzzling people in the room were the Desmonds and Hugh Trevors, who had come up since a late revolution in our sphere. They got into a controversy with the Grandisons, and reduced them sadly to their precedents and authorities. The conclusion of the company seemed to be, that if the world were to be made different from what it is, the change would be effected rather by the philosophies of these gentlemen than the seraphics of the other party; but the general opinion was, that it would be altered by neither, and that in the meantime, " variety was charming ;" a sentiment which the Vicar of Wakefield took care to explain to his wife.

But how are we forgetting ourselves? We have left out, in our divisions, a fifth set, the most delightful of all, one of whom is a whole body of humanity in himself; to-wit, Mr. Abraham Adams, and all whom he loves. We omit his title of Reverend; not because he is not so, but because titles are things exclusive, and our old friend belongs to the whole world.

Bear witness, spirit of everything that is true, that, with the exception of one or two person, only to be produced in these latter times, we love such a man as Abraham Adams better than all the characters in all the histories of the world, orthodox or not orthodox. We hold him to be only inferior to a Shakspeare; and only then. because the latter joins the height of wisdom intellectual to his wisdom cordial. He should have been Shakspeare's chaplain, and played at bowls with him. What a sound heart,—and a list to stand by it! This is better than Sir Charles's fencing, without which his polite person—(virtue included)—would often have been in an awkward way. What disinterestedness! What feeling! What real modesty! What a harmless spice of vanity,—Nature's kind gift,—the comfort we all treasure more or less about us, to keep ourselves in heart with ourselves? In fine, what a regret of his Æschylus! and a delicious forgetting that he could not see to read if he had had it! Angels should be painted with periwigs, to look like him. We confess, we prefer Fanny to Joseph Andrews, which will be pardoned us; but the lad is a good lad; and if poor Molly at the inn has forgiven him (which she ought to do, all things considered), we will forgive him ourselves, on the score of my Lady Booby. It is more than my Lady has done, though she takes a pride in patronizing the "innocent creatures," as she calls them. We are afraid, from what we saw this evening, that poor Joseph is not as well as he would be with his sister Pamela. When the refreshments came in. we observed her blush at his handing a plate of sandwiches to Mr. Adams. She called him to her in a whisper; and asked him. whether he had forgotten that there was a footman in the room?

The arrival of the refreshments divided our company into a variety of small ones. The ladies got more together; and the wines and jellies diffused a benevolent spirit among us all. We forgot our controversies, and were earnest only in the putting of cakes. John Buncle, however, stood talking and eating at a great rate with one of the philosophers. Somebody asked after Lovelace and Clarissa; for the reader need not be told, that it is only in a fictitious sense that these personages are said to have died. They cannot die, being immortal. It seems that Lovelace and Clarissa live in a neighboring quarter, called Romance; a very grave place, where few of the company visited. We were surprised to hear that they lived in the same house; that Lovelace had found out he had a liking for virtue in her own shape as well as Clarissa's, and that Clarissa thought she might as well forget herself so far as to encourage the man not to make a rascal and a madman of himself. This, at least, is the way that Tom Gollogher put it: for Tom undertook to be profound on the subject, and very much startled us by his observations. He made an application of a line in Milton, about Adam and Eve, which the more serious among us thought profane, and which indeed we are afraid of repeating: but Tom's good-nature was so evident, as well as his wish to make the best of a bad case, that we chose to lay the more equivocal part of his logic to the account of his " wild way ;" and for all that we saw to the contrary, he was a greater favorite with the ladies than ever. Desmond's friend Waverley asked us after his celebrated namesake. We told him he was going on very well, and was very like his relation ; a compliment which Mr. Waverley acknowledged by a bow. We related to him the sea-side adventure of Waverley's friend, the Antiquary; at which the other exclaimed, "Good God! how like an adventure which happened to a friend of our acquaintance? Only see what coincidences will take place!" He asked us if the Antiquary had never noticed the resemblance, and was surprised to hear that he had not. "I should not wonder at it," said he, "if the incident had been well known; but these Antiquaries, the best of them, have strange grudging humors, and I will tell him of it," added he, "when I see him." Mr. Waverley anticipated with great delight the society of his namesake with his numerous friends, though he did not seem to expect much from the female part of them.

Before we broke up, tragical doings were likely to have occurred between the housekeeper and Mrs. Humphrey Clinker. Mrs. Slipslop sent up a message apologizing for some of the jellies. She expressed a fear—(which was correctly delivered by an impudent young rogue of a messenger)—that "the *superfluency* of the sugar would take away the *tastality* of the jellies, and render them quite *innoxious*." (If the reader thinks this account overcharged, we have to inform him that he will fall into the error of the audience about the pig.) Mrs. Humphrey was indignant at this "infected nonsense," as she called it; and she was fidgeting out of the room to scold the rhetorician, when her husband called her back, telling her that it was beneath the dignity of a rational soul like hers to fret itself with such matters. Winifred's blood began to rise at the first part of this observation; but the words, "like hers," induced her to sit down, and content herself with an answer to the message. Peregrine Pickle, who was sorry to see affairs end so quietly, persuaded her, however, to put her message in writing ; and Mrs. Slipslop would have inevitably been roused and brought up stairs, had not Sir Charles condescended to interfere. The answer was as follows :—

"MRS. SLIBBERSLOP,—Hit Bing beneath the diggingit of a rasher and sole, to cumfabberrate with sich parsons, I Desire that you wil send up sum geallics Fit for a cristum and a gentile wommun to Heat. We ar awl astonied Att yure niggling gents. The geallys ar Shamful."

Peregrine begged her to add a word of advice respecting the "pompous apology;" upon which she concluded thus :—

"A nuthur tim doant Send up sich pumpers and Polly jeers and stuf; and so no moar at present from
      "Yure wel wisker,
            "WINIFRED CLINKER."

When the ladies had put on their cloaks, and were waiting for their carriages, we could not but remark how well Sophia Western—(we like to call her by her good old name)—looked in any dress and position. She was all ease and good-nature, and had a charming shape. Lady Grandison was a regular beauty ; but did not become a cloak. She was best in full dress. Pamela was a little soft-looking thing, who seemed "as if butter would not melt in her mouth." But she had something in the corner of her eye, which told you that you had better take care how you behaved yourself. She would look all round her at every man in the room, and hardly one of them be the wiser. Pamela was not so splendidly dressed as her friend Lady Grandison ; but her clothes were as costly. The Miss Howes, Lady G.'s, and others of that class, were loud, bright-eyed, raw-boned people, who tossed on their

cloaks without assistance, or commanded your help
with a sarcasm. Camilla, Cecilia, and Evelina, were
all very handsome and agreeable. We prefer, from
what we recollect of them, Camilla and Evelina; but
they say Cecilia is the most interesting. Louisa Mildmay might have been taken for a pale beauty; but her
paleness was not natural to her, and she was resuming
her color. Her figure was luxuriant; and her eyes,
we thought, had a depth in them beyond those of any
person's in the room. We did not see much in Narcissa and Emilia Gauntlett, but they were both good
jolly damsels enough. Of Amelia, we have spoken
already. We have a recollection that Hermsprong's
wife (a Miss Campionet) was a pleasant girl; but somehow she had got out of our sight. The daughters of
the Vicar of Wakefield were fine girls, especially Sophia; for whom, being of her lover Sir William's age,
we felt a particular tenderness.

BEDS AND BEDROOMS.

Intrinsical nature of bed.—Advantage of people in bed over people that are "up."—Dialogue with a person "up."—Feather-beds, curtains, &c.— Idea of a perfect bed-room.—Custom half the secret of content.—Bed- room in a cottage.—Bed at sea.—Beds in presses and alcoves.—Anec- dotes of beds.—The bed of Morpheus in Spenser.

WE have written elsewhere* of "sleep," and of "dreams," and of "getting up on cold mornings," and divers other matters connected with bed ; but, unless we had written volumes on that one subject, it would be hard indeed if we could not find fresh matter to speak of, connected with the bed itself, and the room which it inhabits. We involuntarily use a verb with a human sense,—"inhabits ;" for of all goods and chat- tels, this surely contracts a kind of humanity from the warmth so often given to it by the comfortable soul within. Its pillows—as a philosophic punster might observe—have something in them "next to the human cheek."

"Home is home," says the good proverb, "however homely." Equally certain are we, that bed is bed, however *bedly*. (We have a regard for this bit of parody on the old saying, because we made Charles Lamb laugh one night with it, when we were coming away with him out of a friend's house.) Bed is the home of home ; the innermost part of the content. It

* In the "Indicator."

is sweet within sweet; a nut in the nut; within the
snuggest nest a snugger nest; my retreat from the
publicity of my privacy; my room within my room
walled (if I please) with curtains; a box, a separation,
a snug corner, such as children love when they play
at " house ;" the place where I draw a direct line between me and my cares; where I enter upon a new
existence, free, yet well invested; reposing, but full of
power; where the act of lying down, and pulling the
clothes over one's head, seems to exclude matters that
have to do with us when dressed and on our legs;
where, though in repose, one is never more conscious
of one's activity, divested of those hampering weeds;
where a leg is not a lump of boot and stocking, but a
real leg, clear, natural, fleshy, delighting to thrust itself
hither and thither; and lo ! so recreating itself, it comes
in contact with another; to-wit, one's own. One should
hardly guess as much, did it remain eternally divorced
from its companion,—alienated and altered into leather
and prunella. Of more legs we speak not. The bed
we are at this moment presenting to our imagination,
is a bachelor's; for we must be cautious how we touch
upon others. A married man may, to be sure, conde-
scend, if he pleases, for the trifle's sake, to taste of the
poor bachelor's satisfaction. He has only to go to
bed an hour before his wife. Or the lady may do as
much *vice versa*. And herein we can fancy one gratification, even of the bachelor or spinster order, beyond
what a bachelor or spinster can often be presumed to
realize; which is the pleasure of being in bed at your
ease, united with the highest kind of advantage *over
the person that is up*. Let us not be misunderstood.
The sense of this advantage is not of the malignant
kind. You do not enjoy yourself because others are

in misery; but, because your pleasure at the moment being very much in your bed, and it not being the other's pleasure to come to bed so soon (which you rather wonder at), you are at liberty to make what conclusions you please as to the superior nature of your condition. And there is this consideration besides; namely, that you being in bed, and others up, all cares and attentions naturally fall to the portion of those individuals; so that you are at once the master of your own repose and of their activity. A bachelor, however, may enjoy a good deal of this. He may have kindred in the house, or servants, or the man and woman that keep the lodging; and from his reflections on all, or either of these persons, he may derive no little satisfaction. It is a lordly thing to consider, that others are sitting up, and nobly doing some duty or other with sleepy eyes, while ourselves are exquisitely shutting ours; they being also ready to answer one's bell, bring us our white wine whey, or lamp, or what not, or even to go out in spite of the rain for some fruit, should we fancy it, or for a doctor in case we should be ill, or to answer some question for the mere pleasure of answering it.

"Who's there?"

"Me, sir; Mrs. Jones."

"Oh, I beg your pardon, Mrs. Jones; I merely rang to know if you were up."

"Dear me, yes, sir, and likely to be this hour."

(*Aside and happy*)—"Poor soul!"

"It's Mr. Jones's club-night, sir."

("Poor woman! Capital pillow this!")

"And it's a full hour's walk from the Jolly Gardeners."

("Poor Jones! Very easy mattress.) *Aloud*—

Bless me, that's a bad business; and it rains, doesn't it, Mrs. Jones ?"

" A vile rain, sir, with an east wind."

" (Poor Jones ! Delicious curtains these !) Couldn't the servant sit up, and let Mr. Jones in ?"

" Lord, sir, we're both of us sitting up; for I'm frighted out of my wits, sitting alone ; and Mr. Jones wouldn't be pleased if I didn't see him in myself."

" (Poor woman !) Good night Mrs. Jones : pray don't stand any longer at that cold door."

" Do you want anything, sir ?"

" Nothing, I thank you. I am very comfortable. What o'clock is it ?"

" Just going one, sir."

" (Poor creature !—Poor Susan !—Poor Jones !) *Whew* goes the wind ; *patter* go the windows ; *rumble* goes a coach ; to sleep go I."

This is pretty ;—but a wife, instead of the woman of the house,—a wife up, and going about like one's guardian angel ; we also loving her well, and having entreated her not to sit up, only she is forced to do so for this half hour,—either we know nothing of bliss itself, or the variety—merely *as* a variety—the having a whole bed for half an hour, merely as a *change* from that other super-human elysian state—the seeing even a little pain borne so beautifully by the " partner of one's existence," whom of course we love the better for it, and cannot but rejoice in seeing gifted with such an opportunity of showing herself to advantage—all this, if we mistake not (owing to our present bachelor hallucination), must be a sublimation of satisfaction unknown to sojourners at large, who are but too often accused, with justice, of having more room than they know what to do with.

5*

A bed, to be perfectly comfortable, should be warm, clean, well made, and of a reasonable softness. People differ as to the amount of the softness. The general opinion seems to be in favor of feather-beds. To ourselves (if the fact *must* be publicly torn out of us by a candor trying to the sense of our nothingness), a feather-bed is a Slough of Despond. When we are in the depths of it, we long to be on the heights. When we get on the heights, down they go with us, and turn into depths. The feathers hamper us, obstruct, irritate, suffocate. We lose the sense of repose and independence, and feel ourselves in the hands of a soft lubberly giant. The pleasure of being " tucked up," we can better understand ; but it likes us not. What we require is, that the limbs should be as free as possible from obstruction. We desire to go counter to all that we endure when up and about. We must have nothing constrained about us ;—must be able to thrust arms and legs whithersoever we please. That the bed should be well and delicately tucked up, pleaseth us ; but only that we may have the greater satisfaction in disengaging the clothes on each side with a turn of the foot, and so giving freedom to our borders.

> Upon my resting body,
> Lie lightly, gentle *clothes*.

Warmth, cleanliness, and ease being secured, it is of minor importance what sort of bed we lie in, whether it has curtains, or a canopy, or even legs. We can lie on the floor for that matter, provided the palliasse be of decent thickness. The floor itself then becomes a part of the great field of rest in which we expatiate. There is nothing to bound our right of in-

cumbency ; we can gather the clothes about us, and
roll on the floor if we please. Much greater philosophy does it take, on the other hand, to make us go up
half a dozen steps to our bed,—to climb up to such
lofty absurdities as are shown in old houses for the
beds of James's and Charles's time ; thrones rather,
and canopies for Prester John ;—edifices of beds,
where we make a show of the privatest and humblest
of our pleasures ; contrivances for the magnificent
breaking of our necks ; or, if we are not to die that
way, three-piled hyperboles of beds to ingulf us, like
a slough on the top of a mountain. Fine curtains disgust us by the same uneasy contradiction. We do
not mean handsome ones of a reasonable kind ; but
velvet, and such like cumbrous clouds, lording it over
the sweet idea of rest, and forcing us to think of the
most out-of-door pretensions. And we hate gilding,
and coronets (not having any), and imperial eagles,
and *fleurs de lis,* and all other conspiracies to put out
the natural man in us, and deprive the poor great
human being of the sweet privilege of being on a
level with his reposing fellow-creatures. We are not
sure that we could patronize Cupids, gilt torches,
doves and garlands, &c. Flowery curtains we like ;
but the Cupids and gilt torches are particular. We
are not the fonder of them for being the taste in France.
Curtains, paperings, plates and dishes, everything in
that country, babbles, not of green fields, as with us,
which is pretty, but of gallantry and *la belle passion.*
The French (when they are not afraid of being thought
afraid) are a good-natured people ; and they are much
wiser in this good-nature, than if they took to " heavy
wet," and to being sulky. But in these amatory matters they seem to us never to make out the **proper**

case. There is something ever too cold, or too meretricious, probably both ; for these extremes are too apt
to meet. Cupids and torches might be well enough,
provided we could be secure that none but eyes of
good taste would see them ; but how are they or we
to look, when every idle servant, or the glazier, or the
landlord, or the man that comes to look at the house
when it is to be let, is to gape about him, and make an
impertinence of our loves and graces ?

But we forget our solitary condition.—We should
almost equally dislike the most gorgeous and the most
sorry bedroom, did not the former stand the greater
chance of cleanliness. The Duke of Buckingham,
" gallant and gay," in one of the state beds of Cliefden's
" proud alcove," or reckless and drunk in " the worst
inn's worst room," behind his

> " Tape-tied curtains never meant to draw,"

is, to our mind, in no such difference of condition as
the poet makes him out. And his company were much
like one another in both cases. Nay, that is not true
either ; for it would have been difficult to pick up such
an abomination from a village ale-house as the Countess of Shrewsbury,—a woman, ugly all over with a
hard heart. Commend us (for a climate like ours) to
a bed-chamber of the middle order, such as it was set
out about a hundred years back, and may still be seen
in the houses of some old families ; the room of moderate size ; the four-post bedstead neatly and plentifully,
but not richly, draperied ; the chairs draperied also,
down to the ground ; a drapery over the toilet ; the
carpet, a good old Turkey or Brussels, not covering
the floor, and easily to be taken up and shaken ; the
wardrobe and drawers of old shining oak, walnut, or

mahogany ; a few cabinet pictures, as exquisite as you
please ; the windows with seats, and looking upon
some green place ; two or three small shelves of books ;
and the drawers, when they are opened, redolent of
lavender and clean linen. We dislike the cut-and-dry
look of modern fashions ; the cane chairs, formal-pat-
terned carpets, and flimsy rooms. Modern times (or
till very lately they were so) are all for lightness, and
cheap sufficiency, and what is considered a Grecian
elegance. They realize only an insipid or gaudy anatomy of things, a cold pretension, and houses that will
tumble upon the heads of our grand-children. But
these matters, like others, are gradually improving. If
our bed-room is to be perfect, it should face the east,
to rouse us pleasantly with the morning sun ; and in
case we should be tempted to lie too long in so sweet
a nest, there should be a happy family of birds at the
windows, to salute our rise with songs.

It is a good thing, however, to reflect, that custom
is half the secret of content. The reason why we like
a hard bed is, that we were brought up at a public
school, without any luxuries : and, to this day, we like
just such a sort of bed as we had there. We could
find a satisfaction in having the identical kind of rug
over our sheets ; and sheets, too, of no greater fineness.
And the same reason makes us prefer a coarse towel
to a fine one, and a gown, of some sort, to a coat ; with
a pocket in the same place as the one in which we used
to put our marbles and tops, and our pocket editions
of Gray and Collins. We have since slept in houses
of all sorts—in rich houses and in poor, in cottages, in
taverns, and inns, and public-houses, in palaces (what
at least the Italians call such), and on board ship : yea,
in *bivouacs*—just enough to taste the extremest hard-

ness of the bed military; and for the only contrivance utterly to vitiate our night's rest, commend us to the bed of down. That, and the wooden bed of the guard house, disputed the palm. Habit does the same with kings and popes. Frederick the Second preferred lying in a little tent-bed, such as Voltaire found him in at their first interview, shivering with an ague; and we learn from Horace Walpole's Letters, that the good Pope, Benedict the Fourteenth, lay upon one no better (the palliasse, most probably, of his convent) by the side of the gorgeous canopy prepared for his rank. In truth, luxuriate as we may in this our at-different-times-written article (wherein the indulgences and speculations, though true at the moment, are of many years chance preservation on paper, and therefore may crave excuse if they look a little ultra nice and fanciful, beyond the want of experience), we should be heartily ashamed of ourselves at our present time of life, if we could not sleep happily in any bed (down and *mud* always excepted), provided only it had enough clothes to keep us warm, and were as clean and decent as honest poverty could make it. We talk of fine chambers, and luxurious contrasts of sitters up; but our secret passion is for a homely room in a cottage, with perfect quiet, a book or two, and a sprig of rosemary in the window; not the book or two for the purpose of reading in bed, —(having once received a startling lesson that way, and not choosing to burn down the village,)—but in order that we may see them in the window the first thing in the morning, together with the trees of which they discourse. Add to this, a watch-dog at a distance, and a moaning wind, no matter how "melancholy," provided it does not blow a tempest (for though nature does nothing but for good, the particular suffering

sometimes presses upon the imagination), and we drop
to sleep in a transport of comfort. Compare such a
bed as this with one that we have seen during a storm
of fifty-six hours' duration at sea, the occupant (the
mate of the vessel) with his hands wet, black, blistered,
and smarting with the cold, and the very bed (a hole
in a corner) as wet as his hands! And the common
sailors had worse! And yet the worst of all, shut out
from wet and cold as they were, but not having work
like the seamen to occupy the mind, were the cribs of
a parcel of children tossing about in all this tempest,
and the bed of their parents on the cabin-floor.—With
these recollections (as the whole vessel got safe), we
sometimes think we could find it in our hearts to relish
even a feather-bed.

A very large bedroom in an old country-house is
not pleasant, where the candle shows you the darkness at the other end of it, and you begin to think it
possible for houses to be haunted. And as little comfortable is the bed with a great dusty canopy, such as
they say the Highland laird mistook for the bed itself,
and mounted at top of, while he put his servant into
the sheets, thinking that the loftier stratum was the
place of grandeur. Sometimes these canopies are
domed, and adorned with plumes, which give them a
funereal look; and a nervous gentleman, who, while
getting into bed, is hardly sure that a hand will not
thrust itself out beneath the valance and catch him by
the ankle, does not feel quite so bold in it as the
French general, who, when threatened by some sheet-
ed ghosts, told them to make the best of their way off,
or he would give them a sound thrashing. On the
other hand, unless warranted by necessity and good-
humor, which can reconcile anything, it is very disa-

greeable to see sofa-bedsteads and press-bedsteads in
"stived-up" little rooms, half sitting-room and half
chamber. They look as if they never could be aired.
For a similar reason, an Englishman cannot like the
French beds that shut up into alcoves in the wall.
We do not object to a custom merely because it is
foreign ; nor is it unreasonable, or indeed otherwise
than agreeable, that a bedroom of good dimensions
should include a partial bit of a sitting-room or bou-
doir ; but in that case, and indeed in all cases, it should
be kept scrupulously neat and clean. Order in a
house first manifests itself in the room which the
housewife inhabits ; and every sentiment of the heart,
as well as of the external graces, demands that a very
reverence and religion of neatness should be there exhibited ; not formality—not a want of snugness,—but
all with evidences that the esteem of a life is preferred
to the slatternliness of the moment, and that two hearts
are always reigning together in that apartment, though
one person alone should be visible.

It is very proper that bedrooms, which can afford
it, should be adorned with pictures, with flowers by
day-time, (they are not wholesome at night), and, if
possible, with sculpture. We are among those who
believe, with the old romance of Heliodorus, that, under circumstances which affect the earliest periods of
existence, familiar objects are not without their influence upon the imagination. Besides. it is wholesome to live in the kindly and tranquil atmosphere of
the arts ; and few, even of the right-minded, turn to
half the account they might do the innumerable beauties which Heaven has lavished upon the world, both
in art and nature. Better hang a wild rose over the
toilet, than nothing. The eye that looks in the glass

will see there something besides itself; and it will ac-
quire something of a religious right to respect itself,
in thinking by how many objects in the creation the
bloom of beauty is shared.

The most sordidly ridiculous anecdote we remember of a bed-chamber, is one in the life of Elwes, the
rich miser, who, asking a visitor one morning how he
had rested, and being told that he could not escape
from the rain which came through the roof of the
apartment, till he had found out one particular corner
in which to stow the truckle-bed, said, laughingly,
and without any sense of shame, "Ah! what! you
found it out, did you? Ah! that's a nice corner, isn't
it?" This, however, is surpassed in dramatic effect,
by the story of two ministers of state, in the last century, who were seen one day, by a sudden visitor, fu-
riously discussing some great question out of two
separate beds in one room, by day-time, their arms
and bodies thrust forward towards each other out of
the clothes, and the gesticulation going on accordingly. If our memory does not deceive us, one of
them was Lord Chatham. He had the gout, and his
colleague coming in to see him, and the weather being very cold, and no fire in the room, the noble earl
had persuaded his visitor to get into the other bed.
The most ghastly bed-chamber story, in real life (next
to some actually mortal ones), is that of a lady who
dreamt that her servant-maid was coming into the
room to murder her. She rose in the bed with the
horror of the dream in her face; and sitting up thus
appalled, encountered, in the opening door, the sight
of the no less horrified face of the maid-servant,
coming in with a light to do what her mistress ap-
prehended.

To give this article the termination fittest for it, such as leaves the reader with the most comprehensive sense upon him of profound rest, and of whatsoever conduces to lull and secure it, we shall conclude with a divine passage of Spenser, in which he combines, with the most poetical fiction, the most familiar feeling of truth. Morpheus, the god of sleep, has an impossible bed somewhere, on the borders of the sea, —on the shore of "the world of waters wide and deep," by which its curtains are washed. Observe how this fictitious bed is made real by every collateral circumstance.

> " And more to lulle him in his slumber soft,
> A trickling streame, from high rock tumbling downe,
> And ever-drizzling raine upon the loft,
> Mixed with a murmuring winde, much like the sowne
> Of swarming bees, did cast him in a swowne.
> No other noise, nor people's troublous cries
> As still are wont t' annoy the wallèd towne,
> Might there be heard ;—but carelesse quiet lyes,
> Wrapt in eternal silence—farre from enemyes."
>
> FAERIE QUEENE, Book I. canto i. stanza 41,

THE WORLD OF BOOKS.

Difficulty of proving that a man is not actually in a distant place, by dint of being there in imagination.— Visit of that kind to Scotland.—Suggestion of a Book-Geography; of Maps in which none but poetical or otherwise intellectually-associated places are set down.—Scottish, English, French, and Italian items for such maps.—Local literizations of Rousseau and Wordsworth objected.—Actual enrichment of the commonest places by intellectual associations.

TO THE EDITOR OF TAIT'S MAGAZINE.

Sir,—To write in your Magazine makes me feel as if I, at length, had the pleasure of being personally in Scotland, a gratification which I have not yet enjoyed in any other way. I dive into my channel of communication, like another Alpheus, and reappear in the shop of Mr. Tait; not pursuing, I trust, anything *fugitive*, but behaving very unlike a river-god, and helping to bring forth an Edinburgh periodical.

Nor will you, sir, who enter so much into the interests of your fellow-creatures, and know so well of what their faculties are capable, look upon this kind of presence as a thing so purely unreal as it might be supposed. Our strongest proofs of the existence of anything amounts but to a proportionate belief to that effect; and it would puzzle a wise man, though not a fool, to prove to himself that I was not, in some spiritual measure, in any place where I chose to pitch my imagination. I notice this metaphysical subtlety,

merely, in the first place, to baulk your friend the
Pechler, should he think it a settled thing that a man
cannot be in two places at once (which would be a
very green assumption of his) ; and secondly, the
better to impress a conviction which I have,—that I
know Scotland very well, and have been there many
times.

Whether we go to another country on these occasions, in the manner of a thing spiritual, our souls being
pitched out of ourselves like rockets or meteors ; or
whether the country comes to us, and our large souls
are inhabited by it for the time being, upon the principle of the greater including the less,—the mind of
man being a far more capacious thing than any set of
square miles,—I shall leave the curious to determine ;
but if I am not intimate with the very best parts of
Scotland, and have not seen them a thousand times,
then do I know nothing of Burns, or Allan Ramsay, or
Walter Scott, or Smollett, or Ossian, or James the
First, or Fifth, or snoods, or cockernonies, or gloamin',
or birks and burnies, or plaids, bonnets, and phillabegs,
or John Knox, or Queen Mary, or the Canongate, or
the Calton Hill, or Hume and Robertson, or Tweed-
side, or a haggis, or cakes, or heather, or reels and
strathspeys, or Glengarry, or all the clans, or Auld
Robin Gray, or a mist, or rappee, or second sight, or
the kirk, or the cutty-stool, or golf and hurling, or the
Border, or Bruce and Wallace, or bagpipes, or bonnie
lasses.

" A lover's plaid and a bed of heath," says the right
poetical Allan Cunningham, " are favorite topics with
the northern muse. When the heather is in bloom, it
is worthy of becoming the couch of beauty. *A sea
of brown blossom, undulating as far as the eye can*

reach, and swarming with wild bees, is a fine sight."
Sir, I have seen it a million times, though I never set
eyes on it.

Who that has ever read it, is not put into visual
possession of the following scene in the "Gentle
Shepherd?"

> A flowrie howm between twa verdant braes,
> Where lasses used to wash and spread their claes;
> A trotting burnie, wimpling through the ground,
> Its channel pebbles shining smooth and round:
> Here view twa bare-foot beauties, clean and clear.

Or this?—

> The open field.—A cottage in a glen;
> An auld wife spinning at the sunny en'.

Or this other, a perfect domestic picture?—

> . While Peggy laces up her bosom fair,
> Wi' a blue snood Jenny binds up her hair;
> Glaud by a morning ingle takes a beek,
> The rising sun shines motty through the reek:
> A pipe his mouth, the lasses please his een,
> And now and then a joke maun intervene.

The globe we inhabit is divisible into two worlds;
one hardly less tangible, and far more known than the
other,—the common geographical world, and the
world of books; and the latter may be as geographi-
cally set forth. A man of letters, conversant with
poetry and romance, might draw out a very curious
map, in which this world of books should be delineated
and filled up, to the delight of all genuine readers, as
truly as that in Guthrie or Pinkerton. To give a
specimen, and begin with Scotland.—Scotland would
not be the mere territory it is, with a scale of so many
miles to a degree, and such and such a population.
Who (except a patriot or a cosmopolite) cares for the

miles or the men, or knows that they exist, in any degree of consciousness with which he cares for the
never-dying population of books? How many generations of men have passed away, and will pass, in
Ayrshire or Dumfries, and not all the myriads be as
interesting to us as a single Burns? What have we
known of them, or shall ever know, whether lairds,
lords, or ladies, in comparison with the 'nspired plough-
man? But we know of the bards and the lasses, and
the places which he has recorded in song; we know
the scene of *Tam o'Shanter's* exploit; we know the
pastoral landscapes above quoted, and the scenes im-
mortalized in Walter Scott and the old ballads; and,
therefore, the book-map of Scotland would present us
with the most prominent of these. We should have
the border, with its banditti, towns, and woods; Tweed-
side, Melrose, and Roslin, *Edina*, otherwise called
Edinburgh and Auld Reekie, or the town of Hume,
Robertson, and others; Woodhouselee, and other
classical and haunted places; the bower built by the
fair hands of *Bessy Bell* and *Mary Gray;* the farm-
houses of Burns's friends; the scenes of his loves and
sorrows; the land of *Old Mortality*, of the *Gentle
Shepherd* and of *Ossian*. The Highlands, and the
great blue billowy domains of heather, would be dis-
tinctly marked out, in their most poetical regions; and
we should have the tracks of Ben Jonson to Hawthorn-
den, of *Rob Roy* to his hiding-places, and of *Jeanie
Deans* towards England. Abbotsford, be sure, would
not be left out; nor the house of the *Antiquary*,—almost as real a man as his author. Nor is this all; for
we should have older Scotland, the Scotland of James
the First, and of " Peeblis at the Play," and Gawin
Douglas, and Bruce, and Wallace; we should have

older Scotland still, the Scotland of Ariosto, with his tale of "Ginevra," and the new "Andromeda," delivered from the sea-monster at the Isle of Ebuda (the Hebrides), and there would be the residence of the famous *Launcelot of the Lake*, at Berwick, called the Joyeuse Garde, and other ancient sites of chivalry and romance; nor should the nightingale be left out in Ginevra's bower, for Ariosto has put it there, and there, accordingly, it is and has been heard, let ornithology say what it will; for what ornithologist knows so much of the nightingale as a poet? We would have an inscription put on the spot—"Here the nightingale sings, contrary to what has been affirmed by White and others."

This is the Scotland of books, and a beautiful place it is. I will venture to affirm, sir, even to yourself, that it is a more beautiful place than the other Scotland, always excepting to an exile or a lover; for the former is piqued to prefer what he must not touch; and to the latter, no spot is so charming as the ugliest place that contains his beauty. Not that Scotland has not many places literally as well as poetically beautiful: I know that well enough. But you see that young man there, turning down the corner of the dullest spot in Edinburgh, with a dead wall over against it, and delight in his eyes! He sees No. 4, the house where the girl lives he is in love with. Now what that place is to him, all places are, in their proportion, to the lover of books, for he has beheld them by the light of imagination and sympathy.

China, sir, is a very unknown place to us,—in one sense of the word unknown; but who is not intimate with it as the land of tea, and *china*, and ko-tous, and pagodas, and mandarins, and Confucius, and conical

caps, and people with little names, little eyes, and little
feet, who sit in little bowers, drinking little cups of tea,
and writing little odes? The Jesuits, and the tea-cups,
and the novel of Ju-Kiao-Li, have made us well acquainted with it; better, a great deal, than millions of
its inhabitants are acquainted—fellows who think it in
the middle of the world, and know nothing of themselves. With *one* China they are totally unacquainted,
to-wit, the great China of the poet and old travellers,
Cathay, " seat of Cathian Can," the country of which
Ariosto's *Angelica* was princess-royal; yes, she was a
Chinese, " the fairest of her sex, Angelica." It shows
that the ladies in that country must have greatly de-
generated, for it is impossible to conceive that Ariosto,
and Orlando, and Rinaldo, and King Sacripant. who
was a Circassian, could have been in love with her for
having eyes and feet like a pig. I will deviate here
into a critical remark, which is, that the Italian poets
seem to have considered people the handsomer the farther you went north. The old traveller, it is true,
found a good deal of the beauty that depends on red
and white, in Tartary, and other western regions; and
a fine complexion is highly esteemed in the swarthy
south. But *Astolfo*, the Englishman, is celebrated for
his beauty by the Italian poets; the unrivalled *Angelica*
was a Chinese; and the handsomest of Ariosto's heroes, *Zerbino*, of whom he writes the famous passage
" that nature made him, and then broke the mould," was
a *Scotchman*. The poet had probably seen some very
handsome Scotchman in Romagna. With this piece
of " bribery and corruption" to your national readers, I
return to my subject.

Book-England on the map would shine as the Albion
of the old Giants; as the " Logres" of the Knights of

the Round Table; as the scene of Amadis of Gaul, with its *island* of Windsor; as the abode of fairies, of the Druids, of the divine Countess of Coventry, of Guy, Earl of Warwick, of *Alfred* (whose reality was a romance), of the Fair Rosamond, of the Arcades and "Comus," of Chaucer and Spenser, of the poets of the Globe and the Mermaid, the wits of Twickenham and Hampton Court. Fleet Street would be Johnson's Fleet Street; the Tower would belong to Julius Cæsar; and Blackfriars to Suckling, Vandyke, and the "Dunciad." Chronology, and the mixture of truth and fiction, that is to say, of one sort of truth and another, would come to nothing in a work of this kind; for, as it has been before observed, things are real in proportion as they are impressive. And who has not as "gross, open, and palpable" an idea of *Falstaff* in East Cheap, as of *Captain Grose* himself, beating up his quarters? A map of fictitious, literary, and historical London, would, of itself, constitute a great curiosity. So would one of Edinburgh, or of any other city in which there have been great men and romantic events, whether the latter were real or fictitious. Swift speaks of maps, in which they

> "Place elephants for want of towns."

Here would be towns and elephants too, the popular and the prodigious. How much would not Swift do for Ireland, in this geography of wit and talent! What a figure would not St. Patrick's Cathedral make! The other day, mention was made of a "Dean of St. Patrick's" *now living;* as if there was, or ever could be, more than one Dean of St. Patrick's! In the Irish maps we should have the Saint himself driving out all venomous creatures: (what a pity that the most venomous retain a property as absentees!) and there would be the old Irish kings, and O'Donoghue with his White Horse, and the lady of the "gold wand" who made the miraculous virgin pilgrimage, and all the other marvels of lakes and ladies, and the Round Towers still remaining to perplex the antiquary, and Goldsmith's "Deserted Village," and Goldsmith himself, and the birth-places of Steele and Sterne, and the brief hour of poor Lord Edward Fitzgerald, and Carolan with his harp, and the schools of the poor Latin boys under the hedges, and Castle Rackrent, and Edgeworth's town, and the Giant's Causeway, and Ginleas and other classical poverties, and Spenser's castle on the river Mulla, with the wood-gods whom his pipe drew round him. Ireland is wild ground still; and there are some that would fain keep it so, like a forest to hunt in.

The French map would present us with the woods and warriors of old Gaul, and Lucan's witch; with Charlemaine and his court at Tours; with the siege of Paris by the Saracens, and half the wonders of Italian poetry; with Angelica and Medoro; with the castles of Orlando and Rinaldo, and the traitor Gan; with part of the great forest of Ardenne (Rosalind being in it); with the gentle territory of the Troubadours, and Navarre; with "Love's Labor Lost," and "Vaucluse;" with Petrarch and Laura, and the pastoral scenes of D'Urfé's romance, and the "Men-Wolves" of Brittany, and the "Fairy of Lusignan." Napoleon, also (for he too was a romance), should be drawn as a giant, meeting the allied forces in the neighborhood of Paris.

Italy would be covered with ancient and modern romance; with Homer, Virgil, Ovid, Dante. Boccaccio, &c., with classical villas, and scenes Elysian and infernal. There would be the regions of Saturn, during his Age of Gold, and the old Tuscan cities, and Phæton in the north, and the sirens and fairies at Naples, and Polyphemus in Sicily, with the abodes of Boiardo and Ariosto, and Horace's mount Soracte, and the Cross of St. Peter, and the city in the sea, and the golden scenes of Titian and Raphael, and other names that make us hear the music of their owners: Pythagoras also with his philosophy, and Petrarch with his lute. A circle of stars would tell us where Galileo lived; and the palace of Doria would look more than royal towards the sea.

I dare not, in this hasty sketch, and with limited time before me, indulge myself in other luxuries of recollection, or do anything more than barely mention the names of Spain, Fontarabia, and Cervantes; of Greece; of Persia, and the "Arabian Nights;" of Mount Caucasus and Turkey, and the Gothic north; of El Dorado and Columbus; or the sea-snakes, floating islands, and other marvels of the ocean; not forgetting the Atalantis of Plato, and the regions of Gulliver and Peter Wilkins. Neither can I have the pleasure of being suffocated with contemplating, at proper length, the burning deserts of Africa; or of hearing the ghastly sounds of its old satyrs and Ægipans in their woody hills at night-time, described by Pomponius Mela; or of seeing the stormy Spirit of the Cape, stationed there forever by Camoens, and whose stature on the map would be like a mountain. You will be good enough to take this paper as nothing but a hint of what such a map might contain.

One word, however, respecting a heresy in fictitious belief, which has been uttered by Rousseau, and repeated, I am sorry to say, by our excellent poet Wordsworth, the man of all men who ought not to reduce a matter of fact to what might be supposed to be its poverty. Rousseau, speaking of the banks of the Lignon, where the scene of the old French romance is laid, expresses his disappointment at finding there nothing like the beautiful things he fancied in his childhood; and Mr. Wordsworth in his poem of "Yarrow," Visited and Unvisited, utters a like regret, in speaking of the scene of the "bonny bride—the winsome marrow." I know there is such an opinion abroad, like many other errors; but it does not become men of imagination to give in to it; and I must protest against it, as a flat irreligion. I do not pretend to be as romantic in my conduct as the Genevese philosopher, or as poetical in my nature as the bard of Rydalmount; but I have, by nature, perhaps, greater animal spirits than either; and a bit of health is a fine prism to see fancies by. It may be granted, for the sake of argument, that the book-Lignon and the book-Yarrow are still finer things than the Lignon and Yarrow geographical: but to be actually on the spot, to look with one's own eyes upon the places in which our favorite heroes or heroines underwent the circumstances that made us love them—this may surely make up for an advantage on the side of the description in the book; and, in addition to this, we have the pleasure of seeing how much has been done for the place by love and poetry. I have seen various places in Europe, which have been rendered interesting by great men and their works; and I never found myself the worse for seeing them, but the better. I seem to have made friends with them in their own houses; to have walked, and talked, and suffered, and enjoyed with them; and if their books have made the places better, *the books themselves were*

there which made them so, and which *grew out of them.*
The poet's hand was on the place, blessing it. I can
no more separate this idea from the spot, than I can
take away from it any other beauty. Even in London,
I find the principle hold good in me, though I have
lived there many years, and, of course, associated it
with every commonplace the most unpoetical. The
greater still includes the less: and I can no more pass
through Westminster, without thinking of Milton; or
the Borough, without thinking of Chaucer and Shakspeare: or Gray's Inn, without calling Bacon to mind;
or Bloomsbury Square, without Steele and Akenside—
than I can prefer brick and mortar to wit and poetry,
or not see a beauty upon it beyond architecture, in the
splendor of the recollection. I once had duties to perform, which kept me out late at night, and severely
taxed my health and spirits. My path lay through a
neighborhood in which Dryden lived; and though nothing could be more commonplace, and I used to be
tired to the heart and soul of me, I never hesitated to
go a little out of the way, purely that I might pass
through Gerard Street, and so give myself the shadow
of a pleasant thought.

I am, sir, your cordial well-wisher,
A Lover of Books.

JACK ABBOTT'S BREAKFAST.

Animal spirits.—A Dominie Sampson drawn from the life.—Many things fall out between the (breakfast) cup and the lip.—A magistrate drawn from the life.—Is breakfast ever to be taken, or is it not?—The question answered.

"What a breakfast I *shall* eat !" thought Jack Abbott, as he turned into Middle Temple Lane, towards the chambers of his old friend and tutor, Goodall. "How I shall swill the tea ! how cram down the rolls (especially the inside bits) ! how apologize for 'one cup more !'—But Goodall is an excellent old fellow—he won't mind. To be sure, I'm rather late. The rolls, I'm afraid, wild be cold, or double baked ; but anything will be delicious. If I met a baker, I could eat his basket."

Jack Abbott was a good-hearted, careless fellow, who had walked that morning from Hendon, to breakfast with his old friend by appointment, and afterwards consult his late father's lawyer. He was the son of a clergyman more dignified by rank than by solemnity of manners, but an excellent person too, who had some remorse in leaving a family of sons with little provision, but comforted himself with reflecting that he had gifted them with good constitutions and cheerful natures, and that they would " find their legs somehow," as indeed they all did ; for very good legs they were, whether to dance away care with, or make love with, or walk seven miles to breakfast with, as Jack had done that morning ; and so they all got on accordingly, and clubbed up a comfortable maintenance for the prebendary's widow, who, sanguine and loving as her husband, almost wept out of a fondness of delight, whenever she thought either of their legs or their affection. As to Jack himself, he was the youngest, and at present the least successful, of the brotherhood, having just entered upon a small tutorship in no very rich family ; but his spirits were the greatest in the family (which is saying much), and if he was destined never to prosper so much as any of them in the ordinary sense, he had a relish of every little pleasure that presented itself, and a genius for neutralizing the disagreeable, which at least equalized his fate with theirs.

Well, Jack Abbott has arrived at the door of his friend's room. He knocks ; and it is opened by Goodall himself, a thin grizzled personage, in an old greatcoat instead of a gown, with lantern-jaws, shaggy eyebrows, and a most bland and benevolent expression of countenance. Like many who inhabit Inns of Court, he was not a lawyer. He had been a tutor all his life ; and as he led only a book-existence, he retained the great blessing of it—a belief in the best things which he believed when young. The natural sweetness of his disposition had even gifted him with a politeness of manners which many a better-bred man might have envied ; and though he was a scholar more literal than profound, and, in truth, had not much sounded the depths of anything but his tea-caddy, yet an irrepressible respect for him accompanied the smiling of his friends ; and mere worldly men made no grosser mistake, than in supposing they had a right to scorn him with their uneasy satisfactions and misbelieving success. In a word, he was a sort of better-bred Dominic Sampson—a Goldsmith, with the genius taken out of him, but the goodness left—an angel of the dusty heaven of bookstalls and the British Museum.

Unfortunately for the hero of our story, this angel of sixty-five, unshaved, and with stockings down at heel, had a memory which could not recollect what had been told him six hours before, much less six days. Accordingly, he had finished his breakfast, and given his cat the remaining drop of milk long before his (in every sense of the word) late pupil presented himself within his threshold. Furthermore, besides being a lantern-jawed cherub, he was very short-sighted, and his ears were none of the quickest; so in answer to Jack's " Well—eh—how d' ye do, my dear sir?—I'm afraid I'm very late," he stood holding the door open with one hand, shading his winking eyes with the other, in order to concentrate their powers of investigation, and in the blandest tones of *unawareness* saying—

" Ah, dear me—I'm very—I beg pardon—I really —pray who is it I have the pleasure of speaking to?"

" What! don't you recollect me, my dear sir? Jack Abbott. I met you, you know, and was to come and ——"

"Oh! Mr. Abbott, is it? What—ah—Mr. James Abbott, no doubt—or Robert. My dear Mr. Abbott, to think I should not see you!"

" Yes, my dear sir; and you don't see now that it is Jack, and not James? Jack, your last pupil, who plagued you so in the Terence."

"Not at all, sir, not at all; no Abbott ever plagued me;—far too good and kind people, sir. Come in,

pray; come in and sit down, and let's hear all about
the good lady your mother, and how you all get on,
Mr. James."

"Jack, my dear sir, Jack: but it doesn't signify.
An Abbott is an Abbott, you know; that is, if he is
but fat enough."

Goodall (very gravely, not seeing the joke). " Surely
you are quite fat enough, my dear sir, and in excellent
health. And how is the good lady your mother?"

" Capitally well, sir (*looking at the breakfast table*).
I'm quite rejoiced to see that the breakfast-cloth is not
removed; for I'm horribly late, and fear I must have
put you out; but don't you take any trouble, my good
sir. The kettle, I see, is still singing on the hob. I'll
cut myself a piece of bread and butter immediately;
and you'll let me scramble beside you as I used to do,
and look at a book, and talk with my mouth full."

Goodall. " Ay, ay; what! you have come to breakfast, have you, my kind boy? that is very good of
you, very good indeed. Let me see—let me see—my
laundress has never been here this morning, but you
won't mind my serving you myself—I have everything
at hand."

Abbott (apart, and sighing with a smile). " He has
forgotten all about the invitation! Thank ye, my
dear sir, thank ye—I would apologize, only I know
you wouldn't like it; and to say the truth, I'm very
hungry—hungry as a hunter—I've come all the way
from Hendon."

" Bless me! have you, indeed? and from Wendover
too? Why, that is a very long way, isn't it?"

" Hendon, sir, not Wendover—Hendon."

" Oh, Endor—ah—dear me (*smiling*), I didn't know
there was an Endor in England. I hope there is—

he! he!—no witch there, Mr. Abbott; unless she be some very charming young lady with a fortune."

"Nay, sir, I think you can go nowhere in England, and not meet with charming young ladies."

"Very true, sir, very true—England—what does the poet say? something about 'manly hearts to guard the fair.'—You have no sisters, I think, Mr. Abbott?"

"No; but plenty of female cousins."

"Ah! very charming young ladies, I've no doubt, sir. Well, sir, there's your cup and saucer, and here's some fresh tea, and ——"

"I beg pardon," interrupted Jack, who, in a fury of hunger and thirst, was pouring out what tea he could find in the pot, and anxiously looking for the bread; "I can do very well with this—at any rate to begin with."

"Just so, sir," balmily returned Goodall. "Well, sir, but I am sorry to see—eh, I really fear—certainly the cat—eh—what are we to do for milk? I'm afraid I must make you wait till I step out for some; for this laundress, when once she ——"

"Don't stir, I beg you," ejaculated our hero; "don't think of it, my dear sir. I can do very well without milk—I can indeed—I *often* do without milk."

This was said out of an intensity of a sense to the contrary; but Jack was anxious to make the old gentleman easy.

"Well," quoth Goodall, "I have met with such instances, to be sure; and very lucky it is, Mr.—a— John—James I should say—that you do not care for milk; though I confess, for my part, I cannot do without it. But, bless me! heyday! well, if the sugar-basin, dear me, is not empty. Bless my soul, I'll go

instantly—it is but as far as Fleet Street—and my hat,
I think, must be under those pamphlets."

"Don't think of such a thing, pray, dear sir," cried
Jack, half leaping from his chair, and tenderly laying
his hand on his arm. "You may think it odd; but
sugar, I can assure you, is a thing I don't *at all* care
for. Do you know, my dear Mr. Goodall, I have often
had serious thoughts of leaving off sugar, owing to the
slave-trade?"

"Why that, indeed ——"

"Yes, sir; and probably I should have done it, had
not so many excellent men, yourself among them,
thought fit to continue the practice, no doubt after the
greatest reflection. However, what with these perhaps
foolish doubts, and the indifference of my palate to
sweets, sugar is a mere drug to me, sir—a mere drug."

"Well, but ——"

"Nay, dear sir, you will distress me if you say another word upon the matter—you will indeed : see how
I drink." (And here Jack made as if he took a hasty
gulp of his milkless and sugarless water.) "The bread,
my dear sir—the bread is all I require ; just that piece
which you were going to take up. You remember
how I used to stuff bread, and fill the book I was reading with crumbs? I dare say the old Euripides is
bulging out with them now."

"Well, sir—ah— em—ah—well, indeed, you're very
good, and, I'm sure, very temperate ; but, dear me—
well, this laundress of mine—I must certainly get rid
of her thieving—rheumatism. I should say ; but *butter!*
I vow I do not ——"

"Butter!" interrupted our hero, in a tone of the
greatest scorn. "Why I haven't eaten *butter* I don't
know when. Not a step, sir, not a step. And now

let me tell you I must make haste, for I've got to lunch
with my lawyer, and he'll expect me to eat something;
and in fact I'm so anxious, and feel so hurried, that
now I have eaten a good piece of my hunk, I must be
off, my good sir—I must, indeed."

To say the truth, Jack's hunk was a good three days
old, if an hour ; and so hard,* that even his hunger and
fine teeth could not find it in the hearts of them to relish it with the cold slop ; so he had made up his mind
to seek the nearest coffee-house as fast as possible,
and there have the heartiest and most luxurious breakfast that could make amends for his disappointment.
After reconciling the old gentleman, however, to his
departure, he sat a little longer, out of decency and respect, listening, with a benevolence equal to his appe-
tite, to the perusal of a long passage in Cowley, which
Goodall had been reading when he arrived, and the
recitation of which was prolonged by the inflictor with
admiring repetitions, and bland luxuriations of com-
ment.

"What an excellent good fellow he is !" thought
Jack ; "and what a very unshaved face he has, and
neglectful washerwoman !"

At length he found it the more easy to get away,
inasmuch as Goodall said he was himself in the habit
of going out about that time to a coffee-house to look
at the papers before he went the round of his pupils;
but he had to shave first, and would not detain Mr.
Abbott, if he *must* go.

---

* People of regular comfortable lives, breakfasts, and conveniences,
must be cautious how they take pictures like these for caricatures.
The very letter of the adventure above described, with the exception of
a few words, has actually happened. And so, with the same difference,
has that of the sheep and hackney-coach, narrated in the " Disasters
of Carfington Blundell."

Being once more out of doors, our hero rushes back like a tiger into Fleet Street, and plunges into the first coffee-house in sight.

" Waiter !"

" *Yessir.*"

" Breakfast immediately. Tea, black and green, and all that."

" *Yessir.* Eggs and toast, sir ?"

" By all means."

" *Yessir.* Any ham, sir ?"

" Just so, and instantly."

" *Yessir.* Cold fowl, sir ?"

" Precisely ; and no delay."

" *Yessir.* Anchovy perhaps, sir ?"

" By all—eh ?—no, I don't care for anchovy—but pray bring what you like ; and above all, make haste. my good fellow—no delay—I'm as hungry as the devil."

" *Yessir*—coming directly, sir. ('Good chap and great fool,' said the waiter to himself.) Like the newspaper, sir ?"

" Thankye. Now for Heaven's sake——"

" *Yessir*—immediately, sir—everything ready, sir."

" Everything ready !" thought Jack. " Cheering sound ! Beautiful place a coffee-house ! Fine *English* place—everything so snug and at hand—so comfortable—so easy—have what you like, and without fuss. What a breakfast I *shall* eat ! And the paper too—hum, hum (*reading*)—Horrid Murder—Mysterious Affair—Express from Paris—Assassination—intense. Bless me ! what horrible things—how very comfortable. What toast I——Waiter !"

Waiter, from a distance. " *Yessir*—coming, sir."

In a few minutes everything is served up—the toast hot and rich—eggs plump—ham huge, &c.

"You've another slice of toast getting ready?" said Jack.

"*Yessir.*"

"Let the third, if you please, be thicker; and the fourth."

"Glorious moment!" inwardly ejaculated our hero. He had doubled the paper conveniently, so as to read the "Express from Paris" in perfect comfort; and before he poured out his tea, he was in the act of putting his hand to one of the inner pieces of toast, when—awful visitation!—whom should he see passing the window, with the evident design of turning into the coffee-house, but his too-carelessly and swiftly shaved friend Goodall. He was coming, of course, to read the papers. Yes, such was his horrible inconvenient practice, as Jack had too lately heard him say; and this, of all coffee-houses in the world, was the one he must needs go to.

What was to be done? Jack Abbott, who was not at all a man of manœuvres, much less gifted with that sort of impudence which can risk hurting another's feelings, thought there was nothing left for him but to bolt; and accordingly, after hiding his face with the newspaper till Goodall had taken up another, he did so as if a bailiff was after him, brushing past the waiter who had brought it him, and who had just seen another person out. The waiter, to his astonishment sees him plunge into another coffee-house over the way; then hastens back to see if anything be missing; and finding all safe, concludes he must have run over to speak to some friend, perhaps upon some business suddenly called to mind, especially as he seemed " such a hasty gentleman."

Meanwhile, Jack, twice exasperated with hunger, but congratulating himself that he had neither been seen by Goodall, nor tasted a breakfast unpaid for, has ordered precisely such another breakfast, and has got the same newspaper, and seated himself as nearly as possible in the very same sort of place.

" *Now*," thought he, " I am beyond the reach of chance. No such ridiculous hazard as this can find me here. Goodall cannot read the papers in two coffee-houses. By Jove! was there ever a man so hungry as I am? What a breakfast I *shall* eat!"

Enter breakfast served up as before—toast hot and rich—eggs plump—ham huge, &c. Homer himself, who was equally fond of a repetition and a good meal, would have liked to re-describe it. " Glorious moment!" Jack has got the middle bit of toast in his fingers, precisely as before, when happening to cast his eye at the door, he sees the waiter of the former coffee-house pop his head in, look him full in the face, and as suddenly withdraw it. Back goes the toast on the plate ; up springs poor Abbott to the door, and hardly taking time to observe that his visitant is not in sight, rushes forth for the second time, and makes out as fast as he can for a third coffee-house.

" Am I *never* to breakfast?" thought he. " Nay, breakfast I will. People can't go into three coffee-houses on purpose to go out again. But suppose the dog should have seen me! Not likely, or I should have seen him again. He may have gone and told the people ; but I've hardly got out of the second coffee-house before I've found a third. Bless this confounded Fleet Street—Most convenient place for

diving in and out of coffee-houses! Dr. Johnson's
street—'High tide of human existence'—ready breakfasts.   What a breakfast I *will* eat !"

Jack Abbott, after some delay, owing to the fulness
of the room, is seated as before—the waiter has
yessir'd to their mutual content—the toast is done—
Homeric repetition—eggs plump, ham huge, &c.

"By Hercules, who was the greatest twist of antiquity, what a breakfast I *will*, shall, must, and have
now certainly *got* to eat !   I could not have stood it
any longer.   Now, *now*, now, is the moment of moments."

Jack Abbott has put his hand to the toast.

Unluckily, there were three pair of eyes which had
been observing him all the while from over the curtain
of the landlord's little parlor ; to-wit, the waiter's of
the first tavern, the waiter's of the second, and the
landlord's of the third.   The two waiters had got in
time to the door of tavern the second, to watch his
entrance into tavern the third ; and both communi-
cating the singular fact to the landlord of the same,
the latter resolved upon a certain mode of action,
which was now to develop itself.

" Well," said the first waiter, " I've seen strange
chaps in my time in coffee-houses ; but this going
about, ordering breakfasts which a man doesn't eat,
beats everything ! and he hasn't taken a spoon or anything as I see.   He doesn't seem to be looking about
him, you see ; he reads the paper as quiet as an old
gentleman."

" Just for all the world as he did in our house," said
the second waiter ; "and he's very pleasant and easy-
like in his ways."

" Pleasant and easy !" cried the landlord, whose

general scepticism was sharpened by gout and a late loss of spoons. "Yes, yes; I've seen plenty of your pleasant and easy fellows—palavering rascals, who come, hail-fellow-well-met, with a bit of truth mayhap in their mouths, just to sweeten a parcel of lies and swindling. 'Twas only last Friday I lost a matter of fifty shillings' worth of plate by such a chap; and I vowed I'd nab the next. Only let him eat one mouthful, just to give a right o' search, and see how I'll pounce on him."

But Jack didn't eat one mouthful! No; not even though he was uninterrupted, and really had now a fair field before him, and was in the very agonies of hunger. It so happened, that he had hardly taken up the piece of toast above mentioned, when with a voluntary (as it seemed) and strange look of misgiving, *he laid it down again!*

"I'm blessed if he's touched it, after all," said waiter the first. "Well, this beats everything! See how he looks about him! He's feeling in his pockets though."

"Ah, look at that!" says the landlord. "He's a precious rascal, depend on't. I shouldn't wonder if he whisk'd something out of the next box; but we'll nab him. Let us go to the door."

Mr. Abbott—Jack seems too light an appellation for one under his circumstances—looked exceedingly distressed. He gazed at the toast with a manifest sigh; then glanced cautiously around him; then again felt his pockets. At length, he positively showed symptoms of quitting his seat. It was clear he did not intend eating a bit of this breakfast, any more than of the two others.

" I'll be hanged if he ain't going to bolt again," said the waiter.

" Nab him !" said the landlord.

The unhappy, and, as he thought, secret Abbott makes a desperate movement to the door, and is received into the arms of this triple alliance.

" Search his pockets!" cried the landlord.

" Three breakfasts, and ne'er a one of 'em eaten !" cried first waiter.

" Breakfasts afore he collects his spoons," cried second.

Our hero's pockets were searched almost before he was aware ; and nothing found but a book in an unknown language, and a pocket handkerchief. He encouraged the search, however, as soon as his astonishment allowed him to be sensible of it, with an air of bewildered resignation.

" He's a Frenchman," said first waiter.

" He hasn't a penny in his pockets," said second.

" What a villain !" said the landlord.

" You're under a mistake—you are, upon my soul !" cried poor Jack.   " I grant it's odd ; but ——"

" Bother and stuff !" said the landlord ; " where did you put my spoons last Friday ?"

" Spoons !" echoed Jack ; " why I haven't eaten even a bit of your breakfast."

By this time all the people in the coffee-room had crowded into the passage, and a plentiful mob was gathering at the door.

" Here's a chap has had three breakfasts this morning," exclaimed the landlord, " and eat ne'er a one !"

" Three breakfasts !" cried a broad, dry-looking gentleman in spectacles, with a deposition-taking sort of face; "how could he possibly do that? and why did you serve him?"

"Three breakfasts in three different houses, I tell you," said the landlord; "he's been to *my* house; and to *this* man's house; and to *this* man's; and we've searched him, and he hasn't a penny in his pocket."

"That's it," exclaimed Jack, who had, in vain, tried to be heard; "that's the very reason."

"What's the very reason?" said the gentleman in spectacles.

"Why, I was shock'd to find, just now, that I had left my purse at home, in the hurry of coming out, and ——"

"Oh! oh!" cried the laughing audience; "here's the policeman: he'll settle him."

"But how does that explain the two other breakfasts?" returned the gentleman.

"Not at all," said Jack.

"Impudent rascal!" said the landlord. Here the policeman is receiving a bye explanation, while Jack is raising his voice to proceed.

"I mean," said he, "that *that* doesn't explain it; but I can explain it."

"Well, how, my fine fellow?" said the gentleman, hushing the angry landlord, who had, meanwhile, given our hero in charge.

"Don't lay hands on me, any of you," cried our hero; "I'll go quietly anywhere, if you let me alone; but first let me explain."

"Hear him, hear him!" cried the spectators; "and watch your pockets."

Here Jack, reasonably thinking that nothing would help him out if the truth did not, but not aware that the truth does not always have its just effect, especially

when of an extraordinary description, gave a rapid,
but reverent statement of the character of his friend
in the neighborhood, whose breakfast had been so inefficient; then an account (all which excited laughter
and derision) of his going into the first coffee-house,
and seeing his friend come in (which, nevertheless,
had a great effect on the first waiter, who knew the
old gentleman), and so on of his subsequent proceed-
ings; a development which succeeded in pacifying
both the waiters, who had, in fact, lost nothing; so,
coming to an understanding with one another, they
slipped away, much to the anger and astonishment of
the landlord. This personage, whose whole man,
since he left off their active life, had become affected
with drams and tit-bits, and whose irritability was ag-
gravated by the late loss of his spoons, persisted in
giving poor unbreakfasted Jack in charge, especially
when he found that he would not send for a character
to the friend he had been speaking of, and that he had
no other in town but a lawyer, who lived at the end
of it. And so off goes our hero to the police-office.

" You, perhaps, any more than my irritable friend
here, don't know the sort of literary old gentleman I
have been speaking of," said Jack to the policeman, as
they were moving along.

" Can't say I do, sir," said the policeman, a highly
respectable individual of his class, clean as a pink, and
dull as a pike-staff.

" No, nor no one else ;" said the landlord. " Who's
a man as can't be sent for ? He's neither here nor
there."

" That's true enough," observed Jack ; " he's in
Rome or Greece by this time, at some pupil's house ;
but, wherever he is, I can't send to him. With what

face could I do it, even if possible, in the midst of all
this fuss about a breakfast?"

"Fuss about white broth, you mean?" said the landlord; "my Friday spoons are prettily melted about
this time; but Mr. Kingsley will fetch all that out."

"Then he will be an alchemist, cunninger than
Raymond Lully," said our hero. "But what is your
charge, pray, after all?"

"False pretences, sir," said the policeman.

"False pretences!"

"Yes, sir. You comes, you see, into the gentleman's
house under the pretence of eating breakfast, and has
none; and that's false pretences."

"That is, supposing I intended them to be false."

"Yes, sir. In course I don't mean to say as—I only
says what the gentleman says.—Every man by law is
held innocent till he's found guilty."

"You are a very civil, reasonable man," said our
warm-hearted hero, grateful at this unlooked for ad-
admittance of something possible in his favor; "I respect you. I have no money, nor even a spoon to beg
your acceptance of; but pray take this book. It's of
no use to me; I've another copy."

"Mayn't take anything in the execution of my office," said the man, giving a glance at the landlord, as
if he might have done otherwise, had he been out of
the way; "thank'e all the same, sir; but ain't allowed
to have no *targiwarsation.*"

"Yet your duties are but scantily paid, I believe,"
said Jack. "However, you've a capital breakfast, no
doubt, before you set out?"

"Not by the reg'lations, sir," said the policeman.

"But you have by seven or eight o'clock?" said
Jack, smiling at his joke.

"Oh, yes, tight enough, as to that," answered the policeman, smiling; for the subject of eating rouses the wits of everybody.

" Hot toast, eggs, and all that, I suppose," said Jack, heaving a sigh betwixt mirth and calamity.

" Can't say I take eggs," returned the other; " but I takes a bit o' cold meat, and a good lot o' bread and butter." And here he looked radiant with the reminiscence.

" Lots of bread and butter," thought Jack; " what bliss! I'll have bread and butter when I breakfast, not toast—it's more hearty—and, besides, you get it sooner: bread is sooner spread than toasted—thick, thick—I hear the knife plastering the edge of the crust before it cuts. Agony of expectation! When *shall* I breakfast?"

" The office !" cried the landlord, hurrying forward; and in two minutes, our hero found himself in a crowded room, in which presided the all-knowing and all-settling Mr. Kingsley. This gentleman, who died not long after policemen came up, was the last lingering magistrate of the old school. He was a shortish stout man in powder, with a huge vinous face, a hasty expression of countenance, Roman nose, and large lively black eyes; and he always kept his hat on, partly for the most dignified reason in the world, because he represented the sovereign magistracy, and partly for the most undignified; to wit, a cold in the head; for to this visitation he had a perpetual tendency, owing to the wine he took over-night, and the draughts of air which beset him every morning in the police office. Irritability was his weak side, like the landlord's; but then, agreeably to the inconsistency in that case made and provided, he was very intolerant

of the weakness in others. To sum up his character,
he was very loyal to his king ; had a great reverence
for all the by-gone statesmen of his youth, especially
such as were orators and lords ; indeed, had no little
tendency to suppose all rich men respectable, and to
let them escape too easily if brought before him ; but
was severe in proportion with what are called " decent" men and tradesmen, and very kind to the poor:
and if he loved anything better than his dignity, it was
a good bottle of port, and an ode of Horace. He had
not the wit of a Fielding or Dubois ; but he had a
spice of their scholarship ; and while taking his wine,
would nibble you the beginnings of half the odes of his
favorite poet, as other men do a cake or biscuit.

To our hero's dismay, a considerable delay took
place before the landlord's charge could be heard.
Time flew, hunger pressed, breakfast drew farther off,
and the son of the jovial prebendary learned what it
was to feel the pangs of the want of a penny, for he
could not buy even a roll. " Immortal Goldsmith !"
thought he ; " poor Savage ! amazing Chatterton ! pathetic Otway.! fine, old, lay-bishop Johnson ! venerable, surly man ! is it possible that you ever felt this !
felt it to-morrow too ; and next day ; and next ! Ill
does it become *me* then, Jack Abbott, to be impatient ;
and yet, O table-cloth ! O thick slices ! O tea ! when
shall I breakfast ?"

The case at length was brought on, and the testi-
mony of the absent witnesses admitted by our hero
with a nonchalance which disgusted the magistrate,
and began to rouse his bile. What irritated him the
more was, that he saw there would be no proving anything, unless the criminal (whom for the very innocence of his looks he took for an impudent offender)

should somehow or other commit himself; which he
thought not very likely. In fact, as nothing had been
eaten, and nothing found on the person, there was no
real charge ; and Mr. Kingsley had a very particular
secret reason, as we shall see presently, why he could
not help feeling that there was one point strongly in
the defendant's favor. But this only served to irritate
him the more.

"Well now, you sir—Mr. What'syourname," quoth
he, in a huffing manner, and staring from under his
hat ; "what is your wonderful explanation of this very
extraordinary habit of taking three breakfasts : eh,
sir ? You seem mighty cool upon it."

"Sir," answered our hero, whose good-nature gifted
him with a certain kind of address, "it is out of no disrespect to yourself that I am cool. You may well be
surprised at the circumstances under which I find myself; but in addressing a gentleman and a man of understanding, and giving him a plain statement of the
facts, I have no doubt he will discover a veracity in it
which escapes eyes less discerning."

Here the landlord, who instinctively saw the effect
which this exordium would have upon Kingsley, could
not help muttering the word "palaver," loud enough to
be heard.

"Silence !" exclaimed the magistrate. "Keep your
vulgar words to yourself, sir. And hark'e, sir, take
your hat off, sir ! How dare you come into this office
with your hat on ?"

"Sir, I have a very bad cold, and I thought that in
a public office——"

"Sir," returned Kingsley, who was doubly offended
at this excuse about the cold, "think us none of your
thoughts, sir. Public office ! Public-house, I suppose

you mean. Nobody wears his hat in this office but myself; and I only do it as the representative of a greater power. Hat, indeed! I suppose some day or other we shall all have the privilege of my Lord Kinsale, and wear our hats in the royal presence."

Jack gave his account of the whole matter, which, from a certain ignorance it exhibited of the ways of the town, did appear a little romantic to his interrogator; but the latter, besides knowing our hero's lawyer, was not unacquainted with the character of Goodall, "who," said he, "is known to everybody."

"Probably, sir;" observed the landlord, "but for that reason may not this person have heard of him, and so pretend to be his acquaintance? He calls himself Abbott, but that is not the name in the French book he's got about him."

"Let me see the book," cried Kingsley. "French book! It is a Latin book, and a very good book too, and an Elzevir. '*E libris Caroli Gibson*, 1743.'—A pretty age for the person before us truly—a very hale, hearty young gentleman, some ninety years old, or thereabouts. (Here a laugh all over the office; which, together with the sight of the Horace, put Kingsley into the greatest good-humor.) You are thinking, I guess, Mr.—a—Abbott, of the '*Odi profanum vulgus*,' I take it; and wishing you could add, '*et arceo*.'"*

"Why, to tell the truth," answered Jack, "I cannot deny a wish to that effect; but my main thought, for these five hours past, has been rather of the '*Nunc est bibendum*'†—only substituting teacups for goblets."

"Very good, sir, very good; and doubtless you ad-

---

* I hate the profane vulgar,—and drive them away.
† Now for drinking.

mire the '*Persicos odi*,' and the '*Quid dedicatum*,' and that beautiful ode, the ' *Vides ut altâ?*' "*

"I do, indeed," said Jack ; "and I trust that one of your favorites, like mine, is the ' *Integer vitæ sceleris-que purus?*'"

> " ' *Non eget Mauri jaculis neque arcu* '

(added Kingsley, unable to avoid going on with the quotation)

> " ' *Nec venenatis gravidâ sagittis,*
> *Fusce, pharetrâ.*'

There's something very charming in that ' *Fusce pha-retrâ*'—so short and pithy, and elegant ; and then the pleasant, social familiarity of *Fusce*."

" Just so," said Jack ; " you hit the true relish of it to a nicety ."

"*Fussy fair-eater!*" muttered the landlord. " A great deal more *fuss* than *fair eating*. My time's lost —that's certain."

Kingsley could not resist a few more returns to his favorite pages; but suddenly recollecting himself, he looked grand and a little turbulent, and said—

" Well, Mr.—a—Landlord—What'syourname,— what's the charge here, after all ? for, on my conscience, I cannot see any ; and, for my part, I thoroughly believe the gentleman ; and I'll give you another reason for it, besides knowing this Mr. Goodall. It may not be thought very dignified in me to own it, but dignity must give way to justice—' *Fiat justitia, ruat cœlum*' —and to say the truth I, I myself, Mr. Landlord— whatever you may think of the confession—came from home this morning without remembering my purse."

---

* Various beginnings of other Odes.

In short, the upshot was, that the worthy magistrate, seeing Bidd's impatience at this confession, and warming the more towards his Horatian friend, not only proceeded to throw the greatest ridicule on the charge, but gave Jack a note to the nearest tavern-keeper, desiring him to furnish the gentleman with a breakfast at his expense, and stating the reason why. He then proclaimed aloud, as he was directing it, what he had done; and added, that he should be very happy to see so intelligent and very innocent a young gentleman, whenever he chose to call upon him.

With abundance of acknowledgments, and in raptures at the now certain approach of the bread and butter, Jack made his way out of the office, and proceeded for the tavern.

"At *last* I have thee !" cried he, internally, "O, most fugacious of meals—what a repast I will make of it ! What a breakfast I *shall* have? Never will a breakfast have been so *intensified*."

Jack Abbott, with the note in his hand, arrived at the tavern, went up the steps, hurried through the passage Every inch of the way was full of hope and bliss. He sees the bar in an angle round the corner, and is hastening into it with the magical document, when lo ! whom should his eyes light on but the plaintiff, Bidds himself, detailing his version of the story to the new landlord, and evidently poisoning his mind with every syllable.

Our modest, albeit not timid, hero, raging with hunger as he was, could not stand this. A man of more confident face might not unreasonably have presented his note, and stood the brunt of the uncomfortableness ; but Jack Abbott, with all his apparent thoughtlessness, had one of those natures which feel

for the improprieties of others, even when they themselves have no sense of them ; and he had not the heart
to outface the vindictiveness of Bidds.   To say the
truth, Bidds, who was a dull fellow, had some reason
to be suspicious ; and Jack felt this too, and retreating
accordingly, made haste to take the long step to his
lawyer's.

   " Now the lawyer," quoth he, soliloquizing, " I have
never seen ; but he was an intimate friend of my
father's ; so intimate, that I can surely take a household
liberty with him, and fairly accept his breakfast, if he
offers it, as of course he will ; and I shall plainly tell
him that I prefer breakfast to lunch ; in short, that I
have made up my mind to have it, even if I wait till
dinner-time, or tea-time ; and he'll laugh, and we shall
be jolly, and so I shall get my breakfast at last.   Exquisite moment !   What a breakfast I *shall* have !"   •

   The lawyer, Mr. Pallinson, occupied a good large
house, with the marks of plenty on it.   Jack hailed
the sight of the fire blazing in the kitchen.   " Delicious
spot !" thought he ; " kettle, pantry, and all that—comfortable maid-servant too ; hope she has milk left, and
will cut the bread and butter.   A home too—good
family house.   Sure of being comfortable there.
Taverns not exactly what I took 'em for—not hospi-
table—not *fiducial*—don't trust ; don't know an honest
man when they see him.   What slices !"

   But a little baulk presented itself.   Jack unfortunately rang at the *office*-bell instead of the *house*, and
found himself among a parcel of clerks.   Mr. Pallinson was out—not expected at home till evening—had
gone to Westminster on special business—and at such
times always dined at the Mendip coffee-house.   Jack,
in desperation, fairly stated his case.   No result but

"Strange, indeed, sir," from one of the clerks, and a general look-up from their desks on the part of the others. Not a syllable of " Won't you stop, sir?" or, " The servant can easily give you breakfast;" or any of those fond succedaneums for the master's presence, which our hero's simplicity had fancied. Furthermore, no Mrs. Pallinson existed, to whom he might have applied: and he had not the face to ask for any minor goddess of the household. Blushing, and stammering a " Good-morning," he again found himself in the wide world of pavement and houses. He had got, however, his lawyer's direction at the coffee-house, and thither accordingly he betook himself, retracing great part of his melancholy steps.

Had our hero, instead of having passed his time at college and in the country, been at all used to living in London, he would have set himself down comfortably at once in this or any other coffee-house, ordered what he pleased, and dispatched a messenger in the meanwhile to anybody he wanted. But under all the circumstances, he was resolved, for fear of encountering further disappointment, to endure whatsoever pangs remained to him for the rest of the time, and wait till he saw his solicitor come in to dinner. In vain the waiters gave him all encouragement—" Knew Mr. Pallinson well"—" A most excellent gentleman" —had " recommended many gentlemen to their house." —" Would you like anything, sir, before he comes?"— " Like to look at the paper?" and the paper was laid, huge and crisp, before him.

" Ah!" thought Jack with a sigh, " I know that sound—no, I'll certainly wait. Five o'clock isn't far off, and then I'm certain. What a breakfast I shall now have, when it *does* come. I'll wait, if I die first, so as to have it in perfect comfort."

At length five o'clock strikes, and almost at the same moment enters Mr. Pallinson. He was a brisk, good-humored man, who had the happy art of throwing off business with the occasion for it; and he acknowledged our hero's claims at once, in a jovial voice, "from his likeness to his excellent friend, the prebendary."

"Don't say a word more, my dear sir—not a word; your eyes and face tell all. Here, John, plates for two. You'll dine of course with your father's old friend? or would you like a private room?"

Jack's heart felt itself at home at once with this cordiality. He said he was very thankful for the offer of the private room, especially for a reason which he would explain presently. Having entered it, he opened into the history of his morning; and by laughing himself, warranted Pallinson in the bursts of laughter which he would have had the greatest difficulty to restrain. But the good and merry lawyer, who understood both a joke and a comfort to the depth, entered heartily into Jack's whim of still having his breakfast, and it was accordingly brought up—not, however, without a guarded explanation on the part of the Westminster-hall man, who had a professional dislike to seeing anybody committed in the eyes of the ignorant; so he told the waiter, that "his friend here had got up so late, and kept such fashionable hours, he must needs breakfast while himself was dining." The waiter bowed with great respect; "and so," says the shrewd attorney, "no harm's done; and now, my dear Mr. Abbott, peg away."

Jack needed not this injunction to lay his hand upon the prey. The bread and butter was now actually before him; not so thick, indeed, as he had pictured to himself; but there it was, real, right-earnest bread and butter; and since the waiter had turned his back, three slices could be rolled into one, and half of the coy aggregation clapped into the mouth at once. The lump was accordingly made, the fingers whisked it up, and the mouth was ready opened to swallow, when the waiter again throws open the door—

"Mr. Goodall, sir."

"Breakfast is abolished with me," thought Jack. "there's no such thing. Henceforward I shall not attempt it."

The prebendary, the lawyer, and Goodall were all well known to each other; but this is not what had brought him hither. The waiter at his coffee-house, where he went to read the papers, and where Jack had had his first mischance, had returned home before the old gentleman had finished his morning's journal, and told him what, to his dusty apprehension, appeared the most confused and unaccountable story in the world, of Mr. Abbott having ordered three breakfasts and been taken to jail. In his benevolent uneasiness, he could hardly get through his day's work, which unfortunately called him so far as Hackney; but as soon as it was over, he hastened in a coach to Pallinson's, and coming there just after Jack had gone, had followed him, in less uneasiness of mind, to the tavern.

"Well, sir—eh, sir? why, my dear Mr. Abbott— John—James I should say—why, what a dance you have led me to find you out! and very glad I am, I'm sure, sir, to find you so comfortably situated with our good friend here, after the story which that foolish, half-witted fellow, William, told me at the coffee-house. Well, sir—eh—and now—I beg pardon—but pray

what is it, and can I do anything for you? I suppose
not—eh—ah? for here's our excellent friend Mr. Pallinson—*he* does everything of that sort—bailiff and
house—yes, sir, and no doubt it's all right—only, if I
am wanted, you'll say so, sir—eh—ah—well—but
don't let me interrupt your *tea*, I beg."

"Luckiest of innocent fancies!" thought our hero,
relieved from a load of misgiving. "He thinks I'm at
tea!"

Jack plunged again at the bread and butter, and at
last actually realized it in his mouth. His calamities
were over! He was in the act of breakfasting!

"I'm afraid, too," said Goodall,—"eh, my dear sir?
—that the very sparing breakfast you took at my chambers—eh—ah—my, my dear Mr. John—must have
contributed not a little to—to—yes, sir. Well, but
pray now what was the trouble you had, of which that
foolish fellow told me such flams? I'm afraid—yes,
indeed—I've had great fears sometimes that he ventures to tell me stories—things untrue, sir."

"God bless him and you, both of you," thought Abbott. "You're a delicious fellow.—Why, my dear,
good sir," continued he, always eating, and at the same
time racking his brains for an invention.—"I beg your
pardon—I'm eating a little too fast——"

Here he made signs of uneasiness in the throat.

"The fact is," said Pallinson, coming to the rescue,
(for he knew that the whole business would fade from
Goodall's mind next day, or be remembered so dimly
that the waiter would hear no more of it), "the fact is,
Mr. Abbott met *me* in Temple Lane, where I had been
summoned on business so early, that I had not breakfasted; and he said he would order breakfast for me at

your coffee-house; and I not coming, he came out to look for me, and found me discussing a matter at another tavern-door, with a policeman, who had been sent for to take up a swindler; and hence, my good sir, all this stuff about the jail and the two breakfasts, for there were only two; but you know how stories accumulate."

"Very deplorably, indeed, sir," said Goodall; "it always was so, and—eh—ah—yes, sir—I fear always will be."

"I beg pardon," interrupted Jack; "but may I trouble you for that loaf? These slices are very thin, and I'm so ravenously hungry, that ——"

"Glorious moment!" The inward ejaculation was at last a true one. The sturdy slices beautifully made their appearance from under the sharp, robust-going, and butter-plastering knife of Jack Abbott. Even the hot toast was called for—Goodall having "vowed" he'd take his tea also, since they were all three met. The eggs were also contrived, and plump went the spoon upon their tops in the egg-cup. The huge ham furthermore was not wanting. And then the well-filled and thrice-filled breakfast-cup;—excellent was its strong and well-milked tea, between black and green, " with an eye of tawny in it;" something with a body, although most liquidly refreshing. Jack doubled his thick slices; he took huge bites; he swilled his tea, as he had sworn in thought he would; and he had the eggs on one side of him, and the ham on the other, and his friends before him, and was as happy as a prince escaped into a foreign land (for no prince in possession knows such moments as these); and when he had at length finished, talking and laughing all the while, or hearing talk and laugh, he pushed the breakfast-cup aside, and said to himself,

"I'VE HAD IT !—BREAKFAST hath been mine !—And now, my dear Mr. Pallinson, I'll take a glass of your port."

ON SEEING A PIGEON MAKE LOVE.

Ut albulus columbus, aut Adoneus?

CATULLUS.

Which is he? Pigeon, or Adonis?

French intermixture of prose and verse.—Courtship of Pigeons.—A word in pity for rakes.—Story of one baffled.—Instinctive sameness of the conduct of the lower animals questioned.—Pope's opinion respecting instinct and reason.—Human Improvability.—Fitness of some of the lower animals for going to heaven not less conceivable than that of some others.—Doves at Maiano.—Ovid's Bird-Elysium.

THE French have a lazy way, in some of their compositions, of writing prose and verse alternately. The author, whenever it is convenient for him to be inspired, begins dancing away in rhyme. The fit over, he goes on as before, as if nothing had happened. We have essays in prose and verse by Cowley (a delightful book) in which the same piece contains both; but with one exception, they are rather poems with long prefaces.

If ever this practice is allowable, it is to a periodical writer in love with poetry. He is obliged to write prose; he is tormented with the desire of venting himself in rhyme; he rhymes, and has not leisure to go on. Behold us, as a Frenchman would say, with our rhyme and our reason!

The following verses were suggested by a sight of a pigeon making love. The scene took place in a large sitting-room, where a beau might have followed a lady up and down with as bustling a solicitation: he could not have done it with more. The birds had been brought there for sale; but they knew no more of this than two lovers whom destiny has designs upon. The gentleman was as much at his ease as if he had been a Bond-street lounger pursuing his fair in a solitary street. We must add, as an excuse for the abruptness of the exordium, that the house belonged to a poet of our acquaintance, who was in the room at the same time.*

Is not the picture strangely like?
Doesn't the very bowing strike?
Can any art of love in fashion
Express a more prevailing passion?
That air—that sticking to her side—
That deference, ill concealing pride,—
That seeming consciousness of coat,
And repetition of one note,—
Ducking and tossing back his head,
As if at every bow he said,
" Madam, by Heaven,"—or " Strike me dead."

And then the lady! look at her:
What bridling sense of character!
How she declines, and seems to go,
Yet still endures him to and fro;
Carrying her plumes and pretty clothings,
Blushing stare, and mutter'd nothings,
Body plump, and airy feet,
Like any charmer in a street.

Give him a hat beneath his wing,
And is not he the very thing?
Give her a parasol or plaything,
And is not she the very she-thing?

---

* Lord Byron. The house was the Casa Saluzzi, at Albaro near Genoa.

Our companion, who had run the round of the great world, seemed to be rather mortified than otherwise at this spectacle. It was certainly calculated, at first blush, to damp the pride of the circles; but upon reflection, it seemed to afford a considerable lift to beaux and belles in ordinary. It seemed to show how much of instinct, and of the common unreflecting course of things, there is even in the gallantries of those who flatter themselves that they are vicious. Nobody expects wisdom in these persons; and if they can be found to be less guilty than is supposed, the gain is much: for, as to letting the dignity of human nature depend upon theirs, on the one hand, or expecting to bring about any change in their conduct by lecturing them on their faults, on the other, it is a speculation equally hopeless.

If a man of pleasure "about town" is swayed by anything, it is by a fear of becoming ridiculous. If he must continue in his old courses, it is pleasant to know him for what he is, and that pigeons are not confined to the gaming-table.

We followed once a young man of fashion in and out a variety of streets at the west end of the town, through which he was haunting a poor blushing damsel, who appeared to be at once distressed by him and endangered. We thought she seemed to be wishing for something to turn the scale in favor of her self-denial; and we resolved to furnish it. Could the consequences of his success have rested entirely with himself, we saw enough of the *pigeon* in him not to have been so ill-bred as to "spoil sport;" but considering, as times go, that what is sport to the gentleman in these cases is very often death to the lady, we found ourselves compelled to be rude and conscientious. In

vain he looked round every now and then, putting on
his best astonishment, and cursing, no doubt, "the in-
delicacy of the fellow." There we were, low and in-
solent,—sticking to his skirts, wondering whether he
would think us of importance enough for a challenge,
and by what bon-mot or other ingenious baffling of his
resentment, we should contrive at once to save our life
and the lady. At length, he turns abruptly across the
street, and we followed the poor girl, till she was at a
safe distance. We caught but one other glimpse of her
face, which was as red as scarlet. We fancied, when
all was safe, that some anger against her deliverer
might mingle with her blushes, and were obliged to
encourage ourselves against a sort of shame for our
interference. We wished we could have spoken to
her; but this was impossible; nay, considering the
mutual tenderness of our virtue at that instant, might
have been dangerous. So we made our retreat in the
same manner as our gentleman; and have thought of
her face with kindness ever since.

To return to our pigeons :—the description given in
the verses is true to the letter. The reader must not
think it a poetical exaggeration. If he has ever wit-
nessed an exhibition of the kind, he has no conception
of the high human hand with which these pigeons carry
it. The poets, indeed, time out of mind, have taken
amatory illustrations from them ; but the literal courtship surpasses them all. One sight of a pigeon paying
his addresses would be sufficient to unsettle in our
minds all those proud conclusions which we draw respecting the difference between reason and instinct.
If this is mere instinct as distinguished from reason, if
a bird follows another bird up and down by a simple
mechanical impulse, giving himself all the airs and

graces imaginable, exciting as many in his mistress, and uttering every moment articulate sounds which we are no more bound to suppose deficient in meaning than a pigeon would be warranted in supposing the same of our own speech, then reason itself may be no more than a mechanical impulse. It has nothing better to show for it. Our mechanism may possess a greater variety of movements, and be more adapted to a variety of circumstances; but if there is not variety here, and an adaptation to circumstances, we know not where there is. If it be answered, that pigeons would never make love in any other manner, under any circumstances, we do not know that. Have people observed them sufficiently to know that they always make love equally well? If they have varied at any time, they may vary again. Our own modes of courtship are undoubtedly very numerous; and some of them are as different from others, as the courtship of the pigeon itself from that of the hog. But though we are observers of ourselves, have we yet observed other animals sufficiently to pronounce upon the limits of their capacity? We are apt to suppose that all sheep and oxen resemble one another in the face. The slightest observation convinces us that their countenances are as various as those of men. How are we to know that the shades and modifications of their character and conduct are not as various? A well-drilled nation would hardly look more various in the eyes of a bee, than a swarm of bees does in our own. The minuter differences in our conduct would escape them for want of the habit of observing us, and because their own are of another sort. How are we to say that we do not judge them as ill? Every fresh speculation into the habits and manners of that singular

little people, produces new and extraordinary discoveries. The bees in *Buffon's time* were in the habit,
when they built their hives, of providing for a certain
departure from the more obvious rules of architecture,
which at a particular part of the construction became
necessary. Buffon ingeniously argued, that because
they always practised this secret geometry, and never
did otherwise, their apparent departure itself was but
another piece of instinct ; and he concluded that they
always had done so, and always would. Possibly they
will ; but the conclusion is not made out by his argument. A being who knows how to build better than
we do, might as well assert, that because we have not
arrived at certain parts of his knowledge, we never
shall. Observe the vast time which it takes us, with
all our boasted reason, to attain to improvements in our
own arts and sciences : think how little we know after
all ; what little certainty we have respecting periods
which are but as yesterday, compared with the mighty
lapse of time ; and judge how much right we have to
say, This we never did—This we shall never be able
to do.

We have read of some beavers, that when they were
put into a situation very different from their ordinary
one, and incited to build a house, they set about their
work in a style as ingeniously adapted as possible to
their new circumstances. Buffon might say, they
had been in this situation before ; he might also argue
that they were provided with an instinct against the
emergency. One argument appears to me as good as
the other. But under the circumstances, he might
tell us, that they would probably act with stupidity.
And what is done by many human beings ? Is our
reason as good for us all on one occasion as another ?

The individuals of the same race of animals are not all equally clever, any more than ourselves. The more they come under our inspection (as in the case of dogs), the more varieties we discern in their characters and understandings. The most philosophical thing hitherto said on this subject appears to be that of Pope.

"I shall be very glad," said Spence, "to see Dr. Hales, and always love to see him, he is so worthy and good a man." POPE. " Yes, he is a very good man ; only I'm sorry he has his hands so much imbrued in blood." SPENCE. " What ! he cuts up rats ?" POPE. " Ay, and dogs too ! (With what emphasis and concern, says the relater, he spoke it.) Indeed, he commits most of these barbarities with the thought of being of use to man ; but how do we know that we have a right to kill creatures that we are so little above as dogs, for our curiosity, or even for some use to us?" SPENCE. " I used to carry it too far : I thought they had reason as well as we." POPE. " So they have, to be sure. All our disputes about that are only disputes about words. Man has reason enough only to know what is necessary for him to know, and dogs have just that too." SPENCE. " But then they have souls too, as imperishable in their nature as ours ?" POPE. " And what harm would that be to us?"

All this passage is admirable, and helps to make us love, as we ought to do, a man who has contributed so much to the entertainment of the world.

That dogs, like men, have " reason enough only to know what is necessary for them to know," is, of course, no argument against their acting in a new manner under novel circumstances. It is the same with us. Necessities alter with circumstances. There

is a well-authenticated story of a dog, who, having
been ill-treated by a larger one, went and brought a
still larger dog to avenge his cause, and see justice
done him.   When does a human necessity reason better than this ?   The greatest distinction between men
and other animals appears to consist in this, that the
former make a point of cultivating their reason ; and
yet it is impossible to say that nothing of the kind has
ever been done by the latter.   Birds and beasts in
general do not take the trouble of going out of their
ordinary course ; but is the ambition of the common
run of human beings any greater?   Have not peasants
and mechanics, and even those who flourish and grow
learned under establishments, an equal tendency to
deprecate the necessity of innovation ?   A farmer
would go on with his old plough, a weaver with his
old loom, and a placeman with his old opinions, to all
eternity, if it were not for the restlessness of individuals ;   and these are forced to battle their way
against a thousand prejudices, even to do the greatest
good.   An established critic has not always a right to
triumph over the learned pig.

  We have been told by some, that the " swinish multitude" are better without books.   Now the utmost
which the holders of this opinion can say for the superior reason of their species, is, that pigs dispense
already with a knowledge which is unfit for man.   They
tell us, nevertheless (and we receive the text with reverence), that a day shall come when " the lion will lie
down with the lamb ;" and yet they will laugh in your
face, if you suspect that beasts may be improvable
creatures, or even that men may deserve to be made
wiser.   But they will say, that this great event is not
to be brought about by knowledge.   Some of their

texts say otherwise.   We believe, that all which they
know of the matter is, that it will not be brought about
by themselves.

But we must not be led away from the dignity of
our subject by the natural tendencies of these gentlemen.   Human means are divine means, if the end be
divine.   Without controverting the spirit of the text
in question, it would be difficult, from what we see
already of the power of different animals to associate
kindly with each other, (such as lions with dogs, cats
with birds in the same cages, &c.) to pronounce upon
the limits of improvability in the brute creation, as far
as their organs will allow.   We would not venture to
assert that, in the course of ages, and by the improved
action of those causes which give rise to their present
state of being, the organs themselves will not undergo
alteration.   There is a part in the pectoral conformation of the male human being which is a great puzzle
to the anatomists, and reminds us of one of Plato's
reveries on the original state of mankind.   When the
Divine Spirit acts, it may act through the medium of
human knowledge and will, as well as any other,—
as well as through the trunk of a tree in the pushing
out of a blossom.   New productions are supposed to
take place from time to time in the rest of the creation:
old ones are known to have become extinct.

Be this as it may, we are not to conclude that the
world always was and always will be such as it is,
simply because the little space of time, during which
we know of its existence, offers to us no extraordinary
novelty.   The humility of a philosopher's ignorance
(and there is more humility in his very pride, than
in the "prostration of intellect" so earnestly recommended by some persons) is sufficient to guard him

against this conclusion, setting aside Plato and the mammoth.

With respect to other animals going to heaven, our pride smiles in a sovereign manner at this speculation. We have no objection, somehow, to a mean origin; but we insist that nothing less dignified than ourselves can be immortal. We are sorry we cannot settle the question. We confess (if the reader will allow us to suppose that we shall go to heaven, which does not require much modesty, considering all those who appear to be certain of doing so) we would fain have as much company as possible ; and he was of no different opinion who told us that a time should come when the sucking child should play with the asp. We see, that the poet had no more objection to his dog's company in a state of bliss, than the " poor Indian," of whom he speaks in his Essay.* We think we could name other celebrated authors, who would as lief take their dogs into the next world as a king or a bishop, and yet they have no objection to either. We may conceive much less pleasant additions to our society than a flock of doves, which, indeed, have a certain fitness for an

---

* " Lo! the poor Indian whose untutor'd mind
   Sees God in clouds, or hears him in the wind :
   His soul proud science never taught to stray
   Far as the solar walk, or milky way ;
   Yet simple nature to his hope has given,
   Behind the cloud-topt hill, an humbler heaven ;
   Some safer world in depth of woods embraced,
   Some happier island in the watery waste,
·   Where slaves once more their native land behold,
   No fiends torment, no Christians thirst for gold.
   To be, contents his natural desire,—
   He asks no angel's wings, no seraph's fire ;
   But thinks, admitted to that equal sky,
   His faithful dog shall bear him company."

Elysian state. We would confine our argument to one simple question, which the candid reader will allow us to ask him: " Does not *Tomkins* go to heaven?" Has not the veriest bumpkin of a squire, that rides after the hounds, an immortal soul? If so, why not the whole pack? It may be said, that the pack are too brutal and blood-thirsty: they would require a great deal of improvement. Well, let them have it, and the squire along with them. It has been thought by some, that the brutal, or those who are unfit for heaven, will be annihilated. Others conceive that they will be bettered in other shapes. Whatever be the case, it is difficult to think that many beasts and birds are not as fit to go to heaven at once as many human beings,— people, who talk of their seats there with as much confidence as if they had booked their names for them at a box-office. To our humble taste, the goodness and kindness in the countenance of a faithful dog are things that appear almost as fit for heaven as serenity in a human being. The prophets of old, in their visions, saw nothing to hinder them from joining the faces of other animals with those of men. The spirit that moved the animal was everything.

It was the opinion of a late writer, that the immortality of the soul depended on the cultivation of the intellect. He could not conceive how the sots and fools that abound on this earth could have any pretensions to eternity: or with what feelings they were to enter upon their new condition. There appears to be too much of the pride of intellect in this opinion, and too little allowance for circumstances; and yet, if the dispensation that is to take us to heaven is of the exclusive kind that some would make it, this is surely the more noble dogma. The other makes it depend on the

mere will of the Divinity, or (to speak plainly) upon a
system of favoritism, that would render a human tyranny unbearable. We are not here speaking of the
mild tenets inculcated by the spirit of the Church of
England, but of those of certain sects. In neither case
would the majority of us have much better pretensions
to go to heaven than the multitude of other animals;
nor, perhaps, a jot more, if we knew all their thoughts
and feelings. But we shall stray from our subject, and
grow more positive than becomes a waking dream.

To conclude with the pleasant animals with whom
we commenced, there is a flock of pigeons in the
neighborhood where we are writing,* whom we might
suppose to be enjoying a sort of heaven on earth.
The place is fit to be their paradise. There is plenty
of food for them, the dove-cots are excellent, the scene
full of vines in summer-time, and of olives all the year
round. It happens, in short, to be the very spot where
Boccaccio is said to have laid the scene of his Decameron. He lived there himself. Fiesole is on the
height ; the Valley of Ladies in the hollow ; the brooks
are all poetical and celebrated. As we behold this
flock of doves careering about the hamlet, and whiten-
ing in and out of the green trees, we cannot help fan-
cying that they are the souls of the gentle company
in the Decameron, come to enjoy in peace their old
neighborhood. We think, as we look at them, that
they are now as free from intrusion and scandal as
they are innocent ; and that no falcon will touch them,
for the sake of the story they told of him.†

* At Maiano, near Florence.

† The well-known and beautiful story of the Decameron. Mr. Proc-
ter has touched it in a high and worthy strain of enthusiasm in his
" Dramatic Sketches."

Ovid, in one of his elegies,* tells us, that birds have a Paradise near Elysium. Doves, be sure, are not omitted. But peacocks and parrots go there also. The poet was more tolerant in his *orni-theology* than the priests of Delphos, who, in the sacred groves about their temple, admitted doves, and doves only.

* *Amorum*, lib. ii. eleg. 6.

THE MONTH OF MAY.

Might not the May-holidays be restored?—Melancholy remnant of them —Recollections of a May-morning in Italy.

THOSE who reasonably object to the feudality of the old times, or the extreme inequalities of their condition, think that the old holidays were essentially connected with these inequalities, and that we could not have them again without renewing the ancient dependency of the poorer classes upon the givers of Christian dinners, and the beggings from door to door for the May garland. But this does not follow. We may surely rejoice in similar ways, by other means. The object of all true advancement is not to get rid of bad and good together, but to retain or restore the good, to increase it. and enjoy it all better than before. The songs of May have been suspended, not merely because the intercourse has grown less between landlord and tenant, or the lord of the manor and the villagers, but because the singers have had to " pay the piper" for very different tunes blown by trumpets, and blown by their own connivance too, as well as that of the rich. They have grown wiser : all are grown wiser : we blame nobody in these our philosophical pages, any more than we desire ourselves to be blamed. All have had something to be sorry for, during contests carried on with partial knowledge ; and all will doubtless do away the wrong part of contest, in proportion as knowledge increases. We blame not even the contests themselves ; which in the mysterious working of the operations of this world may have been necessary, for aught we know, to the speedier abolition of the evils mixed up with them. All we mean to say is, that as knowledge and comfort advance, there is no reason whatever why old good things should not revive, as well as new good ones be created ; and, for our parts, if society were wise, comfortable, and in a condition to enjoy itself without hurting the feelings of any portion of it, we do not see how it could *help* renewing its bursts of delight and congratulation amidst the beauties of new seasons, any more than it could help seeing them, and knowing how beautiful they are.

Meantime, as certain patient and hopeful politicians, not long ago, kept a certain small fire alive, in the midst of everything that threatened to put it out, which is now lighting all England, and promising better times to the very seasons we speak of, so shall we persist, as we have for these twenty years past,* in keeping up a certain fragrant and flowery belief on the altars of May and June, in these sequestered corners of literature, ready against those better times, and already rewarding us for our perseverance, because the belief is spreading, and the corners beginning to lose their solitude.

> Huc ades :—tibi lilia plenis
> Ecce ferunt Nymphæ calathis ; tibi candida Nais
> Pallentes violas et summa papavera carpens,
> Narcissum et florem jungit bene olentis anethi ;
> Tum casia atque aliis intexens suavibus herbis,
> Mollia luteola pingit vaccinia caltha.—VIRGIL.

---

* Now seven-and-thirty. This article was written in 1834.

Come, take the presents which the nymphs prepare.
White lilies in full canisters they bring,
With all the purple glories of the spring.
The daughters of the flood have search'd the mead
For violets pale, and cropp'd the poppy's head,
The brief narcissus and fair daffodil,
Pansies to please the sight, and cassia sweet to smell.
                                    DRYDEN.

But where shall we begin, or what authors quote,
on the much quoted subject of May? It is a principle
with us, in making a selection from our writings, to
repeat as little as possible of what has been extracted
into other publications; and thus we are cut off from a
heap of books which have contributed their stores to
the illustration of the season. We cannot quote
Brady; we cannot quote Brand; we cannot quote
Aikin; nor Hone, nor Howitt, nor ourselves (which is
hard), nor the venerable Stowe, nor Forster, nor Pat-
more; nor again, in poetry, may we repeat the quotation from Chaucer about May and the Daisy; nor
Milton's Ode to May-morning; nor Spenser's joyous
dunce on the subject (in his Eclogues); nor his divine
personification of the month in the Faerie Queene, Book
VI.; nor Shakspeare's passage in Henry the Eighth,
about the impossibility of keeping people in their beds
on May-morning; nor Moore's " Young May-moon,"
(" young" moon for "new," thus prettily turning Luna
into a girl of fifteen;) nor Thomson's rich landscape
in the Castle of Indolence " atween June and May;"
nor Mr. Loviband's " Tears of old May-day;" nor Gay
on the May-pole; nor Wordsworth's bit about the
month, nor Dr. Darwin's ode (which, luckily, is not
worth quoting), nor twenty other poets, great and
small; nor Keats (one of the first), who has described
a May bush " with the bees about it." And so with

this we conclude our list of negations; for even out of things negative, we would show how a positive pleasure may be extracted.

But the poets are not yet exhausted on this subject, —nor a fiftieth part of them. How could they be, and May be what it is, especially in the south? We only wish we had time and space, and a huge library, and could quote all we could think of, the reader should feel as if our pages scented of May-blossom, and ran over with milk and honey. We hope, however, to give him a specimen or two before we close our article. Meantime, in order to get rid of all the melancholy that will force itself into the subject, and make a clear field for our true May-time, we have two observations to make; first, that if the first of the month turn out badly, it is not the fault of the May-day of our ancestors, which was twelve days later, or what is now called Old May-day (the day otherwise does not much signify; for it is a sentiment and not a date, which is the thing concerned); and second, that the only remnant of the old festivities now left us, like a sorry jest and a smeared face, is that melancholy burlesque the chimney-sweepers,—melancholy, however, not to themselves, and so far, to nobody else; neither would we have them brow-beaten, but made as merry as possible on this their only holiday ;—but it is melancholy to think, that all the mirth of the day is left to their keeping. If their trade were a healthy one, it would be another matter; if we were even sure that they were not beaten and bruised when they got home, it would be something. As it is, we can only give money to them (if one has it) and wish them a less horrible mixture of tinsel, dirty skin, dance, and disease. Nevertheless, the dance is something: sacred be the dance, and the

desecration thereof; and sacred the laugh of the frightfully red lips amidst that poisonous black.   Give them
money, for God's sake, all you that inhabit squares
and great streets, and then do your utmost, from that
day forward, never again to let May-day blossom into
those funereal flowers of living and fantastic death.

The last pleasant remnant of a town exhibition in
connection with the old May holidays, was the milk-
maids' garland.   There was something in that.   A set
of buxom lasses, breathing of the morning air and the
dairy, were a little more native to the purpose than
these poor devils of the chimney.   But even these
have long vanished.   They are rarely to be found,
even in the exercise of their daily calling.   Milk-maids
have been turned into milk-men; and when the latter,
in their transference of the virgin title to the buyers
instead of the sellers of milk, call out (as they do in
some quarters of the town) "Come, pretty maids,"
nine old women issue out of the areas in the street,
milk-jug in hand, and all hobbling;—all rheumatic, in
consequence of not having been in the fields these
twenty years.

"My soul, turn from them."   Get not rheumatic
thyself, nor do thou, dear reader, consent to be old before thy time, and oppressed with cough and chagrin,
especially in spring weather; but get up betimes on a
May morning, if it be only in fancy, and send your
thoughts wandering among the dewy May-bushes, and
the songs of birds.   Nay, if you live in the country,
or on the borders of it, and if the morning itself be not
ungenial, it will do you no harm to venture personally,
as well as spiritually, among the haunts of your jovial
ancestors,—the men. who helped to put blood and
spirit into your race; or if cosy old habit is too strong

for you to begin at so short a notice, and the united
charms of bed and breakfast prevail over the "raw"
air, you are a man too masculine at heart, and too
generous, not to wish that your children may grow up
in better habits than yourself, or recall the morning
hours of your own childhood ; and *they* can go forth into
the neighborhood, and see what is to be seen,—what
beauteous and odorous May-boughs they can bring
home, young and fair as themselves—the flowery
breath of morning—the white virgin blossom—the
myrtle of the hedges. The voices of children seem as
natural to the early morn as the voice of the birds.
The suddenness, the lightness, the loudness, the sweet
confusion, the sparkling gayety, seem alike in both.
The sudden little jangle is now here, and now there ;
and now a single voice calls out to another voice, and
the boy is off like the bird.

When we had the like opportunities, not a May did
we pass, if we could help it, without keeping up the
good old religion of the season, and heaping ourselves
and our children with blossom enough to make a bower
of the breakfast room : so that we only preach what
we have practised. If we were happy, it added to our
happiness, and was like a practical hymn of gratitude.
If we were unhappy, it helped to save our unhappiness
from the addition of impatience and despair. We
looked round upon the beautiful country, and the
world of green and blossom, and said to ourselves,
"We can still enjoy these. We still belong *to the paradise of good-will.*"

Therefore we say to all good-willers, "Enjoy what
you can of May-time, and help others to enjoy it, if it
be but with a blossom, or a verse, or a pleasant thought.
Let us all help, each of us, to keep up our spark of the

sacred fire—the same, we may dare to believe, which
fires the buds themselves, and the song of the birds, and
puts the flush into the cheek of delight; and hope, faith,
and charity into the heart of man; for if one great cause
of love and good-will does not do this, what does, or
what can?

May, or the time of the year analogous to it in different countries, is more or less a holiday in all parts
of the civilized world, and has been such from time im-
memorial. Nothing but the most artificial state of
life can extinguish or suspend it: it is always ready to
return with the love of nature. Hence the vernal
holidays of the Greeks and Romans, their songs of the
Swallow, and vigils of the Goddess of Love; hence the
Beltein of the Celtic nations, and the descent of the god
Krishna upon the plains of Indra, where he sported,·
like a proper Eastern prince, with sixteen thousand
milk-maids; a reasonable assortment.

In no place in the world perhaps but in England
(which is another reason why so great and beautiful a
country should get rid of the disgrace), is the remnant
of 'the May-holyday reduced to so melancholy a burlesque as our soot and tinsel. The necessities of war
and trade may have produced throughout Europe a
suspension of the main spirit of the thing, and a consciousness that the means of enjoyment must be restored before there can be a proper return to it. We
hope and believe, that when they are restored, the enjoyment will be greater than ever, through the addition of taste and knowledge. But meanwhile, we do
not believe that the sense of its present imperfection
has been suffered anywhere else to fall to a pitch so
low. In Tuscany, where we have lived, it has still its
guitar and its song; and its jokes are on pleasant sub-

jects, not painful ones. We remember being awakened
on May-day morning, at the village of Maiano near
Fiesole, by a noise of instruments and merry voices in
the court of the house in which we lodged,—a house
with a farm and vineyard attached to it, where the
cultivator, or small farmer, lived in a smaller detached
dwelling, and accounted to the proprietor for half the
produce—a common arrangement in that part of the
world. The air which was played and sung was a
sort of merry chaunt, as old perhaps as the time of
Lorenzo de Medici; the words to it were addressed to
the occupiers of the mansion, to the neighbors, or to
anybody who happened to show their face; and they
turned upon an imaginary connection between the
qualities of the person mentioned, and the capabilities
of the season. We got up, and looked out of the window; and there, in the beautiful Italian morning, under
a blue sky, amidst grass and bushes, and the white out-
houses of the farm, stood a group of rustic guitar-players, joking good-humoredly upon every one who appeared, and welcomed as good-humoredly by the person joked on. The verses were in homely couplets;
and the burden or leading idea of every couplet was
the same. A respectable old Jewish gentleman, for
instance, resided there; and he no sooner showed his
face, than he was accosted as the patron of the corn-
season.—as the genial influence without whom there
was to be no bread.

Ora di Maggio fiorisce il grano,
Ma non puo estrarsi senza il Sior Abramo.

Now in May-time comes the corn; but, quoth he, though come I am,
I should never have been here, but for Signor Abraham.

A lady put forth her pretty laughing face (and a most

good-tempered woman she was).   She is hailed as the
goddess of the May-bush.

> Ora di Maggio viene il fior di spina,
> Ma non viene senza la Signora Allegrina.

> Now in May-time comes the bush, all to crown its queen-a ;
> But it never would without Signora Allegrina.

A poor fellow, a servant named Giuseppino or Pep-
pino (Joe) who was given to drinking (a rare thing in
Italy), and was a great admirer of the fair sex (a thing
not so uncommon), crosses the court with a jug in his
hand.   It was curious to see the conscious, but not re-
sentful face, with which he received the banter of his
friends.

> Ora di Maggio fiorisce amor e vino,
> Ma ni l'un ni l'altro senza il Sior Peppino.

> Now in May-time comes the flower of love and wine also ;
> But there's neither one nor t' other, without Signor Joe.

With this true bit of a taste of May for the reader's
ruminations, we close our present article.   It would be
an "advancement" to look out of a May-morning in
England, and see guitar-players instead of chimney-
sweeps.*

* Since this article was written, the condition of the chimney-sweepers has been greatly mitigated.

THE GIULI TRE.*

Specimen of Sonnets written on this subject by the Abate Casti.

THE Giuli Tre (Three Juliuses, so called from a head of one of the Popes of that name) are the se pieces of money, answering to about fifteen pence of our coin, for which the Italian poet, Casti, says he was pestered from day to day by an inexorable creditor. The poet accordingly had his revenge on him and incarcerated the man in immortal amber, by devoting to the subject no less than two hundred sonnets, which he published under the above title. The Abate Casti is known to the English public, by means of Mr. Stewart Rose's pleasant abridgement, as the author of the Animali Parlanti; and he is also known to what we suppose must be called the English private, as the writer of a set of Tales in verse, which an acquaintance of ours says "everybody has read, and nobody acknowledges to have read." The Animali Parlanti is celebrated throughout Europe. The Tales have the undeniable merit which a man of genius puts into whatever work he condescends to write; but they are a gross mistake in things amatory, and furnish one of those portentous specimens of excess on the side of free writing, which those who refer every detail of

* Pronounced ("For the benefit of the country-gentlemen," and for the sake of the euphony in the perusal of our versions) *Joolce Tray.*

8*

the world to Providence could only account for by supposing, that some such addition of fuel was necessary to the ordinary inflammability of the young and unthinking.

The work before us, as the Florentine editor observes, is in every respect unexceptionable. He informs us, that it is not liable to a charge brought against the Abate's other works, of being too careless in point of style, and un-idiomatic. The Giuli Tre, according to him, speak the true Italian language ; so that the recommendation they bring with them to foreigners is complete.

We proceed to give some specimens. The fertility of fancy and learned allusion, with which the author has written his two hundred sonnets on a man coming to him every day and asking him for Tre Giuli, is inferior only to what Butler or Marvell might have made of it. The very recurrence of the words becomes a good joke.

Nobody that we have met with in Italy could resist the mention of them. The priest did not pretend it. The ladies were glad they could find something to approve in a poet of so erroneous a reputation. The man of the world laughed as merrily as he could. The patriot was happy to relax his mustachios. Even the bookseller, of whom we bought them, laughed with a real laugh, and looked into the book as if he would fain have sat down and read some of it with us, instead of going on with his business.

We shall notice some of the principal sonnets that struck us throughout the work, and wish we could review them all, partly that we might give as much account of it as possible, and partly because the jest is concerned in showing to what a length it is carried.

But we are compelled to be brief. It may be as well to mention, that the single instead of double rhymes which the poet uses, and which render the measure exactly similar to that of the translation, have a ludicrous effect to an Italian ear.

In this third sonnet, the poet requests fables and dreams to keep their distance :—

> Lungi, o favole, o sogni, or voi da me,
> Or che la Musa mia tessendo va
> La vera istoria delli Giuli Tre.

> Ye dreams and fables, keep aloof, I pray,
> While this my Muse keeps spinning, as she goes,
> The genuine history of the Giuli Tre.

Son. 8.—His Creditor, he says, ought not to be astonished at his always returning the same answer to his demand for the Giuli Tre, because if a man who plays the organ or the hautboy were always to touch the same notes, the same sounds would always issue forth.

SONNET 10.

> Ben cento volte ho replicato a te
> Questa istessa infallibil verità,
> Che a conto mio, da certo tempo in quà,
> La razza de' quattrini si perdè.
> Tu non ostante vieni intorno a me
> Con insoffribile importunità,
> E per quei maledetti Giuli Tre
> Mi perseguiti senza carità.

> Forse in disperazion ridur mi vuo',
> Ond' io m'appichi, e vuoi vedermi in giù
> Pender col laccio al collo ? Oh questo no.
> Risolverommi a non pagarti più,
> E in guisa tal te disperar farò,
> E vo' puittosto che ti appichi tu.

> I've said for ever, and again I say,
> And it's a truth as plain as truth can be,

That from a certain period to this day,
Pence are a family quite extinct with me.
And yet you still pursue me, and waylay,
With your insufferable importunity,
And for those d———d infernal Giuli Tre
Haunt me without remorse or decency.

Perhaps you think that you'll torment me so,
You'll make me hang myself? You wish to say
You saw me *sus. per coll.*—No, Giuli, no.
The fact is, I'll determine not to pay;
And drive *you*, Giuli, to a state so low,
That you shall hang yourself, and I be gay.

Son. 13.—The poet does not know whether there is a plurality of worlds, whether the moon is inhabited, etc. He is inclined to doubt whether there can be a people who had not Adam for their father. But if there is, he longs to go up there and live among them. Nevertheless, he fears it would be of no avail, as his Creditor would get Father Daniel to show him the way, and come after him.*

Son. 31.—When an act has been very often repeated, he says that the organs perform it of their own accord, without any attention on the part of the will. Thus mules go home to the stable, and parrots bid one good-morning; and, thus, he says, the Creditor has a habit of asking him for the Giuli Tre, and he has a habit of answering, "I haven't got 'em."

SONNET 35.

Mai l' uom felice in vita sua non fu.
Fanciullo un guardo soi tremar lo fa
Quindi trapassa la più fresca età
Intento alle bell' arti e alle virtù.
Poi nel fiero bollor di gioventù
Or d' amore or di sdegno ardendo va;

---

* Father Daniel is author of a work entitled "Travels through the World of Des Cartes."

Di quà malanni, e cancheri di là,
E guai cogli anni crescon sempre più.

Alfin vengono i debiti; e allor sì
Che più speme di ben allor non v'è,
E anch' io la vita mia trassi così:
E il dibito fatal de' Giuli Tre
Ora ai malanni che passai fin quì
Solennemente il campimento diè.

No: none are happy in this best of spheres.
Lo: when a child, we tremble at a look:
Our freshest age is wither'd o'er a book;
The fine arts bite us, and the great characters.
Then we go boiling with our youthful peers
In love and hate, in riot and rebuke;
By hook misfortune has us, or by crook,
And griefs and gouts come thick'ning with one's years.

In fine, we've debts:—and when we've debts, no ray
Of hope remains to warm us to repose.
Thus has my own life pass'd from day to day;
And now, by way of climax, though not close,
The fatal debit of the Giuli Tre
Fills up the solemn measure of my woes.

Son. 41.—He says, that as the sun with his genial energy strikes into the heart of the mountains of Golconda and Peru, and hardens substances there into gold and gems, so the hot activity of his Creditor has hardened the poet's heart, till at length it has produced that hard, golden, and adamantine No! which has rendered the Giuli Tre precious.

Son. 44.—He says, that he was never yet bound to the conjugal yoke,—a yoke which is as pleasant to those who have it not, as it is disagreeable to those who have: but that if he were married, his children would certainly resemble the proprietor of the Giuli Tre, and that he should see Creditor-kins, or little Creditors, all about him;—*Creditorelli.*

Son. 72.—If a man has a little tumor or scratch on

his leg or arm, and is always impatiently touching it, the little wound will become a great one. So, he says, it is with his debt of the Giuli Tre. The debt, he allows, is in itself no very great thing, but the intolerable importunity of his Creditor,—

Considerabilissimo lo fa,—
Makes it a very considerable one.

Son. 78.—As various climates and countries give rise to a variety of characters among mankind,—as the Assyrian and Persian has been accounted luxurious, the Thracian fierce, and the Roman was once upon a time bold and magnanimous, so he suspects that the climate in which he lives must be eminent for producing hard Creditors.

Son. 79.—He wishes that some logician, who understands the art of persuading people, would be charitable enough to suggest to him some syllogism or other form of argument, which may enable him to prove to his Creditor the impossibility of paying money when a man has not got it.

Son. 89.—Philosophers maintain, he says, that if two bodies stand apart from each other, and are distinct, it is impossible they can both stand in the same place. Otherwise one body also might be in several places at once. He therefore wonders how it is, that his Creditor is to be found here and there and everywhere.

Son. 96.—He tells us, that his Creditor is fond of accosting him on physical subjects, and wishes to know the nature of lightning, of the winds, colors, &c., and whether the system of Tycho Brahe is better than that of Pythagoras. The poet answers that it is impossible to get at the secrets of Nature; and that all that he knows upon earth is, that a man is perpetually asking him for Tre Giuli, and he has not got them.

SONNET 98.

Non poche volte ho inteso dir da chi
E Galeno ed Ippocrate studió
Che vi sono fra l'anno alcuni dì,
Ne' quali cavar sangue non si può.
Se ragione vi sia di far così,
Se'l vedano i Dottori, io non lo so;
E luogo non mi par questo ch'è quì
Di dire il mio parer sopra di ciò.

So ben che il Creditor de' Giuli Tre
Tanti riguardi e scrupoli non ha,
Nè osserva queste regole con me;
Ch'anzi ogni giorno procurando va
Da me trarre il denar, ch'è un non so che
Ch' ha col sangue una qualche affinità.

Often and often have I understood
From Galen's readers and Hippocrates's,
That there are certain seasons in diseases
In which the patient oughtn't to lose blood.
Whether the reason that they give be good,
Or doctors square their practice to the thesis,
I know not; nor is this the best of places
For arguing on that matter, as I could.

All that I know is this,—that Giuli Tre
Has no such scruple or regard with me,
Nor holds the rule himself: for every day
He does his best, and that most horribly,
To make me lose my cash: which I must say,
Has with one's blood some strange affinity,

Son. 101.—The poet alludes to the account of words freezing at the pole; and says, that if he were there with his Creditor, and a thaw were to take place, nothing would be heard around them but a voice calling for the Giuli Tre.

SONNET 113.

Si mostra il Creditor spesso con me
Piacevole ed affabile così,
Come fra amici suol farsi ogni dì,
E par che più non pensi a' Giuli Tre ;
E solo vuol saper, se il Prusso Re
Liberò Praga, e di Boemia uscì ;
Se l'armata naval da Brest partì ;
Se Annover prese il marescial d' Etrè.

E poiche da lontano la pigliò,
A poco a poco al *quia* calando va,
E dice,—" Ebben, quando i Tre Giuli avrò ?"
Così talor col sorcio il gatto fa ;
Ci ruzza, e scherza, e l'intrattiene un po',
E la fatal graffiata alfin gli dà.

My Creditor seems often in a way
Extremely pleasant with me, and polite ;
Just like a friend :—you'd fancy, at first sight,
He thought no longer of the Giuli Tre.
All that he wants to know is, what they say
Of Frederick now ; whether his guess was right
About the sailing of the French that night ;
Or, What's the news of Hanover and D'Estrees.

But start from whence he may, he comes as truly,
Bẏ little and little, to his ancient pass,
And says, " Well—when am I to have the Giuli ?"
'Tis the cat's way.   She takes her mouse, alas !
And having purred, and eyed, and tapp'd him duly,
Gives him at length the fatal *coup de grace*.

SONNET 122.

Oh quanto scioccamente vaneggiò
Chi Arnaldo, e Lullo, ed il Gebèr seguì,
E lavorò nascosto e notte e dì,
Ed i metalli trasformar pensò :
E intorno ad un crocciuol folle sudò,
In cui mercuri, e solfi, e sali unì,
Ne finalmente mai gli riuscì
Coll'arte oprar ciò che natura oprò.

Ma oh ! perchè si bell'arte in noi non e ?
Perchè all'uom d'imitar vietato fu

I bei lavori che natura fe !
Studiar vorrei la chimica virtù,
E fatto il capital de' Giuli Tre,
Rompere il vaso, e non pensarvi piu.

Oh, with what folly did they toil in vain,
Who thought old Arnald, Lully, or Geber wise,
And night and day labor'd with anxious eyes
To turn their metals into golden grain !
How did their pots and they perspire again
Over their ·lphurs, salts, and mercuries,
And never, after all, could see their prize,
Or do what Nature does, and with no pain !

Yet oh, good heavens ! why, why, dear Nature say,
This lovely art—why must it be despis'd ?
Why mayn't we follow this thy noblest way ?
I'd work myself; and having realiz'd,
Good God ! a capital of Giuli Tre,
Break up my tools, content and aggrandiz'd.

Son. 124.—He supposes that there was no such
Creditor as his in the time of David, because in the
imprecations that are accumulated in the hundred and
eighteenth psalm, there is no mention of such a person.

Son. 127.—His Creditor, he tells us, disputed with
him one day, for argument's sake, on the immortality
of the soul ; and that the great difficulty he started
was, how anything that had a beginning could be
without an end. Upon which the poet asked him,
whether he did not begin one day asking him for the
Giuli Tre, and whether he has left off ever since.

Son. 128.—He says that as Languedoc is still so
called from the use of the affirmative particle *oc* in
that quarter, as writers in other parts of France
used to be called writers of *oui*, and as Italy is de-
nominated the lovely land of *si*, so his own language,
from his constant habit of using the negative particle
to the Creditor of the Giuli Tre, ought to be called
the language of *no*.

Son. 134.—He informs us, that his Creditor has lately taken to learning French; and conjectures, that finding he has hitherto asked for the Giuli Tre to no purpose in his own language, he wishes to try the efficacy of the French way of dunning.

SONNET 140.

Armato tutto il Creditor non già
Di quell'armi che Achille o Enea vestì,
Onde di tanta poi mortalità
La Frigia l'un, l'altro l'Italia empì;
Ne di quelle onde poscia in altra età
D'estinti corpi Orlando il suol coprì:
Ma di durezza e d'importunità
E d'aspri modi armato ei m'assali.

Ed improvviso in contro mi lanciò
La richiesta mortal di Giuli Tre;
Io mi schermisco, indi gli scaglio un Nò:
Seguia la pugna ed inficria; ma il piè
Da lui volgendo alfin ratto men vò,
E vincitor la fuga sol mi fe'.

My Creditor has no such arms, as he
Whom Homer trumpets, or whom Virgil sings,
Arms which dismiss'd so many souls in strings
From warlike Ilium and from Italy.
Nor has he those of later memory,
With which Orlando did such heaps of things;
But with hard hints, and constant botherings,
And such rough ways,—with these he warreth me.

And suddenly he launcheth at me, lo!
His terrible demand, the Giuli Tre;
I draw me back, and thrust him with a No!
Then glows the fierce resentment of the fray,
Till turning round, I scamper from the foe;
The only way, I find, to gain the day.

Son. 142.—The first time the seaman hears the horrible crashing of the tempest, and sees the fierce and cruel rising of the sea, he turns pale, and loses both his courage and his voice; but if he lives long enough

to grow gray in his employment, he sits gayly at the
stern, and sings to the accompaniment of the winds.
So it is with the poet. His Creditor's perpetual song
of the Giuli Tre frightened him at first; but now that
his ears have grown used to it, he turns it into a musical accompaniment like the billows, and goes singing
to the sound.

Son. 148.—A friend takes him to see the antiquities
in the Capitol, but he is put to flight by the sight of a
statue resembling his Creditor.

Son. 185.—He marks out to a friend the fatal place
where his Creditor lent him the Giuli Tre, showing
how he drew out and opened his purse, and how he
counted out to him the Giuli with a coy and shrinking
hand. He further shows, how it was not a pace distant from this spot that the Creditor began to ask him
for the Giuli: and finishes with proposing to purify
the place with lustral water, and exorcise its evil
genius.

Son. 189.—He laments that happy age of the world,
in which there was a community of goods; and says
that the avidity of individuals and the invention of
meum and *tuum* have brought an immense number of
evils among mankind, his part of which he suffers by
reason of the Giuli Tre.

Son. 200.—Apollo makes his, appearance, and re-
bukes the poet for wasting his time, advising him to
sing of things that are worthy of immortality. Upon
which the poet stops short in a song he was chanting
upon his usual subject, and bids good-night for ever to
his Creditor and the Giuli Tre.

Not a word of payment.

A FEW REMARKS ON THE RARE VICE
CALLED LYING;

OR,

AN APPEAL TO THE MODESTY OF ANTI-BALLOTMEN.

Impossibility of finding a liar in England.—Lying, nevertheless, allowed and organized as a mutual accommodation, except in the case of voters at elections.—Reason of this, a wish to have all the lies on one side.—The right of lying arrogated by the rich as a privilege.—Vindication, nevertheless, of the rich as human beings.—Social root of apparently unsocial feelings.—Conventional liars not liars out of the pale of conventionality.—Falsehood sometimes told for the sake of truth and good.—Final appeal to the consciences of anti-ballotmen.

THE great argument against the Ballot is, that it teaches people duplicity,—that the elector will promise his vote to one man, and give it to another. In short, that he will lie. Lying is a horrid vice,—*un*-English. It must not be suffered to pollute our shores. People lie in France. They lie in Italy. They lie in Spain and Portugal. They lie in Africa, in Asia, and America. But in England, who ever heard of such a thing ?

" What *is* lying ?" says the English courtier.

" Can't say indeed, sir," says the footman.

"Nor I," says the government spy.

" Never heard of it," says the tradesman.

" Never borough-mongered with it," says the peer.

" Never bribed with it," says the member of parliament.

" Never subscribed the 39 articles with it," says the collegian.

" Never pretended to a call with it," says the clergyman.

" Never *nolo-episcopari'd* with it," says the bishop.

" Never played a *ruse de guerre* with it," says the general.

" Never told it to a woman," says the man of gallantry.

" Never argued for it," says the barrister.

" Never sent in a medicine with it," says the apothecary.

" Never jockeyed with it," says the turf-man.

" Never dealt with it," says the man at Crockford's.

" Never wrote great A with it," says the underwriter.

" Never took in the custom-house with it," says the captain.

" Never doctor'd my port with it," says the wine-merchant.

" Never praised or condemned with it," says the critic.

" Never concealed a motive with it," says the partisan.

" Never puff'd with it," says the bookseller.

" Nor I," says the manager.

" Nor I," says the auctioneer.

" Nor I," says the quack-doctor.

" Never used it in my bread," says the baker.

" Nor I in a bill," says the tailor.

" Nor I in a measure," says the coalman.

" Can't conceive how anybody ever thought of it," says the innkeeper.

" Never made an excuse with it," says the fine lady.

" Nor I," says the lady's maid.

" Nor I," says the milliner.

" Am a horrible sinner, but never went so far as that," says the Methodist.

" Never uttered one to my wife, pretty jealous soul," says the husband.

" Nor I to my husband, poor man," says the wife.

" Nor I to my mother," says the little boy.

" Nor I in one of my speeches," says the king.

" Nor I in mine," says the minister.

" Nor I at a foreign court," says the diplomatist.

" Should never forgive myself such a thing," says the pickpocket.

" Couldn't live under it," says the beggar.

" Never saved myself from starvation by it," says the Irishman.

" Nor I got a bawbee," says the Scotchman.

" Nor I a penny," says ALL ENGLAND.

O spirits of Lucian, of Rabelais, of Molière, of Henry Fielding, of Sterne,—look down upon borough-mongers and their anti-ballot men, in the shopkeeping nation of England, and in the nineteenth century, protesting against the horrible innovation of encouraging *the bribed and misrepresented to say one thing in self-defence and intend another!*

Lying is the commonest and most conventional ot all the vices. It pervades, more or less, every class of the community, and is fancied to be so necessary to the carrying on of human affairs, that the practice is tacitly agreed upon; nay, in other terms, openly avowed. In the monarch, it is *king-craft*. In the statesman, *expediency*. In the churchman, *mental reservation*. In the lawyer, *the interest of his client*. In the merchant, manufacturer, and shopkeeper, *secrets of trade*. It was the opinion of King James, that without the art of lying, a king was not worthy to reign. This was his boasted "king-craft," which brought his son to the block; for if poor Charles was a "martyr," it was certainly not to the spirit of truth. Lord Bacon was of opinion that lying, like alloy in metals, was a debasement, but good for the working. It worked him, great as he was, into a little and ruined man. Pleasant Sir Henry Wotton (himself an ambassador) defined an ambassador to be "an honest man sent to *lie* abroad for the good of his country." Paley openly defends the "mental reservation" of the churchman,—of the subscriber to the thirty-nine articles, &c.; and his is the great text-book of the universities. If you go into a shop for any article, you know very well that you cannot be secure of having it genuine; nor do you expect the shopkeeper to tell you the truth. The grocer notoriously sells Jamaica coffee for Mocha, the tobacconist his own snuff for Latakia and Macubau, the linen-draper cotton for thread, and British goods for India.

Well, granting all this,—says the boroughmonger, —don't you see that it overdoes your argument, and that if we all lie and cheat one another at this rate,

we in reality do not cheat, and that the practice becomes comparatively innocent?

Excuse me—we answer—you *are* cheated, or how
could you cheat? and what would be the use of the
practice? You know the fact is general, and may
often detect it in the particular; but still you are cheated in the gross. And supposing the case to be otherwise, or that the practice becomes comparatively innocent by its universality (which is to be granted), *why
not make the duplicity charged against the Ballot
equally innocent, by the same process, and for the same
general accommodation?*

If it were understood that the elector had the same
right and necessity to prevaricate for *his* convenience,
as the candidate has to bribe or cajole for his,—if the
thing were understood on both sides, and the voter's
promise came to be of no more account than the great
man's, or than the pretty things said to the voter's wife
and children, *where would be the harm of it,* ACCORDING
TO YOUR OWN SHOWING? or where the greater vice of
it than that of the famous "king-craft," or of the minister's "expediency," or of the thirty-nine article-man's
"mental reservation?"

The truth is, that such would and *will* be the result;
so much so, that candidates will at last cease to prac-
tise their tricks and tell *their* lies, out of a hopeless-
ness of doing anything with the voters. But we will
tell the anti-balloter, what the harm will be in the meanwhile. The harm will be that *lies will no longer be
told for his sake exclusively;* AND THIS IS THE WHOLE
REAL AMOUNT OF HIS GRIEVANCE. His grievance is precisely what the prince's is, who likes to have all the
"craft" to himself, and not be deceived by his ministers.
It is what the minister's is, who complains of want of

truth in the opposition ;—what the opposition's is, when they cry "Oh! oh!" against the same things which they did when in place ;—what the wholesale dealer's cry is against the retail, and the master manufacturer's against the workman. The weapons of state and expediency will at length be turned against expediency itself,—against power and monopoly,—and used in behalf of the Many ; and this is what the virtuous indignation of the Few cannot bear.

But an insidious compliment may be paid to "us youth" of the press,—us "philosophic radicals ;" and it may be asked us, "What! do *you* advocate lying? You advocate it under *any* circumstances? *You* wish a man to say one thing and intend another? Is the above *your* picture of society and of human nature? We thought you had a better opinion of it ;—were believers in the goodness of the human heart, and did not take all your fellow-creatures for such a parcel of hypocrites."

"My dear sir," we answer, " we do not see you, and we know not who you may be. We know not whether you are one of the greatest liars under the sun, or only a conventional liar, like our friends the statesman and the baker (good and true fellows perhaps out of the pale of their offices and bake-houses). We are also totally ignorant whether you are a man who has a regard for truth at the expense of conventionalities. Perhaps you are. Perhaps you are even a martyr to those virtues, with the possession of which you are pleased to compliment ourselves. But this we can tell you; first, that if you were the greatest liar that ever breathed, and ourselves were lovers of the truth to an extent of which you have no conception, and if you were to come to us for help against a murderer, or a bailiff, or a tax-gatherer, or a lying boroughmonger, we should make no scruple to tell a lie for your sake; and we can tell you, secondly, that our above picture of society and our opinion of human nature, are two very different things; because we believe the vices of society to result entirely from its imperfect knowledge, education, and comfort; whereas we believe human nature to be capable of all good and true things, and to be ever advancing in them, the Ballot itself notwithstanding; for the very 'worst of the Ballot is, that it exchanges a lie for the sake of an individual, into a lie for the sake of the country; and the best of it is, that it will ultimately do away the necessity of either. With the Ballot must come extended suffrage (*that* is what you are afraid of). From extended suffrage must come Universal Suffrage. And from Universal Suffrage must come universal better treatment of man by his fellows;—universal *wiser* treatment;—universal comforts;—food for all, fire and clothing for all; education for all, monopolies for *none;*—hence no necessity for lying; which is only the resource of the unequally treated against those whose lies, in pretending a right so to treat them, are far greater and more vicious.

O love of truth! believer in all good and beautiful things! believer even in one's self, and therefore believer in others, and such as are far better than one's self! putter of security into the heart, of solidity into the ground we tread upon, of loveliness into the flowers, of hope into the stars! retainer of youth in age, and of comfort in adversity! bringer of tears into the eyes that look upon these imperfect words, to think how large and longing the mind of man is, compared with his frail virtues and his transitory power, and what mornings of light and abundance thou hast in store

nevertheless, for the whole human race, preparing to
ripen for them in accordance with their belief in its
possibility, and their resolution to work for it in loving
trust! Oh! shall they be thought guilty of deserting
thee, because, out of the very love of truth they feel
themselves bound to proclaim to what extent it does
not exist? because, out of the very love of truth, they
will not suffer those who care nothing for it to pretend
to a religious zeal in its behalf, when the lie is to be
turned against themselves?

One of the bitterest sights in the world to a lover of
equal dealing, is the selfish and conceited arrogance
*with which the rich demand virtues on the side of the
poor, which they do not exercise themselves.* The rich
man lies through his lawyer—through his dependent
—through his footman; lies when he makes *civil
speeches ;*—lies when he subscribes articles;—lies when
he goes to be married (vide marriage service);—lies
when he takes "the oaths and his seat;"—but that the
poor man should lie! that *he* should give a false promise!—that he should risk the direful, and unheard-of,
and unparliamentary crime of political perjury! Oh,
it is not to be thought of! Think of the example—
think of the want of principle—think of the harm done
to the poor man's "own mind"—to his sense of right
and wrong—to his eternal salvation. Nay, not that
either:—they have seldom the immodesty to go as far
as that. But what enormous want of modesty to go
so far as they do! Why should the poor man be expected to have scruples which the rich laugh at? Why
deny him weapons which they make use of against
himself?—in this respect, as in too many others, resembling their "noble" feudal ancestors, who had the

nobleness to fight in armor, while the common soldier was allowed none.

Yet let us not be supposed to think ill of the rich or of anybody, beyond the warrant of humanity—beyond all modesty of our own, or sense of the frailties which we possess plentifully in common with our fellow-creatures. We think ill, in fact, of no one, in the only bad and deplorable sense of the term,—that sense which would make him out to be something wicked from sheer preference of evil to good, or of harm to others without impulse or excuse. We are of opinion, that all classes and descriptions of men are modified as they are by circumstances; and instead of lamenting that there is so much vice during their advancement towards a wiser condition, we rejoice that there is so much virtue,—so much indelible and hopeful good. Nay, we can see a certain large and gallant healthiness of social constitution in man, in the very circumstance of vice's taking so gay or indifferent an air during what it supposes to be a necessity, or a condition of human nature; and the gayer it is, in some respects, the better; not only because of its having the less uneasy or mean conscience, but because it is the less given to cant and hypocrisy, and is ashamed of putting on a grave face of exaction upon others. The very worst of all vices (cruelty excepted)—that pride which seems to make the rich and prosperous hold their fellow-creatures in such slight regard,—is often traceable only to a perverted sense of that identical importance in their eyes, which is grounded in a social feeling, and which, under a wiser education, would make them proud of sympathizing with the humblest. Those courtiers—those Whigs and Tories—those lawyers—those tradesmen we have been talking of,—how shocked would not

many, perhaps most of them be, and what a right
would they not have to resent it,—if you treated them
as liars beyond the pale of their conventional duplicity ?
Take the grocer or the linen-draper from behind his
counter—apply to him in any concern but that of his
shop,—and most likely he is as great a truth-teller as
the rest. There is nothing you may not take his word
for. And then see what affections all these people
have; what lovers they are of their familes; what
anxious providers for their children; what " good fellows" as friends and helpers; and what a fool and
coxcomb you ought to consider yourself, if you dared
to set yourself up, and pretend that you were a bit
better than any one of them, even though circumstances might enable you to be free from some of their
errors,—perhaps with greater of your own. Falsehood itself is sometimes almost pure virtue,—at least
it contemplates anything but the ordinary and unjust
results of falsehood; as in the case of a jury, who de-
liberately tell a lie when, in order to save a man from
transportation, or a poor child from the jail, they bring
in a verdict of Not Guilty on the principal charge,
.knowing him to be otherwise. Here the law is violated
for the sake of justice, and a lie told for the sake of the
beautiful truth that we ought to be humane to one another. But the law should be changed ? True : and
so should ALL LAWS be changed which force just feelings upon falsehood in self-defence ;—and as the rich
advance in their notions of justice, and the poor get
better fed and taught, all such laws WILL be changed.

In short, dear anti-Ballot people, whoever you are,
and granting, for the sake of the argument, that all
which you say about the voter's prevarication will be
rue (for in innumerable instances we deny that it will,

and in all it must eventually come to nothing in the hope-
lessness of applying to him), but granting, for the sake
of the argument, that all which you anticipate in that
respect will come to pass, we have two short things to
say to you, which appear to us to sum up all that is
necessary for the refutation of your reasoning : first,
that before you have a right to ask the voter not to be
false to you, you must get rid of your own falsehoods,
great and small ; and second, that when you do get
rid of them, *you will be such very conscientious men,
that you will not have the face to ask him to violate
his conscience.*

CRITICISM ON FEMALE BEAUTY.

I.—HAIR, FOREHEAD.

Fault-finding of the old style of criticism ridiculed.—Painting with the pen.—Ugliness of beauty without feeling.—The hand of the poisoner.—Hair.—Under what circumstances it is allowable to use artificial helps to beauty.—Red and golden hair.—Hair of Lucretia Borgia.—Forehead.

CRITICISM, for the most part, is so partial, splenetic, and pec untic, and has such little right to speak of what it unde akes to censure, that the words " criticism on beauty' sound almost as ill as if a man were to announce something unpleasant upon something pleasant.

And, certainly, as criticism, according to its general practice, consists in an endeavor to set the art above its betters, and to render genius amenable to want of genius (particularly in those matters which, by constituting the very essence of it, are the least felt by the men of line and rule), so critics are bound by their trade to object to the very pleasantest things. Delight, not being their business, " puts them out." The first reviewer was Momus, who found fault with the Goddess of Beauty.*

* Since the remarks in this exordium were written, periodical criticism has for the most part wholly changed its character. Instead of fault-finding, it has become beauty-finding. This extreme, of course, has also its wrong side ; but, upon the whole, is unquestionably on the higher side of the art. There are few poor books, however indulgently

We have sometimes fancied a review set up by this anti-divinity in heaven. It would appear, by late discoveries in the history of the globe, that, as one species of production has become extinct, so new ones may have come into being. Now, imagine the gods occasionally putting forth some new work, which is criticised in the " Olympian Review." Chloris, the goddess of flowers, for instance, makes a sweet-brier :—

" The Sweet-Brier, a new bush, by Chloris, Goddess of Flowers. Rain and Sun, 4104.

" This is another hasty production of a lady, whom we are anxious to meet with a more satisfied face. Really, we must say, that she tires us. The other day we had the *pink*. It is not more than a year ago that she flamed upon us with the *hearts-ease* (pretty names these) ; then we were all to be sunk into a bed of luxury and red leaves by the *rose;* and now, *ecce iterum Rosina,* comes a new edition of the same effeminate production, altered, but not amended, and made careless, confused, and full of harsh points. These the fair author, we suppose, takes for a dashing variety ! Why does she not consult her friends ? Why must we be forced to think that she mistakes her talents, and that she had better confine herself to the production of daisies and dandelions ? Even the *rose,* which has been so much cried up in certain quarters, was not original. It was clearly suggested by that useful production of an orthodox friend of ours,—the *cabbage;* which has occasioned it to be pretty generally called the *cabbage-rose.* The *sweet-brier,* therefore, is imitation upon imitation, *crambe* (literally) *bis cocta ;** a

treated, that will not soon die ; but the very best books sometimes require aid, because of their depth and originality. It is observable that the indulgent spirit of criticism has increased with its profundity.

thing not to be endured. To say the truth, which we wish to do with great tenderness, considering the author's sex, this *sweet brier bush* is but a *rifaccimento* of the *rose-bush*. The only difference is, that everything is done on a pettier scale, the flowers hastily turned out, and a superabundance of those startling points added, which so annoyed us in the *rose* yclept *moss* ; for there is no end to these pretty creatures the *roses*. Let us see. There is the *cabbage-rose*, the *moss-rose*, the *musk-rose*, the *damask-rose*, the *hundred-leaved rose*, the *yellow rose*, and earth only knows how many more. Surely these were enough, in all conscience. Most of them rank little above extempore effusions, and were hardly worth the gathering; but after so much trifling, to go and alter the style of a commonplace is a spirit of mere undoing and *embrouillement*, and then palm it upon us for something *free*, forsooth, and original, is a desperate evidence of falling off! We cannot consent to take mere wildness for invention ; a hasty and tangled piece of business, for a regular work of art. What is called nature will never do. Nature is unnatural. The best production by far of the fair author, was the *auricula*, one of those beautiful and regular pieces of composition, the right proportions of which are ascertained, and reducible to measurement. But *tempora mutantur*. Our fair florist has perhaps got into bad company. We have heard some talk about zephyrs, bees, wild birds, and such worshipful society. Cannot this ingenious person be content with the hot-house invented by Vulcan and Co. without gadding abroad in this disreputable manner? We have heard that she speaks with disrespect of ourselves ; but we need not assure

* Cabbage twice cooked.

the reader that this can have no weight with an honest critic. By-the-by, why this brier is called sweet, we must unaffectedly and most sincerely say, is beyond our perceptions."

We were about to give a specimen of another article, by the same reviewer, on the subject of our present paper:—"WOMAN, being a companion to MAN," &c. But the tone of it would be intolerable. We shall therefore proceed with a more becoming and grateful criticism, such as the contemplation of the subject naturally produces. Oh, Pygmalion, who can wonder (no artist surely) that thou didst fall in love with the work of thine own hands! Oh, Titian! Oh, Raphael! Oh, Apelles! We could almost fancy this sheet of paper to be one of your tablets, our desk an easel, our pen a painting-brush; so impossible does it seem that the beauty we are about to paint should not inspire us with a *gusto* equal to your own!

"Come, then, the colors and the ground prepare."

This ink-stand is our palette. We handle our pen as if there were the richest bit of color in the world at the end of it. The reds and whites look as if we could eat them. Look at that pearly tip at the end of the ear. The very shade of it has a glow. What a light on the forehead! What a moisture on the lip! What a soul, twenty fathom deep, in the eyes! Look at us, madam, if you please. The eye right on ours. The forehead a little more inclined. Good. What an expression! Raphael,—it is clear to me that you had not the feeling we have: for you could paint such a portrait, and we cannot. We cannot paint after the life. Titian, how could you contrive it? Apelles, may we trouble you to explain yourself? It is lucky

9*

for the poets that their mistresses are not obliged to sit
to them.   They would never write a line.   Even a
prose-writer is baffled.   How Raphael managed in the
Palazzo Chigi,—how Sacchini contrived, when he wrote
his "Rinaldo and Armida," with Armida by his side,
—is beyond our comprehension.   We can call to mind,
but we cannot copy.   Fair presence, avaunt!   We
conjure you out of our study, as one of our brother
writers, in an agony of article, might hand away his
bride, the printer having sent to him for copy.   Come
forth, our tablets.   Stand us instead of more distract-
ing suggestions, our memorandums.

It has been justly observed, that heroines are best
painted in general terms, as in "Paradise Lost,"

> " Grace was in all her steps, heaven in her eye," &c.

or by some striking instance of the effects of their
beauty, as in Homer, where old age itself is astonished
at the sight of Helen, and does not wonder that Paris
has brought a war on his country for her sake.   Particular description divides the opinion of the readers,
and may offend some of them.   The most elaborate
portrait of the heroine of Italian romance could say
nothing for her, compared with the distractions that
she caused to so many champions, and the millions that
besieged her in Albracca.

> " Such forces met not, nor so wide a camp,
> When Agrican with all his northern powers
> Besieged Albracca, as romances tell,
> The city of Gallaphrone, from whence to win
> The fairest of her sex, Angelica."

Even Apuleius, a very "particular fellow," who is an
hour in describing a chambermaid, enters into no details respecting Psyche.   It was enough that the people worshipped her.

The case is different when a writer describes a real person, or chooses to acquaint us with his particular taste. In the "Dream of Chaucer" is an admirable portrait of a woman, supposed to be that of Blanche, Duchess of John of Gaunt. Anacreon gives us a whole length of his mistress, in colors as fresh as if they were painted yesterday. The blue eye is moist in its sparkling ; the cheek, which he compares to milk with roses in it, is young for ever. Oh, Titian, even thy colors are dry compared with those of poetry !

It happens luckily for us, on the present occasion, that we can reconcile particulars with generals. The truth is, we have no particular taste. We only demand that a woman should be womanly ; which is not being exclusive. We think also that anybody who wishes to look amiable, should be so. The detail, with us, depends on a sentiment. For instance, we used to think we never could tolerate flaxen hair ; yet meeting one day with a lovely face that had flaxen locks about it, we thought for a good while after, that flaxen was your only wear. Harriet O—— made us take to black ; and yet, if it had not been for a combination of dark browns, we should the other night have been converted to the superiority of light brown by Harriet D——. Upon the whole, the dark browns, chestnuts, &c., have it with us ; but this is because the greatest number of kind eyes that we have met, have looked from under locks of that color. We find beauty itself a very poor thing unless beautified by sentiment. The reader may take the confession as he pleases, either as an instance of abundance of sentiment on our part, or as an evidence of want of proper ardor and impartiality ; but we cannot (and that is the plain truth) think the most beautiful creature beautiful, or be at all

affected by her, or long to sit next her, or go to a theatre with her, or listen to a concert with her, or walk
in a field or a forest with her, or call her by her Christian name, or ask her if she likes poetry, or tie (with
any satisfaction) her gown for her, or be asked whether
we admire her shoe, or take her arm even into a din-
ing-room, or kiss her at Christmas, or on April-fool
day, or on May-day, or on any other day, or dream of
her, or wake thinking of her, or feel a want in the
room when she is gone, or a pleasure the more when
she appears,—unless she has a heart as well as a face,
and is a proper good-tempered, natural, sincere, honest girl, who has a love for other people and other
things, apart from self-reference and the wish to be admired. Her face would pall upon us in the course of
a week, or even become disagreeable. We should
prefer an enamelled tea-cup; for we should expect
nothing from it. We remember the impression made
on us by a female plaster-cast hand, sold in the shops
as a model. It is beautifully turned, though we thought
it somewhat too plump and well-fed. The fingers,
however, are delicately tapered : the outline flowing
and graceful. We fancied it to have belonged to some
jovial beauty, a little too fat and festive, but laughing
withal, and as full of good-nature. The possessor told
us it was the hand of Madame Brinvilliers, the famous
poisoner. The word was no sooner spoken, than we
shrank from it as if it had been a toad. It was now
literally hideous ; the fat seemed sweltering and full of
poison. The beauty added to the deformity. You
resented the grace : you shrank from the look of
smoothness, as from a snake. This woman went to
the scaffold with as much indifference as she distributed
her poisons. The character of her mind was insensi-

bility. The strongest of excitements was to her what a cup of tea is to other people. And such is the character, more or less, of all mere beauty. Nature, if one may so speak, does not seem to intend it to be beautiful. It looks as if it were created in order to show what a nothing the formal part of beauty is, without the spirit of it. We have been so used to it with reference to considerations of this kind, that we ha[.]re met with women generally pronounced beautiful, and spoken of with transport, who took a sort of ghastly and witch-like aspect in our eyes, as if they had been things walking the earth without a soul, or with some evil intention. The woman who supped with the Goule in the "Arabian Nights," must have been a beauty of this species.

But to come to our portrait. Artists, we believe, like to begin with the eyes. We will begin, like Anacreon, with the hair.

Hair should be abundant, soft, flexible, growing in long locks, of a color suitable to the skin, thick in the mass, delicate and distinct in the particular. The mode of wearing it should differ. Those who have it growing low in the nape of the neck, should prefer wearing it in locks hanging down, rather than turned up with a comb. The gathering it, however, in that manner is delicate and feminine, and suits many. In general, the mode of wearing the hair is to be regulated according to the shape of the head. Ringlets hanging about the forehead suit almost everybody. On the other hand, the fashion of parting the hair smoothly, and drawing it tight back on either side, is becoming to few. It has a look of vanity instead of simplicity. The face must do everything for it, which is asking too much; especially as hair, in its freer state, is the ornament in-

tended for it by nature. Hair is to the human aspect,
what foliage is to the landscape. This analogy is so
striking, that it has been compared to flowers, and even
to fruit. The Greek and other poets talk of hyacinthine
locks, of clustering locks (an image taken from grapes).
of locks like tendrils. The favorite epithet for a Greek
beauty was "well-haired;" and the same epithet was
applied to woods. Apuleius says, that Venus herself,
if she were bald, would not be Venus. So entirely do
we agree with him, so much do we think that the sentiment of anything beautiful, even where the real
beauty is wanting, is the best part of it, that we prefer
the help of artificial hair to an ungraceful want of it.
We do not wish to be deceived. We should like to
know that the hair was artificial; or at least that the
wearer was above disguising the fact. This would
show her worthy of being allowed it. We remember,
when abroad, a lady of quality, an English-woman,
whose beauty was admired by all Florence; but never
did it appear to us so admirable, as when she observed
one day, that the ringlets that hung from under her
cap were not her own. Here, thought we, it is not
artifice that assists beauty; it is truth. Here is a woman
who knows that there is a beauty in hair beyond the
material of it, or the pride of being thought to possess
it. Oh, wits of Queen Anne's day, see what it is to live
in an age of sentiment, instead of your mere periwigs,
and reds and whites!—The first step in taste is to dislike all artifice; the next is to demand nature in her
perfection; but the best of all is to find out the hidden
beauty, which is the soul of beauty itself, to-wit, the
sentiment of it. the loveliest hair is nothing, if the
wearer is incapable of a grace. The finest eyes are
not fine, if they say nothing. What is the finest harp

to us, strung with gold, and adorned with a figure of
Venus, if it answer with a discordant note, and hath
no chords in it fit to be awakened? Long live, therefore, say we, lovely natural locks at five-and-twenty,
and lovely artificial locks, if they must be resorted to,
at five-and-thirty or forty. Let the harp be new strung,
if the frame warrant it, and the sounding-board hath a
delicate utterance. A woman of taste should no more
scruple to resort to such helps at one age, than she
would consent to resort to them at an age when no
such locks exist in nature. Till then, let her not cease
to help herself to a plentiful supply. The spirit in
which it is worn gives the right to wear it. Affectation and pretension spoil everything: sentiment and
simplicity warrant it. Above all things, cleanliness.
This should be the motto of personal beauty. Let a
woman keep what hair she has, clean, and she may
adorn or increase it as she pleases. Oil, for example,
is two different things, on clean hair and unclean. On
the one, it is but an aggravation of the dirt: to the
other, if not moist enough by nature, it may add a
reasonable grace. The best, however, is undoubtedly
that which can most dispense with it. A lover is a
little startled, when he finds the paper, in which a lock
of hair has been enclosed, stained and spotted as if it
had wrapped a cheesecake. Ladies, when about to
give away locks, may as well omit the oil that time,
and be content with the washing. If they argue that
it will not look so glossy in those eyes in which they
desire it to shine most, let them own as much to the
favored person, and he will never look at it but their
candor shall give it a double lustre.

" Love adds a precious seeing to the eye;"

and how much does not sincerity add to love! One
of the excuses for oil is the perfume mixed with it.
The taste for this was carried so far among the ancients, that Anacreon does not scruple to wish that the
painter of his mistress's portrait could convey the odor
breathing from her delicate oiled tresses. Even this
taste seems to have a foundation in nature. A little
black-eyed relation of ours (often called Molly, from a
certain dairy maid turn of hers, and our regard for old
English customs) has hair with a natural scent of spice.

The poets of antiquity, and the modern ones after
them, talk much of yellow and golden tresses, tresses
like the morn, &c. Much curiosity has been evinced
respecting the nature of this famous poetical hair; and
as much anxiety shown in hoping that it was not red.
May we venture to say, in behalf of red hair, that we
are not of those in whose eyes it is so very shocking?
Perhaps, as " pity melts the soul to love," there may be
something of such a feeling in our tenderness for that
Pariah of a color. It must be owned that hair of this
complexion appears never to have been in request;
and yet, to say nothing of the general liking of the
ancients for all the other shades of yellow and gold, a
good red-headed commentator might render it a hard
matter to pronounce, that Theocritus has not given two
of his beautiful swains hair amounting to a positive
fiery. *Fire-red* is the epithet, however it may be understood.

> " Both fiery-tressed heads, both in their bloom."*

We do not believe the golden hair to have been
red; but this we believe, that it was nearer to it than

* Αμφω τωγ' ητην πυρροτριχω, αμφω αναβω.

IDYLL. 7.

most colors, and that it went a good deal beyond what it is sometimes supposed to have been, auburn. The word yellow, a convertible term for it, will not do for auburn. Auburn is a rare and glorious color, and we suspect will always be more admired by us of the north, where the fair complexions that recommended golden hair are as easy to be met with, as they are difficult in the south. Both Ovid and Anacreon, the two greatest masters of the ancient world in painting external beauty, seem to have preferred it to golden, notwithstanding the popular cry in the other's favor; unless, indeed, the hair they speak of was too dark in its ground for auburn. The Latin poet, in his fourteenth love-elegy, speaking of tresses which he says Apollo would have envied, and which he prefers to those of Venus as Apelles painted her, tells us, that they were neither black nor golden, but mixed, as it were, of both. And he compares them to cedar on the declivities of Ida, with the bark stripped. This implies a dash of tawny. We have seen pine-trees in a southern evening sun take a lustrous burnished aspect between dark and golden, a good deal like what we conceive to be the color he alludes to. Anacreon describes hair of a similar beauty. His touch, as usual, is brief and exquisite :—

> " Deepening inwardly, a dun ;
> Sparkling golden, next the sun."*

Which Ben Jonson has rendered in a line,

> " Gold upon a ground of black."

Perhaps, the true auburn is something more lustrous throughout, and more metallic than this. The cedar

* Τα μεν ενδοθεν, μελαινας,
Τα δ' ες ακρον, ήλιωσας.

with the bark stripped looks more like it. At all events, that it is not the golden hair of the ancients has been proved in our opinion beyond a doubt, by a memorandum in our possession, worth a thousand treatises of the learned. This is a solitary hair of the famous Lucretia Borgia, whom Ariosto has so praised for her virtues, and whom the rest of the world is so contented to think a wretch.* It was given us by a lamented friend† who obtained it from a lock of her hair preserved in the Ambrosian library at Milan. On the envelope he put a happy motto—

> " And beauty draws us with a single hair."

If ever hair was golden, it is this. It is not red, it is not yellow, it is not auburn ; it is golden, and nothing else : and, though natural-looking too, must have had a surprising appearance in the mass. Lucretia, beautiful in every respect, must have looked like a vision in a picture, an angel from the sun. Everybody who sees it, cries out, and pronounces it the real thing. We must confess, after all, we prefer the auburn, as we construe it. It forms, we think, a finer shade for the skin ; a richer warmth ; a darker lustre. But Lucretia's hair must have been still divine. Mr. Landor, whom we had the pleasure of becoming acquainted with over it, as other acquaintances commence over a bottle, was inspired on the occasion with the following verses :—

> " Borgia, thou once wert almost too august,
> And high for adoration ;—now thou 'rt dust !

---

* Mr. Roscoe must be excepted, who has come into the field to run a tilt for her. We wish his lance may turn out to be the Golden Lance of the poet, and overthrow all his opponents. The greatest scandal in the world, is the readiness of the world to believe scandal.

† Lord Byron.

All that remains of thee these plaits infold—
Calm hair, meand'ring with pellucid gold!"

The sentiment implied in the last line will be echoed
by every bosom that has worn a lock of hair next it,
or longed to do so.   Hair is at once the most delicate
and lasting of our materials ; and survives us, like love.
It is so light, so gentle, so escaping from the idea of
death, that with a lock of hair belonging to a child or a
friend, we may almost look up to heaven, and compare
notes with the angelic nature ; may almost say, "I
have a piece of thee here, not unworthy of thy being
now."

FOREHEAD.   There are fashions in beauty as well
as dress.   In some parts of Africa, no lady can be
charming under twenty stone.

> " King Chihu put nine queens to death ;
> Convict on Statute, *Ivory Teeth.*"

In Shakspere's time, it was the fashion to have high
foreheads, probably out of compliment to Queen Elizabeth.   They were thought equally beautiful and in-
dicative of wisdom : and if the portraits of the great
men of that day are to be trusted, wisdom and high
foreheads were certainly often found together.   Of
late years, physiognomists have declared for the wisdom of strait and compact foreheads, rather than high
ones.   We must own we have seen very silly persons
with both.   It must be allowed, at the same time, that
a very retreating forehead is apt to be no accompaniment of wit.   With regard to high ones, they are often
confounded with foreheads merely bald ; and baldness,
whether natural or otherwise, is never handsome ;
though in men it sometimes takes a character of sim-

plicity and firmness. According to the Greeks, who
are reckoned to have been the greatest judges of
beauty, the high forehead never bore the palm. A
certain conciseness carried it. "A forehead," says
Junius, in his Treatise on Ancient Art, "should be
smooth and even, white, delicate, short, and of an
open and cheerful character." The Latin is briefer.*
Ariosto has expressed it in two words, perhaps in one.

> "Di *terso* avorio era la fronte lieta."
>> ORLAN. FUR. Canto VII.

> "Terse ivory was her forehead glad."   •

A large bare forehead gives a woman a masculine and
defying look. The word effrontery comes from it.
The hair should be brought over such a forehead, as
vines are trailed over a wall.

* "Frons debet esse plana, candida tenuis, breuis, pura."—Junius
De Pictura Veterum, Lib. iii. cap. 9. The whole chapter is very curious
and abundant on the subject of ancient beauty. Yet it might be rendered a good deal more so. A treatise on Hair alone might be collected
out of Ovid.

CRITICISM ON FEMALE BEAUTY.

II.—EYES, EYEBROWS, NOSE.

Eyes.—Eyebrows.—Frowning without frowning.—Eyebrows meeting.— Shape of head, face, ears, cheeks, and ear-rings.—Nose.—A perplexity to the critics.—Question of aquiline noses.—Angels never painted with them.

EYES.—The finest eyes are those that unite sense and sweetness. They should be able to say much, and all charmingly. The look of sense is proportioned to the depth from which the thought seems to issue ; the look of sweetness to an habitual readiness of sympathy, an unaffected willingness to please and be pleased. We need not be jealous of—

> " Eyes affectionate and glad,
> That seem to love whate'er they look upon."
> *Gertrude of Wyoming.*

They have always a good stock in reserve for their favorites : especially if, like those mentioned by the poet, they are conversant with books and nature. Voluptuaries know not what they talk about, when they profess not to care for sense in a woman. Pedantry is one thing : sense, taste, and apprehensiveness, are another. Give us an eye that draws equally from head above and heart beneath ; that is equally full of ideas and feelings, of intuition and sensation. If either must predominate, let it be the heart. Mere beauty

is nothing at any time but a doll, and should be packed
up and sent to Brobdignag.   The color of the eye is
a very secondary matter.   Black eyes are thought the
brightest, blue the most feminine, gray the keenest.
It depénds entirely on the spirit within.   We have
seen all these colors change characters; though we
must own, that when a blue eye looks ungentle, it
seems more out of character than the extremest contradiction expressed by others.   The ancients appear
to have associated the idea of gladness with blue eyes;
which is the color given to his heroine's by the
author just quoted.   Anacreon attributes a blue or a
gray eye to his mistress, it is difficult to say which:
but he adds, that it is tempered with the moist delicacy
of the eye of Venus.   The other look was Minerva's,
and required softening.   It is not easy to distinguish the
shades of the various colors anciently given to eyes;
the blues and grays, sky-blues, sea-blues, sea-gray,
and even cat-grays.*   But it is clear that the expression
is everything.   The poet demanded this or that color,
according as he thought it favorable to the expression
of acuteness, majesty, tenderness, or a mixture of all.
Black eyes were most lauded; doubtless, because in a
southern country the greatest number of beloved eyes
must be of that color.   But on the same account of
the predominance of black, the abstract taste was in
favor of lighter eyes and fair complexions.   Hair being of a great variety of tint, the poet had great license
in wishing or feigning on that point.   Many a head of

* *Cæsio veniam obvius leoni.*   Catullus.   See *glaucus cæruleus*, &c.
and their Greek correspondents.   Χαροπος, glad-looking, is also rendered
in the Latin, blue-eyed: and yet it is often translated by *ravus*, a word
which at one time is made to signify blue, and at another something ap-
proximating to hazel.   *Cæsius*, in like manner, appears to signify both
gray and blue, and a tinge of green.

hair was exalted into gold, that gave slight color for
the pretension; nor is it to be doubted that auburn,
and red, and yellow, and sand-color, and brown with
the least surface of gold, all took the same illustrious
epithet on occasion. With regard to eyes, the ancients insisted much on one point, which gave rise to
many happy expressions. This was a certain mixture of pungency with the look of sweetness. Sometimes they call it severity, sometimes sternness, and
even acridity, and terror. The usual word was gor-
gon-looking. Something of a frown was implied,
mixed with a radiant earnestness. This was commonly spoken of men's eyes. Anacreon, giving direc-
tions for the portrait of a youth, says—

> " Μελαν ομμα γοργον εστω,
>   Κεκρασμενον γαληνη."
>
> " Dark and *gorgon* be his eye,
>   Tempered with hilarity."

A taste of it, however, was sometimes desired in the
eyes of the ladies. Theagenes, in Heliodorus's " Ethi-
opics," describing his mistress Chariclea, tells us, that
even when a child, something great, and with a divinity
in it, shone out of her eyes, and encountered his, as he
examined them, with a mixture of the *gorgon* and the
alluring.* Perhaps the best word for translating *gorgon* would be *fervent:* something earnest, fiery, and
pressing onward. Anacreon, we see, with his usual
exquisite taste, allays the fierceness of the term with
the participle " tempered." The nice point is, to see
that the terror itself be not terrible, but only a poig-
nancy brought in to assist the sweetness. It is the
salt in the tart; the subtle sting of the essence. It is

* ' Æthiop.' Lib. 11, apud Junium.

to the eye intellectual, what the apple of the eye is to
the eye itself,—the dark part of it, the core, the innermost look; the concentration and burning-glass of the
rays of love. We think, however, that Anacreon did
better than Heliodorus, when he avoided attributing
this look to his mistress, and confined it to the other
sex. He tells us, that she had a look of Minerva as
well as Venus; but it was Minerva without the gorgon. There was sense and apprehensiveness, but nothing to alarm.

Large eyes were admired in Greece, where they
still prevail. They are the finest of all, when they
have the internal look; which is not common. The
stag or antelope eye of the Orientals is beautiful and
lamping, but is accused of looking skittish and indifferent. "The epithet of stag-eyed," says Lady Wort-
ley Montague, speaking of a Turkish love song, "pleases
me extremely; and I think it a very lively image of
the fire and indifference in his mistress's eyes." We
lose in depth of expression when we go to inferior
animals for comparisons with human beauty. Homer
calls Juno ox-eyed; and the epithet suits well with
the eyes of that goddess, because she may be supposed,
with all her beauty, to want a certain humanity. Her
large eyes look at you with a royal indifference. Shakspeare has kissed them, and made them human. Speaking of violets, he describes them as being—

" Sweeter than the lids of Juno's eyes."

This is shutting up their pride, and subjecting them to
the lips of love. Large eyes may become more touching under this circumstance than any others, because
of the field which the large lids give for the veins to
wander in, and the trembling amplitude of the ball be-

neath.   Little eyes must be good-tempered or they are
ruined.   They have no other resource.   But this will
beautify them enough.   They are made for laughing,
and should do their duty.   In Charles the Second's
time, it was the fashion to have sleepy, half-shut eyes,
sly and meretricious.   They took an expression,
beautiful and warrantable on occasion, and made a
commonplace of it, and a vice.   So little do "men of
pleasure" understand the business from which they
take their title.   A good warm-hearted poet shall shed
more light upon voluptuousness and beauty in one
verse from his pen, than a thousand rakes can arrive
at, swimming in claret, and bound on as many voyages
of discovery.

In attending to the hair and eyes, we have forgotten
the eyebrows, and the shape of the head.   They shall
be dispatched before we come to the lips; as the table
is cleared before the dessert.   This is an irreverent
simile, nor do we like it; though the pleasure even of
eating and drinking, to those who enjoy it with temper-
ance, may be traced beyond the palate.   The utmost
refinements on that point are, we allow, wide of the
mark on this.   The idea of beauty, however, is lawfully associated with that of cherries and peaches; as
Eve set forth the dessert in Paradise.

EYEBROWS.—Eyebrows used to obtain more applause
than they do.   Shakespeare seems to jest upon this
eminence, when he speaks of a lover

> " Sighing like furnace, with a woful ballad
> Made to his mistress' eyebrow."

Marot mentions a poem on an eyebrow, which was the

talk of the court of Francis the First.*   The taste of
the Greeks on this point was remarkable.   They
admired eyebrows that almost met.   It depends upon
the character of the rest of the face.   Meeting eyebrows may give a sense and animation to looks that
might otherwise be too feminine.   They have certainly
not a foolish look.   Anacreon's mistress has them :—

> " Taking care her eyebrows be
> Not apart, nor mingled neither,
> But as hers are, stol'n together;
> Met by stealth, yet leaving too
> O'er the eyes their darkest hue.

In the Idyl of Theocritus before mentioned, one of the
speakers values himself upon the effect his beauty has
had on a girl with joined eyebrows.

> " Κημ' εκ τῳ αντρῳ συνοφρυς κηρα εχθες ιδοισα
> Τας δαμαλας παρελευντα, καλον κυλον ημις εφασκεν·
> Ου μεν ουδε λογων εκριθην απο τον πικρον αυτα,
> Αλλα κατω βλεψας ταν ἁμετεραν ὁδϳν ειρπον."

> Passing a bower last evening with my cows,
> A girl look'd out,—a girl with meeting brows.
> " Beautiful! beautiful!" cried she.   I heard,
> But went on, looking down, and gave her not a word.

This taste in female beauty appears to have been confined to the ancients.   Boccaccio, in his " Ameto," the
precursor of the " Decameron," where he gives several
pictures of beautiful women, speaks more than once
of disjoined eyebrows.†   Chaucer, in the " Court of
Love," is equally express in favor of " a due distance."
An arched eyebrow was always in request ; but we
think it is doubtful whether we are to understand that

----

* In one of his Epistles, beginning—

> " Nobles esprits de France poétiques."

† L'Ameto di Messer Giovanni Boccaccio, pp. 31, 32, 39.   Parma,
1802.

the eyebrows were always desired to form separate
arches, or to give an arched character to the brow
considered in unison. In either case the curve should
be very delicate. A straight eyebrow is better than a
very arching one, which has a look of wonder and
silliness. To have it immediately over the eye, is
preferable, for the same reason, to its being too high
and lifted. The Greeks liked eyes leaning upwards
towards each other; which indeed is a rare beauty,
and the reverse of the animal character. If the brows
over these took a similar direction, they would form
an arch together. Perhaps a sort of double curve was
required, the particular one over the eye, and the
general one in the look altogether.* But these are
unnecessary refinements. Where great difference of
taste is allowed, the point in question can be of little
consequence. We cannot think, however, with Ariosto,
that fair locks with black eyebrows are desirable.
We see, by an article in an Italian catalogue, that the
taste provoked a discussion.† It is to be found, however, in "Achilles Tatius," and in the poem beginning

> " Lydia, bella puella, candida,"

attributed to Gallus. A moderate distinction is desirable, especially where the hair is very light. Hear
Burns, in a passage full of life and sweetness,

> " Sae flaxen were her ringlets,
> Her eyebrows of a darker hue,
> Bewitchingly o'er-arching
> Twa laughing een o' bonny blue."

It is agreed on all hands that a female eyebrow ought

* See the " Ameto," p. 32.
† Barrotti, Gio. Andrea; Le Chiome Bionde e Ciglia Nere d'Alcina,
Discorso Accademico. Padova, 1746.

to be delicate, and nicely pencilled.   Dante says of his
mistress's, that it looked as if it was painted.

> " Il ciglio
> Pulito, e brun, talchè dipinto pare."
> *Rime*, Lib. V.

> The eyebrow,
> Polished and dark, as though the brush had drawn it.

Brows ought to be calm and even.

> " Upon her eyelids many graces sat,
> Under the shadow of her even brows."
> *Faery Queen.*

Eyelids have been mentioned before.   The lashes are
best when they are dark, long, and abundant without
tangling.

Shape of Head and Face, Ears, Cheeks, &c.—
The shape of the head, including the face, is handsome
in proportion as it inclines from round into oval.   This
should particularly appear, when the face is looking
down.   The skull should be like a noble cover to a
beautiful goblet.   The principal breadth is at the
temples, and over the ears.   The ears ought to be
small, delicate, and compact.   We have fancied that
musical people have fine ears in that sense, as well as
the other.   But the internal conformation must be the
main thing with them.   The same epithets of small,
delicate, and compact, apply to the jaw; which loses
in beauty, in proportion as it is large and angular.
The cheek is the seat of great beauty and sentiment.
It is the region of passive and habitual softness.
Gentle acquiescence is there; modesty is there; the
lights and colors of passion play tenderly in and out
its surface, like the Aurora of the northern sky.   It

has been seen how Anacreon has painted a cheek.
Sir Philip Sidney has touched it with no less delicacy,
and more sentiment:—"Her cheeks blushing, and
withal, when she was spoken to, a little smiling, were
like roses when their leaves are with a little breath
stirred."—"Arcadia," Book I.   Beautiful-cheeked is a
favorite epithet with Homer.   There is an exquisite
delicacy, rarely noticed, in the transition from the
cheek to the neck, just under the ear.   Akenside has
observed it; but he hurts his feeling, as usual, with
commonplace epithets:—

> " Hither turn
> Thy graceful footsteps; hither, gentle maid,
> Incline thy polish'd forehead; let thy eyes
> Effuse the mildness of their azure dawn;
> And may the fanning breezes waft aside
> Thy radiant locks, disclosing, as it bends
> With airy softness from the marble-neck,
> The cheek fair blooming."
>> *Pleasures of Imagination.*

The "marble neck" is too violent a contrast; but the
picture is delicate.

> " Effuse the mildness of their azure dawn"

is an elegant and happy verse.

We may here observe, that rakes and men of sentiment appear to have agreed in objecting to ornaments
for the ears.   Ovid, Sir Philip Sidney, and, we think,
Beaumont and Fletcher, have passages against ear-
rings; but we cannot refer to the last.

> " Vos quoque non caris aures onerate lapillis,
> Quos legit in viridi decolor Indus aqua."
>> *Artis Amor.* Lib. III.

> Load not your ears with costly jewelry,
> Which the swart Indian culls from his green sea.

This, to be sure, might be construed into a warning

against the abuse, rather than the use, of such ornaments; but the context is in favor of the latter supposition. The poet is recommending simplicity, and ex-
tolling the age he lives in for being sensible enough to
dispense with show and finery. The passage in Sidney is express, and is a pretty conceit. Drawing a
portrait of his heroine, and coming to the ear, he tells
us, that

> " The tip no jewel needs to wear;
> The tip is jewel to the ear."

We confess that when we see a handsome ear without
an ornament, we are glad it is not there; but if it has
an ornament, and one in good taste, we know not how
to wish it away. There is an elegance in the dangling
of a gem suitable to the complexion. We believe the
ear is better without it. Akenside's picture, for instance, would be spoiled by a ring. Furthermore, it
is in the way of a kiss.

Nose.—The nose in general has the least character
of any of the features. When we meet with a very
small one, we only wish it larger; when with a large
one, we would fain request it to be smaller. In itself
it is rarely anything. The poets have been puzzled to
know what to do with it. They are generally contented with describing it as straight, and in good proportion. The straight nose, quoth Dante,—" *Il dritto
naso.*" " Her nose directed streight," saith Chaucer.
" Her nose is neither too long nor too short," say the
" Arabian Nights." Ovid makes no mention of a nose.
Ariosto says of Alcina's (not knowing what else to
say), that envy could not find fault with it. Anacreon
contrives to make it go shares with the cheek. Boccaccio, in one of his early works, the "Ameto" above-

mentioned, where he has an epithet for almost every noun, is so puzzled what to say of a nose, that he calls it *odorante*, the smelling nose. Fielding, in his contempt for so unsentimental a part of the visage, does not scruple to beat Amelia's nose to pieces, by accident ; in order to show how contented her lover can be, when the surgeon has put it decently to rights. This has been reckoned a hazardous experiment. Not that a lover, if he is worth anything, would not remain a lover after such an accident, but that it is well to have a member uninjured, which has so little character to support its adversity. The commentators have a curious difficulty with a line in Catullus. They are not sure whether he wrote

> " Salve, nec *nimio* puello naso—
> Hail damsel, with by no means too much nose."

or,

> " Salve, nec *minimo* puella naso—
> Hail, damsel, with by no means nose too little."

It is a feature generally to be described by negatives. It is of importance, however, to the rest of the face. If a good nose will do little for a countenance otherwise poor, a bad one is a great injury to the best. An indifferent one is so common that it is easily tolerated. It appears, from the epithets bestowed upon that part of the face by the poets and romance writers, that there is no defect more universal than a nose a little wry, or out of proportion. The reverse is desirable, accordingly. A nose should be firmly, yet lightly cut, delicate, spirited, harmonious in its parts, and proportionate with the rest of the features. A nose merely well-drawn and proportioned, can be very insipid. Some little freedom and delicacy is required to give it character. The character which most becomes it is that of taste and apprehensiveness. And a perfectly elegant face has a nose of this sort. Dignity, as regards this feature, depends upon the expression of the rest of the face. Thus a large aquiline nose increases the look of strength in a strong face, and of weakness in a weak one. The contrast,—the want of balance,—is too great, Junius adduces the authority of the sophist, Philostratus, for *tetragonal* or *quadrangular noses*,—noses like those of statues; that is to say, broad and level in the bridge, with distinct angles to the parallelogram. These are better for men than women. The genders of noses are more distinct than those of eyes and lips. The neuter are the commonest. A nose a little aquiline has been admired in some women. Cyrus's Aspasia had one, according to Ælian. "She had very large eyes," quoth he, "and a nose somewhat aquiline." ολιγον δε ην και επιγρυπος.* The less the better. It trenches upon the other sex, and requires all the graces of Aspasia to carry it off. Those, indeed, will carry off anything. There are many handsome and even charming women with aquiline noses; but they are charming in spite of them, not by their assistance. Painters do not give them to their ideal beauties. We do not imagine angels with aquiline noses. Dignified men have them. Plato calls them royal. Marie Antoinette was not the worse for an aquiline nose; at least in her triumphant days, when she swam through an antechamber like a vision and swept away the understanding of Mr. Burke. But if a royal nose has anything to do with a royal will, she would have been the better, at last, for one of a less dominant description. A Roman nose may establish

* "Var. Hist." Lib. 12, Cap. 1.

a tyranny :—according to Marmontel, a little turn-up
nose overthrew one.   At all events, it is more feminine ; and La Fontaine was of Marmontel's opinion.
Writing to the Duchess of Bouillon, who had expressed
a fear that he would grow tired of Chateau Thierry,
he says,—

" Peut-on s'ennuyer en des lieux
    Honorés par les pas, éclairés par les yeux
        D'une aimable et vive Princesse,
    A pied blanc et mignon, à brune et longue tresse ?
Nez troussé, c'est un charme encor selon mon sens,
    C'en est même un des plus puissants.
Pour moi, le temps d'aimer est passé, je l'avoue ;
        Et je mérite qu'on me loue
        De ce libre et sincère aveu,
    Dont pourtant le public se souciera très peu.
Que j'aime ou n'aime pas, c'est pour lui même chose.
    Mais s'il arrive que mon cœur
    Retourne à l'avenir dans sa première erreur,
Nez aquilins et longs n'en seront pas la cause."

How can one tire in solitudes and nooks,
Graced by the steps, enlighten'd by the looks,
    Of the most piquant of Princesses,
    With little darling foot, and long dark tresses ?
    A turn-up nose, too, between you and me,
    Has something that attracts me mightily.
My loving days, I must confess, are over,
A fact it does me honor to discover ;
    Though, I suppose, whether I love or not
    That brute, the public, will not care a jot :—
The dev'l a bit will their hard hearts look to it.
    But should it happen, some fine day,
    That anything should lead me round that way,
A long and beaky nose will certainly not do it.

10*

CRITICISM ON FEMALE BEAUTY.

Mouth and chin.—Mouth the part of the face the least able to conceal the expression of temper, &c.—Handsome smiles in plain faces.—Teeth.—Dimples.—Neck and shoulders.—Perfection of shape.—Bosom.—Caution against the misconstruction of the coarse-minded.

MOUTH AND CHIN.—The mouth, like the eyes, gives occasion to so many tender thoughts, and is so apt to lose and supersede itself in the affectionate softness of its effect upon us, that the first impulse, in speaking of it, is to describe it by a sentiment and a transport. Mr. Sheridan has hit this very happily—see his " Rivals :"—

> " Then, Jack, such eyes! Such lips! Eyes so

We never met with a passage in all the poets that gave us a livelier and softer idea of this charming feature, than a stanza in a homely old writer of our own country. He is relating the cruelty of Queen Eleanor to the Fair Rosamond :—

> " With that she dash'd her on the lips,
>   So dyed double red :
> Hard was the heart that gave the blow,
>   Soft were those lips that bled."
> WARNER'S ALBION'S ENGLAND, Book viii. chap. 41.

Sir John Suckling, in his taste of an under lip, is not to be surpassed :—

" Her lips were red, and one was thin
   Compared with that was next her chin,
   Some bee had stung it newly."

The upper lip, observe, was only comparatively thin. Thin lips become none but shrews or niggards. A rosiness beyond that of the cheeks, and a good-tem pered sufficiency and plumpness, are the indispensable requisites of a good mouth. Chaucer, a great judge, is very peremptory in this matter :—

" With pregnant lippès, thick to kiss percase ;
   For lippès thin, not fat, but ever lean,
   They serve of naught ; they be not worth a bean ;
   For if the base be full, there is delight."
                          THE COURT OF LOVE.

For the consolation, however, of those who have thin lips, and are not shrews or niggards, we must give it here as our opinion, founded on what we have observed, that lips become more or less contracted, in the course of years, in proportion as they are accustomed to express good-humor and generosity, or peevishness and a contracted mind. Remark the effect which a moment of ill-temper or grudgingness has upon the lips, and judge what may be expected from an habitual series of such moments. Remark the reverse, and make a similar judgment. The mouth is the frankest part of the face. It can the least conceal the feelings. We can hide neither ill-temper with it nor good. We may affect what we please ; but affectation will not help us. In a wrong cause, it will only make our observers resent the endeavor to impose upon them. The mouth is the seat of one class of emotions, as the eyes are of another ; or rather, it expresses the same emotions but in greater detail, and with a more irrepressible tendency to mobility. It is

the region of smiles and dimples, of a trembling tenderness, of sharp sorrow, of a full and breathing joy,
of candor, of reserve, of a carking care, of a liberal
sympathy.   The mouth, out of its many sensibilities,
may be fancied throwing up one great expression into
the eyes; as many lights in a city reflect a broad lustre into the heavens.   On the other hand, the eyes
may be supposed the chief movers, influencing the
smaller details of their companion, as heaven influences
earth.   The first cause in both is internal and deep-
seated.

The more we consider beauty, the more we recognize its dependence on sentiment.   The handsomest
mouth, without expression, is no better than a mouth
in a drawing-book.   An ordinary one, on the other
hand, with a great deal of expression, shall become
charming.   One of the handsomest smiles we ever
saw in a man, was that of a celebrated statesman who
is reckoned plain.   How handsome Mrs. Jordan was
when she laughed; who, nevertheless, was not a
beauty.   If we only imagine a laugh full of kindness
and enjoyment, or a "little giddy laugh," as Marot
calls it,—*un petit ris folâtre*,—we imagine the mouth
handsome as a matter of course; at any rate, for the
time.   The material obeys the spiritual.   Anacreon
beautifully describes a lip as "a lip like Persuasion's,"
and says it calls upon us to kiss it.   "Her lips," says
Sir Philip Sidney, "though they were kept close with
modest silence, yet with a pretty kind of natural swel-
ling, they seemed to invite the guests that looked on
them."—*Arcadia*, Book I.

Let me quote another passage from that noble romance, which was written to fill a woman's mind with
all beautiful thoughts, and which we never met with

a woman that did not like, notwithstanding its faults, and in spite of the critics. " Her tears came dropping down like rain in sunshine ; and she not taking heed to wipe the tears, they hung upon her cheeks and lips, as upon cherries, *which the dropping tree bedeweth.*" —Book the Third. Nothing can be more fresh and elegant than this picture.

A mouth should be of good natural dimensions, as well as plump in the lips. When the ancients, among their beauties, make mention of small mouths and lips, they mean small only as opposed to an excess the other way ; a fault very common in the south. The sayings in favor of small mouths, which have been the ruin of so many pretty looks, are very absurd. If there must be an excess either way, it had better be the liberal one. A petty, pursed-up mouth is fit for nothing but to be left to its self-complacency. Large mouths are oftener found in union with generous dispositions, than very small ones. Beauty should have neither ; but a reasonable look of openness and delicacy. It is an elegance in lips, when, instead of making sharp angles at the corner of the mouth, they retain a certain breadth to the very verge, and show the red. The corner then looks painted with a free and liberal pencil.

Beautiful teeth are of a moderate size, even, and white, not a dead white, like fish-bones, which has something ghastly in it, but ivory or pearly white with an enamel. Bad teeth in a handsome mouth present a contradiction, which is sometimes extremely to be pitied ; for a weak or feverish state of body may occasion them. Teeth, not kept as clean as possible, are unpardonable. Ariosto has a celebrated stanza upon a mouth :—

" Sotto quel sta, quasi fra due vallette,
 La bocca, sparsa di natio cinabro:
 Quivi due filze son di perle elette,
 Che chiude ed apre un bello e dolce labro ;
 Quindi escon le cortesi parolette
 Da render molle ogni cor rozzo e scabro ;
 Quivi si forma quel soave riso,
 Ch'apre a sua posta in terra il paradiso."
                              ORLAN. FUR. Canto 7.

Next, as between two little vales appears
The mouth, where spices and vermilion keep:
There lurk the pearls, richer than sultan wears,
Now casketed, now shown, by a sweet lip :
Thence issue the soft words and courteous prayers,
Enough to make a churl for sweetness weep :
And there the smile taketh its rosy rise,
That opens upon earth a paradise.

To the mouth belong not only its own dimples, but
those of the cheek :—

" Le pozzette
Che forma un dolce riso in bello guancia."
                              TASSO.
" The delicate wells
 Which a sweet smile forms in a lovely cheek."

The chin, to be perfect, should be round and delicate, neither advancing nor retreating too much. If
it exceed either way, the latter defect is on the side
of gentleness. The former anticipates old age. A
rounded and gentle prominence is both spirited and
beautiful ; and is eminently Grecian. It is an elegant
countenance (affectation of course apart), where the
forehead and eyes have an over-looking aspect, while
the mouth is delicately full and dimpled, and the chin
supports it like a cushion leaning a little upward. A
dimple in the chin is almost invariably demanded by
the poets, and has a character of grace and tenderness.

NECK AND SHOULDERS.—The shoulders in a female

ought to be delicately plump, even, and falling without
suddenness. Broad shoulders are admired by many.
It is difficult not to like them when handsomely turned.
It seems as if "the more of a good thing the better."
At all events, an excess that way may divide opinion,
while of the deformity of pinched and mean-looking
shoulders there can be no doubt. A good-tempered
woman, of the order yclept buxom, not only warrants
a pair of expansive shoulders, but bespeaks our appro-
bation of them. Nevertheless they are undoubtedly a
beauty rather on the masculine than feminine side.
They belong to manly strength. Achilles had them.
Milton gives them to Adam. His

> " Hyacinthine locks
>   Round from his parted forelock manly hung
>   Clustering; but not beneath his shoulders broad."

Fielding takes care to give all his heroes huge calves
and Herculean shoulders,—graces, by the way, conspicuous in himself. Female shoulders ought rather
to convey a sentiment of the gentle and acquiescent.
They should lean under those of the other sex, as under
a protecting shade. Looking at the male and female
figure with the eye of a sculptor, our first impression
with regard to the one should be, that it is the figure
of a noble creature, prompt for action, and with shoulders full of power;—with regard to the other, that it is
that of a gentle creature, made to be beloved, and
neither active nor powerful, but fruitful:—the mould
of humanity. Her greatest breadth ought not to appear to be at the shoulders. The figure should resemble the pear on the tree,—

> " Winding gently to the waist."

Of these matters, and of the bosom, it is difficult to

speak: but *Honi soit qui mal y'pense.* This essay is
written neither for the prudish nor the indelicate; but
for those who have a genuine love of the beautiful, and
can afford to hear of it. It is not the poets and other
indulgers in a lively sense of the beautiful that are deficient in a respect for it; but they who suppose that
every lively expression must of necessity contain a
feeling of the gross and impertinent. We do not regard these graces, as they pass in succession before us,
with the coarse and cunning eye of a rake at a tavern-
door. We will venture to say that we are too affectionate and even voluptuous for such a taste; and that
the real homage we pay the sex deserves the very best
construction of the best people, and will have it.—

> " Fathers and husbands, I do claim a right
> In all that is called lovely. Take my sight
> Sooner than my affection from the fair.
> No face, no hand, proportion, line, or air
> Of Beauty, but the muse hath interest in."
>   BEN JONSON.

A bosom is most beautiful when it presents *none* of
the extremes which different tastes have demanded
for it. Its only excess should be that of health. This
is not too likely to occur in a polite state of society.
Modern customs and manners too often leave to the
imagination the task of furnishing out the proper quantity of beauty, where it might have existed in perfection. And a tender imagination will do so. The only
final ruin of a bosom in an affectionate eye, is the want
of a good heart. Nor shall the poor beauty which the
mother has retained by dint of being no mother, be
lovely as the ruin. O Sentiment! Beauty is but the
outward and visible sign of thee; and not always there,
where thou art most. Thou canst supply her place

when she is gone.   Thou canst remain, and still make
an eye sweet to look into; a bosom beautiful to rest
the heart on.

A favorite epithet with the Greek poets, lyrical, epic,
and dramatic, is *deep-bosomed.*   A Greek meant to say,
that he admired a chest truly feminine.   It is to be
concluded, that he also demanded one left to its natural state, as it appeared among the healthiest and
loveliest of his countrywomen; neither compressed,
as it was by the fine ladies; nor divided and divorced
in that excessive manner, which some have accounted
beautiful.*   It was certainly nothing contradictory to
grace and activity which he demanded.

> " Crown me, then, I'll play the lyre,
>   Bacchus, underneath thy shade :
> Heap me, heap me, higher and higher;
> And I'll lead a dance of fire,
>   With a dark deep-bosom'd maid."
>   ANACREON, Ode V.

Rosy-bosom'd is another Greek epithet.   Milton
speaks in " Comus" of

> " The Graces and the rosy-bosom'd Hours."

Virgil says of Venus,

>   —— She said,
> And turn'd, refulgent, with a rosy neck.*

> " O'er her warm neck and rising bosom move
> The bloom of young Desire, and purple light of Love;"
>   GRAY.

which is a couplet made up of this passage in Virgil and another.   Virgil follows the Greeks, and the
Greeks followed nature.   All this bloom and rosy re-
fulgence, which are phrases of the poets, mean nothing

---

* See an epigram in the Greek Anthology, beginning
> " Εχμαινει χειλη μη ροδοκρυα, ποικιλοριθα."

† " Dixit; et avertens, rosea cervice refulsit."

more than that healthy color which appears in the finest
skin.   We shall see more of it when we come to speak
of Hands and Arms.

A writer in the Anthology makes use of the pretty
epithet, "*vernal-bosom'd.*"*   The most delicate painting of a vernal bosom is in Spenser:—

> " And in her hand a sharp boar-spear she held,
> And at her back a bow and quiver gay
> Stuft with steel-headed darts, wherewith she quell'd
> The salvage beasts in her victorious play,
> Knit with a golden bauldric, which forelay
> Athwart her snowy breast, and did divide
> Her dainty paps; which, like young fruit in May,
> Now little gan to swell; and being tied,
> Through their thin weeds their places only signified."

Dryden copies after Spenser, but not with such refinement.   His passage, however, is so beautiful, and
has a gentleness and movement so much to the purpose, that I cannot resist the pleasure of quoting it.
He is describing Boccaccio's heroine in the story of
" Cymon and Iphigenia:"—

> " By chance conducted, or by thirst constrain'd,
> The deep recesses of the grove he gain'd;
> Where, in a plain defended by the wood,
> Crept through the matted grass a crystal flood,
> By which an alabaster fountain stood:
> And on the margin of the fount was laid,
> Attended by her slaves, a sleeping maid;
> Like Dian and her nymphs, when, tired with sport,
> To rest by cool Eurotas they resort,
> The dame herself the goddess well express'd
> Not more distinguish'd by her purple vest,
> Than by the charming features of her face,
> And e'en in slumber a superior grace.
> Her comely limbs composed with decent care,
> Her body shaded with a slight cymar,
> Her bosom to the view was only bare;

---

* Ειαρομασθος.

Where two beginning paps were scarcely spied,
For yet their places were but signified.
The fanning wind upon her bosom blows; .
To meet the fanning wind the bosom rose;
The fanning wind, and purling streams, continue her repose."

This beautiful conclusion, with its repetitions, its play
to and fro, and the long continuous line with which it
terminates, is delightfully soft and characteristic. The
beauty of the sleeper and of the landscape mingle with
one another. The wind and the bosom are gentle
challengers.

"Each softer seems than each, and each than each seems smoother."

Even the turn of Dryden's last triplet is imitated from
Spenser.—See the divine passage of the concert in
the " Bower of Bliss, Faery Queen," book ii. canto 12,
stanza 71. "The sage and serious Spenser," as Milton called him, is a great master of the beautiful in all
its branches. He also knew, as well as any poet, how
to help himself to beauty out of others. The former
passage imitated by Dryden was, perhaps, suggested
by one in Boccaccio.* The simile of " young fruit in
May" is from Ariosto.

" Bianca neve è il bel collo, e'l petto latte ;
Il collo tondo, il petto colmo e largo :
Due pome acerbe, e pur d'avorio fatte,
Vengono e van, come onda al primo margo,
Quando piacevole aura il mar combatte."
ORLAN. FUR. Canto 7.

Her bosom is like milk, her neck like snow ;
A rounded neck ; a bosom, where you see
Two crisp young ivory apples come and go,
'. Like waves that on the shore beat tenderly,
When a sweet air is ruffling to and fro.

But Ariosto has been also to Boccaccio, and he to
Theocritus; in whom, we believe, this fruitful meta-

* " L'Ameto," as above, p. 31, 33.

phor is first to be met with. It is very suitable to his shepherds, living among the bowers of Sicily.—See "Idyl" xxvii. v. 49.   Sir Philip Sidney has repeated it in the "Arcadia."   But poets in all ages have drawn similar metaphors from the gardens.   "Solomon's Song" abounds with them.   There is a hidden analogy, more than poetical, among all the beauties of nature.

We quit this tender ground, prepared to think very ill of any person who thinks we have said too much of it. Its beauty would not allow us to say less; but not the less do we " with reverence deem" of those resting-places for the head of love and sorrow—

> " Those dainties made to stir an infant's cries."

CRITICISM ON FEMALE BEAUTY.

IV.—HAND, ARM, WALK, VOICE.

*Hand and arm.—Italian epithet " Morbida."—Figure.—Carriage, &c.
—Perils of fashion.—Vice of tight-lacing—Hips.—Legs and feet.—
Walk.—Carriage of Roman and Italian women.—That of English
preferred.—Voice ditto.—Reason why the most beautiful women are in
general not the most charming.*

HAND AND ARM.—A beautiful arm is of a round
and flowing outline, and gently tapering; the hand
long, delicate, and well turned, with taper fingers,
and a certain buoyancy and turn upwards in their
very curvature and repose. We fear this is not well
expressed. We mean, that when the hand is at rest
on its palm, the wrist a little bent, and the other part
of it, with the fingers, stretching and dipping for-
wards with the various undulations of the joints, it
ought, however plump and in good condition, to retain
a look of promptitude and lightness. The spirit of the
guitar ought to be in it; of the harp and the pianoforte, of the performance of all elegant works, even
to the dairy of Eve, who " tempered dulcet creams."
See a picture in Spenser, not to be surpassed by any
Italian pencil :—

> " In her left hand a cup of gold she held,
>   And with her right the riper fruit did reach,
>   Whose sappy liquor, that with fulness swell'd

> Into her cup she scruzed with dainty breach
> Of her fine fingers, without foul impeach,
> That so fair wine-press made the wine more sweet."
>
> Book ii. canto 12.

It is sometimes thought that hands and arms cannot be too white. A genuine white is very beautiful, and is requisite to give them perfection; but shape and spirit are the first things in all beauty. Complexion follows. A hand and arm may be beautiful, without being excessively fair; they may also be very fair and not at all beautiful. Above all, a sickly white is not to be admired, whatever may be thought of it by the sallow Italian, who praises a white hand for being *morbid.* We believe, however, he means nothing more than a contradiction to his yellow. He would have his mistress's complexion unspoilt by oil and macaroni. These excessive terms, as we have before noticed, are not to be taken to the letter. A sick hand has its merits, if it be an honest one. It may excite a feeling beyond beauty. But sickliness is not beauty. In the whitest skin there ought to be a look of health.* The nails of the fingers ought to be tinged with red. When the Greeks spoke of the *rosy-fingered* Morn, it was not a mere metaphor, alluding to the ruddiness of the time of day. They referred also to the human image. The metaphor was founded in Nature, whether the goddess's office or person was to be considered.

Wherever a genuine and lasting beauty is desired, the blood must be circulated.

FIGURE, CARRIAGE, &c.—The beauty of the female

---

* "Candidis tamen manibus rosei ruboris aliquid suffundatur."—JUNIUS, Cap. ix. sect. 26.

figure consists in being gently serpentine. Modesty and luxuriance, fulness and buoyancy; a rising, as if to meet; a falling, as if to retire; spirit, softness, apprehensiveness, self-possession, a claim on protection, a superiority to insult, a sparkling something enshrined in gentle proportions and harmonious movement, should all be found in that charming mixture of the spiritual and material. Mind and body are not to be separated, where real beauty exists. Should there be no great intellect, there will be an intellectual instinct, a grace, an address, a naturally wise amiableness. Should intellect unite with these, there is nothing upon earth so powerful, except the spirit whom it shall call master.

Beauty too often sacrifices to fashion. The spirit of fashion is not the beautiful, but the wilful; not the graceful but the fantastic; not the superior in the abstract, but the superior in the worst of all concretes, the vulgar. It is the vulgarity that can afford to shift and vary itself, opposed to the vulgarity that longs 'to do so, but cannot. The high point of taste and elegance is to be sought for, not in the most fashionable circles, but in the best-bred, and such as can dispense with the eternal necessity of never being the same thing. Beauty there, both moral and personal, will do all it can to resist the envy of those who would deface, in order to supersede it. The highest dressers, the highest face-painters, are not the loveliest women, but such as have lost their loveliness, or never had any. The others know the value of their natural appearance too well. It is these that inspire the mantua-maker or milliner with some good thought. The herd of fashion take it up, and spoil it. A hundred years ago it was the fashion for ladies to have long waists like a funnel.

Who would suppose that this originated in a natural
and even rustic taste? And yet the stomachers of
that time were only caricatures of the bodice of a
country beauty. Some handsome women brought the
original to town; fashion proceeded to render it ugly
and extravagant; and posterity laughs at the ridiculous portraits of its grandmothers. The poet might
have addressed a beauty forced into this fashion, as he
did his heroine in the celebrated lines:

> " No longer shall the bodice, aptly laced,
> From thy full bosom to thy slender waist,
> •   That air and harmony of shape express,
> Fine by degrees, and beautifully less."
>
> PRIOR'S HENRY AND EMMA.

No: it was

> " Gaunt all at once, and hideously little."

It was like a pottle of strawberries, instead of a human
waist. Some years ago it was the fashion for a lady
to look like an hour-glass, or a huge insect, or anything
else cut in two, and bolstered out at head and feet. A
fashion that gracefully shows the figure is one thing:
a fashion that totally conceals it, may have its merits;
but voluntarily to accept puffed shoulders in lieu of
good ones, and a pinch in the ribs for a body like that
of Venus de Medici, is what no woman of taste should
put up with who can avoid it. They are taking her
in. The levelling rogues know what they are about,
and are for rendering their crooked backs and unsatis-
factory waists indistinguishable. If the levelling
stopped here, it might be pardonable. Fair play is a
jewel that one wishes to see everybody enriched by.
But as fashion is too often at variance with beauty, it
is also at variance with health. The more a woman

sacrifices of the one, the more she loses of the other. Thick legs are the least result of these little waists. Bad lungs, bad livers, bad complexions, deaths, melancholy, and worse than all, rickety and melancholy children, are the consequences of the tricks that fashion plays with the human body.

It is a truism to say that a waist should be neither pinched in nor shapeless, neither too sudden nor too shelving, &c., but a natural, unsophisticated waist, properly bending when at rest, properly falling in when the person is in motion. But truisms are sometimes as necessary to repeat in writing, as to abide by in painting or sculpture. The worst of it is, they are not always allowed to be spoken of. For instance, there is a truism called a hip. It is surely a very modest and respectable joint, and of great use to the rising generation. A sculptor could no more omit it in a perfect figure, than he could omit a leg or an arm. And yet, by some very delicate train of reasoning, known only to the double-refined, not merely the word, but the thing, was suppressed about twenty years back. The word vanished : the joint was put under the most painful restrictions ; it seemed as if there was a Society for the Suppression of Hips. The fashion did not last, or there is no knowing what would have become of us. We should have been the most melancholy, hipped, unhipped generation, that ever walked without our proper dimensions. Moore's Almanac would have contained new wonders for us. Finally, we should have gone out, have wasted, faded, old maided-and-bachelored ourselves away, grown

" Fine by degrees and beautifully less,"

till a Dutch jury (the only survivors) brought in the
11

verdict of the polite world.—Died for want of care in the mother. At present a writer may speak of hips, and live. Nay, the fancies of the men seem to have been so wrought upon by the recollection of those threatening times, that they have amplified into hips themselves, and even grown pigeon-breasted. Such are the melancholy consequences of violating the laws of Nature.

A true female figure, then, is falling and not too broad in the shoulders; moderate, yet inclining to fulness rather than deficiency, in the bosom; gently tapering, and without violence of any sort, in the waist; naturally curving again in those never-to-be-without-apology-alluded-to hips; and, finally, her buoyant lightness should be supported upon natural legs, not at all like a man's; and upon feet, which, though little, are able to support all the rest.

Ariosto has described a foot,—

" Il breve, asciutto, e ritondetto piede."
"The short, and neat, and little rounded foot."

The shortness, however, is not to be made by dint of shoes. It must be natural. It must also be not too short. It should be short and delicate, compared with that of the other sex; but sufficient for all purposes of walking and running, and dancing, and dispensing with tight shoes; otherwise it is neither handsome in itself, nor will it give rise to graceful movements. It is better to have the sentiment of grace in a foot, than a forced or unnatural smallness. The Chinese have three ideas in their heads:—tea, the necessity of keeping off ambassadors, and the beauty of small feet. The way in which they caricature this beauty is a warning to all dull un-

derstandings. We make our feet bad enough already
by dint of squeezing. Nations with shoes have no
proper feet, like those who wear sandals. But the
Chinese out-pinch an inquisitor. We have seen a
model of a lady's foot of that country, in which the toes
were fairly turned underneath. They looked as if they
were almost jammed into and made part of the sole.
In the British Museum, if we remember, there is a
pair of shoes that belonged to such a foot as this, which
are shown in company with another pair, the property
of Queen Elizabeth. Her Majesty stood upon no ceremony in that matter, and must have stamped to some
purpose.

But what are beautiful feet, if they support not, and
carry about with them, other graces? What are the
most harmonious proportions, if the soul of music is
not within? Graceful movement, an unaffected elegance of demeanor, is to the figure what sense and
sweetness are to the eyes. It is the soul looking out.
It is what a poet has called the "thought of the body."
The ancients, as the moderns do still in the south, admired a stately carriage in a woman: though the taste
seems to have been more general in Rome than in
Greece. It is to be observed, that neither in Greece
nor Rome had the women at any time received that
truly feminine polish, which renders their manners a
direct though not an unsuitable contrast to those of the
other sex. It was reserved for the Goths and their
chivalry to reward them with this refinement; and
their northern descendants have best preserved it. The
walk which the Latin poets attribute to their beauties,
is still to be seen in all its stateliness at Rome. "Shall
I be treated in this manner?" says Juno, complaining

of her injured dignity,—"I, who *walk* the queen of the gods, the sister and the wife of Jove ?"*—Venus, meeting Æneas, allows herself to be recognized in departing :—

—————— " Pedes vestis defluxit ad imos,
Et vera incessu patuit Dea."
" In length of train descends her sweeping gown,
And by her graceful walk the queen of love is known."

DRYDEN.

A stately verse ;—but *known* is not strong enough for *patuit*, and Virgil does not say "the queen of love," but simply the goddess—the divinity. The walk included every kind of superiority. It is the step of Homer's ladies—

" Of Troy's proud dames whose garments sweep the ground."

POPE.

The painting has more of Rubens than Raphael, and we could not help thinking, when in Italy, that the walk of the females had more spirit than grace. They know nothing of the swimming voluptuousness with which our ladies at court used to float into the drawing-room with their hoops ; or the sweet and modest sway hither and thither, a little bending, with which a young girl shall turn and wind about a garden by herself, half serious, half playful. Their demeanor is sharper and more vehement. The grace is less reserved. There is, perhaps, less consciousness of the sex in it, but it is not the most modest or touching on that account. The women in Italy sit and sprawl about the doorways in the attitudes of men. Without being viragos, they swing their arms as they walk. There is infinite self-possession, but no subjection of it to a sentiment. The most graceful and modest have a certain want of re-

* " Ego, quæ divum *incedo* regina," &c.

tirement. Their movements do not play inwards, but
outwards: do not wind and retreat upon themselves,
but are developed as a matter of course.   If thought
of, they are equally suffered to go on, with an unaffected and crowning satisfaction, conquering and to
conquer.   This is the walk that Dante admired :—

> " Soave a guisa va di un bel pavone ;
>   Diritta sopra se, come una grua."

> Sweetly she goes, like the bright peacock ; straight
> Above herself, like to the lady crane.

This is not the way we conceive Imogen or Desde-
mona to have walked.

The carriage of Laura, Petrarch's mistress, was
gentle ; but she was a Provençal, not an Italian.   He
counts it among the four principal charms which rendered him so enamored.   They were all identified with
a sentiment.   There was her carriage or walk ; her
sweet looks ; her dulcet words ; and her kind, modest,
and self-possessed demeanor.

> " E con l'ander, e col soave sguardo,
>   S'accordan le dolcissime parole,
>   E l'atto mansueto, umile, e tardo.
>   Di tai quattro faville, e non già sole,
>   Nasce 'l gran foco di ch' io vivo ed ardo :
>   Che son fatto un augel notturno al sole."
> Sonnet 131.

> From these four sparks it was, nor those alone
> Sprung the great fire that makes me what I am,
> A bird nocturnal, warbling to the sun.

In this sonnet is the origin of a word of Milton's, not
noticed by the commentators.

> " With store of ladies, whose bright eyes
>   Rain influence."
> L'ALLEGRO.

> " Da begli occhi un piacer sì caldo *piove*."
> " So warm a pleasure *rains* from her sweet eyes."

And in another beautiful sonnet, where he describes her sparkling with more than her wonted lustre, he says,

> " Non era l'andar suo cosa mortale,
>   Ma d' angelica forma."
>
> Sonnet 68.
>
> Her going was no mortal thing ; but shaped
> Like to an angel's.

Now this is the difference between the walk of the ancient and modern heroine ; of the beauty classical and Provençal, Italian and English.   The one was like a goddess's, stately, and at the top of the earth ; the other is like an angel's, humbler, but nearer heaven.

It is the same with the voice.   The southern voice is loud and uncontrolled ; the women startle you, bawling and gabbling in the summer air.   In the north, the female seems to bethink her of a thousand delicate restraints ; her words issue forth with a sort of cordial hesitation.   They have a breath and apprehensiveness in them, as if she spoke with every part of her being.

> " Her voice was ever soft, gentle, and low,
>   An excellent thing in woman."
>
> SHAKSPEARE.

As the best things, however, are the worst when spoiled, it is not easy to describe how much better the unsophisticated bawling of the Italian is, than the affectation of a low and gentle voice in a body full of furious passions.   The Italian nature is a good one, though run to excess.   You can pare it down.   A good system of education would make it as fine a thing morally, as good training renders Italian singing the

finest in the world.   But a furious English woman
affecting sweet utterance!—"Let us take any man's
horses," as Falstaff says.

It is an old remark, that the most beautiful women
are not always the most fascinating.   It may be added,
we fear, that they are seldom so.   The reason is obvious.   They are apt to rely too much on their beauty,
or to give themselves too many airs.   Mere beauty
ever was, and ever will be, but a secondary thing, except with fools.   And they admire it for as little time
as anybody else ; perhaps not so long.   They have no
fancies to adorn it with.   If this secondary thing fall
into disagreeable ways, it becomes but a fifth or sixth-
rate thing, or nothing at all, or worse than nothing.
We resent the unnatural mixture.   We shrink from it,
as we should from a serpent with a beauty's head.
The most fascinating women are those that can most
enrich the every-day moment of existence.   In a particular and attaching sense, they are those that can
partake our pleasures and our pains in the liveliest and
most devoted manner.   Beauty is little without this.
With it, she is indeed triumphant.

OF STATESMEN WHO HAVE WRITTEN VERSES.

Universality of Poetry, and consequent good effects of a taste for it.—The greater the statesman, the more universal his mind.—Almost all great British Statesmen have written verses.—Specimen of verses by Wyatt, by Essex, by Sackville, Raleigh, Marvell, Peterborough, and Lord Holland.

THE love of moral beauty, and that retention of the spirit of youth, which is implied by the indulgence of a poetical taste, are evidences of good disposition in any man, and argue well for the largeness of his mind in other respects. For this is the boast of poetry above all other arts ; that, sympathizing with everything, it leaves no corner of wisdom or knowledge unrecognized ; which is a universality that cannot be predicated of any science, however great. But in a statesman, this regard for the poetical is doubly pleasing, from the supposed dryness of his studies, and the character he is apt to obtain for worldliness. We are delighted to see, that, sympathizing with poetry, he sympathizes with humanity, and that, in attributing to him a mere regard for expedience and success, we do him injustice. In truth, most men do injustice to one another, when they think ill of what is at their heart's core ; nay, even when they take for granted those avowals of cunning and misbelief, which are themselves generated by an erroneous principle of sociality, and a regard for what

their neighbors will think of them. If it were suddenly to become the fashion for men to have faith in one
another, Bond Street and Regent Street would be
crowded to-morrow with poetry and sentiment; not
because fashion is fashion (for that is a child's reason),
but because fashion itself arises from the social principle, however narrowly exercised, and goes upon the
ground of our regard for one another's opinion. Statesmen are too often unjustly treated in men's minds, as
practisers of mere cunning and expedience, and lovers
of power. Much self-love is doubtless among them,
and much love of power. Where is it not? But
higher aspirations are oftener mingled with the very
cunning and expedience, than the narrow-minded suppose. Indeed, the very position which statesmen occupy, and the largeness of the interests in which they
deal, tend to create such aspirations where they do not
very consciously exist; for a man cannot be habitually
interested, even on his own account, with the concerns
of nations and the welfare of his fellow-creatures, without having his nature expanded. Statesmen learn to
feel as " England," and as " France," or at least as the
influential portion of the country, and not as mere heads
of a party, however the partisanship may otherwise
influence them, or be identified with their form of policy. By-and-by we hope they may feel, not as " England" or as " France," but as the whole world; and
they will do, as the world advances in knowledge and
influence. Now poetry is the breath of beauty, flowing around the spiritual world, as the winds that wake
up the flowers do about the material; and in proportion as statesmen have a regard for poetry, and for
what the highest poetry loves, they " look abroad," as
Bacon phrases it, " into universality," and the universe

11*

partakes of the benefit. Bacon himself wrote verses, though he had not heart enough to write good ones; but his great knowledge told him, that verses were good things to write.

We most compress our recollections on this tempting subject into the smallest possible compass, and therefore shall confine ourselves to the most truly poetical instances we can call to mind; that is to say, such as imply the most genuine regard for what is imaginative and unworldly,—the most child-like spirit retained in the maturest brains and manliest hearts. We must confine ourselves also to our own country. For it is a very curious and agreeable fact, that scarcely any name of eminence can be mentioned in the political world, from Solon and Lycurgus down to the present moment, that has not, at one period of the man's life or another, been connected with some tribute to the spirit of grace and fancy in the shape of verse. Perhaps there is not a single statesman in the annals of Great Britain, that will not be found to have written something in verse,—some lines to his mistress, compliment to his patron, jest on his opponent, or elegy or epithalamium on a court occasion. Even Burleigh, in his youth, wrote verses in French and Latin: Bacon versified psalms:* and Clarendon, when he was Mr. Hide, and one of the "wits about town," wrote complimentary verses to his friends the poets. There are some on a play of Randolph's—the concluding couplet of which may be thought ominous, or auspicious (as the reader pleases), of the future historian's royalism,—

* Here is one of the couplets, not to be surpassed in the annals of Grub street :—

"With wine, man's spirit *for to* recreate;
And oil, man's face *for to* exhilarate!!"

" **Thus much**, where *King* applauds" [that is to say, *the* king !] " **I dare**
   be bold
To say,—'Tis petty treason to withhold.
                                        EDWARD HIDE."

Wyatt, Essex, Sackville, Raleigh, Falkland, Marvell,
Temple, Somers, Bolingbroke, Pulteney, Burke, Fox,
Sheridan, Canning, &c., &c., all wrote verses; many
of them late in life. Pope's Lord Oxford wrote some,
and very bad they were. They were suggested by
some displeasure with the court after his attempted
assassination by Guiscard.

       " To serve with *love*,
           And shed your *blood*,
         Approvèd is *above;*
         But here below,
         The examples show,
       'Tis fatal to be good !"

Lord Chatham wrote Latin verses at college. Pitt,
his son, wrote English ones in his youth, and assisted
his brothers and sisters in composing a play. Even
that caricature of an intriguing and servile statesman,
Bubb Dodington, had a poetical vein of tender and
serious grace.
   Our first statesman, whose verses are worth quoting,
is Sir Thomas Wyatt, a diplomatist of exquisite address in the service of Henry the Eighth. He was
rather a great man than a great poet, and his most important pieces in verse are imitations from other languages. But he was very fond of the art, and was
accounted a rival in his day of his illustrious friend, the
Earl of Surrey. The following " *Description*" is in
the highest moral taste, and reminds us of some of the
sweet quiet faces' in the Italian masters, or the exqui

site combination of "glad and sad" in the female countenances of Chaucer :—

DESCRIPTION OF SUCH A ONE AS HE WOULD LOVE.

" A face that shonld content me wond'rous well,
   Should not be fair, but lovely to behold ;
With gladsome chere, all grief for to expell ;
   With sober looks so would I that it should
Speak without words, such words as none can tell ;
   The tress also should be of crisped gold.
With wit, and these, might chance I might be tied,
And knit again the knot that should not slide."

The reader may be amused with the following specimen of the pleasantness with which a great man can
trifle. It is

A RIDDLE OF A GIFT GIVEN BY A LADY.

" A lady gave me a gift she had not ;
   And I received her gift I took not ;
She gave it me willingly, and yet she would not ;
   And I received it, albeit I could not.
If she give it me, I force not ;
   And if she take it again, she cares not ;
Construe what this is, and tell not ;
   For I am fast sworn, I may not."

The solution is understood to be a Kiss.

Our next poetical statesman is Queen Elizabeth's
Earl of Essex ; and of a truly poetical nature was he,
though with this unfortunate drawback,—that he had
a will still stronger in him than love, and thrusting
itself in front of his understanding,—to the daring of
all opposition, good as well as bad, and downbreak of
himself and fortunes. He was more of a lover of
poets, it is true, than a poet ; but he himself was a
poem and a romance. The man who could even think
that he could wish to " hold in his heart the sorrows
of all his friends," (for such is a beautiful passage in

one of his letters) must have had a noble capability in his nature, that makes us bleed for his bleeding, and wish that he had partaken less of the stormier passions. He died on the scaffold for madly attempting to dictate to his sovereign by force of arms; and Elizabeth, as fierce as he, and fuller of resentment, is thought by some to have broken her heart for the sentence. Here follow some most curious verses, which show the simplicity, and love of gentleness, in one of the corners of the man's mind. They were the close of a dispatch he sent to Elizabeth, when he was Lord Lieutenant of Ireland! Imagine such a winding up of a state paper now!

> " Happy is he could finish forth his fate
>   In some unhaunted desert most obscure,
>   From all society, from love and hate,
>   Of worldly folk; then should he sleep secure;
>   Then wake again, and yield God ever praise,
>   Content with hips and haws and bramble-berry,—
>   In contemplation passing out his days,
>   And change of holy thoughts to make him merry;
>   Who when he dies, his tomb may be a bush
>   Where harmless robin dwells with gentle thrush."

We could never understand how it was, that Sackville, Lord Dorset (in the time of Elizabeth), who wrote the fine Induction to the " Mirror of Magistrates," as well as the tragedy of " Gorboduc," never wrote anything more,—at least of any consequence, and as far as we know. It is true, he became a busy statesman; but what surprises us is, that so genuine a poet could refrain from his poetical vocation. We have made up our minds that he must have written a good deal which is lost; for we can as little imagine a poet passing the greater part of his life without writing poetry, as a lark who never sings.

The Induction to the "Mirror of Magistrates" is a *look in* at the infernal regions, and is like a portal to the allegorical part of the Fairy Queen, or rather to the sadder portion of that part; for it has none of the voluptuousness, and but little imitation of the beauty; nor is the style anything nearly so rich. Perhaps a better comparison would be that of the quaint figures of the earliest Italian painters, compared with those of Raphael. Or it is a bit of a minor Dante. But the poetry is masterly of its kind,—full of passion and imagination,—true, and caring for nothing but truth. The poet's guide in his visit is Sorrow—

> Ere I was ware, into a desart wood
> We now were come; where hand in hand embraced,
> She led the way, *and through the thick so traced*
> As, but I had been guided by her might,
> *It was no way for any mortal wight.*
>
> But lo! while thus amidst the desart dark
> We passed on, with steps and pace unmeet,
> A rumbling roar, confused with howl and bark
> Of dogs, *shook all the ground under our feet,*
> *And struck the din within our ears so deep,*
> As, half distraught, unto the ground I fell,
> Besought return, *and not to visit hell.*
> But she, forthwith, uplifting me apace,
> Removed my dread, and with a steadfast mind,
> Bade me come on, for here was now the place.
>   *   *   *   *
> Next saw we Dread, all trembling how he shook,
> With foot uncertain, *proffered* here and there;
> Benummed of speech, and with a ghastly look,
> Searched every place, all pale and dead with fear,
> *His cap borne up with staring of his hair.*
>   *   *   *   *
> By him lay heavy Sleep, cousin of Death,
> Flat on the ground, and still as any stone;
> A very corpse save yielding forth a breath.—
> The body's rest, the quiet of the heart,

The travail's case, the still night's feer* was he,
And of our life in earth the better part,
Reaver of sight, and yet in whom we see
Things oft that tide, and oft that never be ;
Without respect esteeming equally
King Crœsus' pomp, and Irus' poverty.

     *   *   *   *

On her (Famine) while we thus firmly fixed our eyes,
That bled for ruth of such a dreary sight,
Lo ! suddenly she shrieked in so huge wise,
As made hell gates to shiver with the might.

Observe the line marked in italics in the following passage. It may be called the sublime of mud and dirt! Perhaps Shakspeare took from it his "hell-broth" that "boils and bubbles;" but the consistency is here thicker and more horrid,—a bog of death :—

Hencefrom when scarce I could mine eyes withdraw
That filled with tears as doth the springing well,
We passed on so far forth till we saw
Rude Acheron, a loathsome lake to tell,
That boils and bubs up swelth as black as hell.

     *   *   *   *

Thence came we *to the horror and the hell,*
The *large great* kingdoms, and the dreadful reign
Of Pluto in his throne where he did dwell,
The wide waste places, and the *hugie* plain,
The wailings, shrieks, and sundry sorts of pain,
The sights, the sobs, the deep and deadly groan,
Earth, air, and all, resounding plaint and moan.

Sackville has been gathered into collections of British poetry. So ought Sir Walter Raleigh, whose poems have been lately re-published. Raleigh was a genuine poet, spoilt by what has spoilt so many men otherwise great,—his rival Essex included,—the ascendency of his will. His will thrust itself before his understanding,—the imperious part of his energy before

---

* Companion.

the rational or the loving ; and hence the failure, even
in his worldly views, of one of the most accomplished of
men. We cannot say that, like Bacon, he had no heart ;
otherwise he could not have been a poet ; But like Bacon, he over-estimated worldly cunning ; which is a
weapon for little men, not for great ; and like Bacon
he fell by it. In short, he wanted the highest point of
all greatness,—truth. Raleigh's poems contain some
interesting cravings after that repose and quiet, which
great restlessness so often feels, and to which the poetical part of his nature must have inclined him ; but a
writer succeeds best in that which includes his entire
qualities ; and the best production of this lawless and
wilful genius is the fine sonnet on the Fairy Queen of
his friend Spenser ; which not content with admiring
as its greatness deserved, he violently places at the
head of all poems, ancient and modern, sweeping Petrarch into oblivion, and making Homer himself tremble. It is one of the noblest sonnets in the language.
Warton justly remarks, that the allegorical turn of it
gives it a particular beauty, as a compliment to Spenser.—Petrarch's paragon of fame and chastity, it is to
be observed, is displaced for Queen Elizabeth ; who is
implied in the character of the " Fairy Queen.

> Methought I saw the grave where Laura lay
> Within that temple, where the vestal flame
> Was wont to burn ; and passing by that way
> *To see that buried dust of living fame,*
> Whose tomb fair Love and fairer Virtue kept,
> All suddenly I saw the Fairy Queen ;
> At whose approach the *soul of Petrarch wept,*
> And from henceforth those Graces were *not seen,*
> For they this Queen attended ; in whose stead
> *Oblivion laid him down on Laura's hearse ;—*
> Hereat the hardest stones *were seen to bleed,*
> And groans of buried ghosts the heavens did perse ;

> Where Homer's spright did tremble all for grief,
> *And curst the access of that celestial thief.*

We have marked some of these lines in Italics ; but indeed the whole might have been so marked.

Sir Henry Wotton, James the First's ambassador to Venice, afterwards Provost of Eton College, really united those two extremes of a taste for business and retirement, which Sir Walter's less tender nature could only combine in fancy. He was author of the famous definition of an ambassador ("An honest man sent to *lie abroad* for the good of his country,") and of the no less true epitaph which he desired to be put on his tombstone, *Hic jacet hujus sententiæ*, &c. Here lies the first author of this sentence, " The itch of disputation is the scab of the church;"—one of those rare sayings, the apparent coarseness of which is vindicated by the refinement and worthiness of the feeling. This statesman, who was among the first to hail the genius of Milton, was author of several graceful poems, touching for their thoughtfulness and goodness. One of the most admired, which is to be found in many collections, begins

> How happy is he born and taught,
> Who serveth not another's will.

Lord Falkland, the romantic adherent of Charles the First, but friend of all parties, and tender-hearted desirer of peace, left some poems which are to be found in Nichols's Collection, vol. i. p. 236, and vol. viii. p. 217. The memory of Sir Richard Fanshaw's diplomatic talents would have been swallowed up in the reputation of the translator of Guarini's "Pastor Fido," had not an account of him been written by that sweet amazon, his wife, who (unknown to him) fought by his side on board ship in the disguise of a cabin-boy. But we now come to the great wit and partisan, Andrew Marvell, whose honesty baffled the arts of the Stuarts, and whose pamphlets and verses had no mean hand in helping to put an end to their dynasty. Marvell unites wit with earnestness and depth of sentiment, beyond any miscellaneous writer in the language. His firm partisanship did not hinder him being of the party of all mankind, and doing justice to what was good in the most opposite characters. In a panegyric on Cromwell he has taken high gentlemanly occasion to record the dignity of the end of Charles the First.

So restless Cromwell could not cease
In the inglorious arts of peace,
  Bur through adventurous war
  Urgèd his active star;

And, like the three-fold lightning, first
Breaking the clouds where it was nurst,
  Did thorough his own side
  His fiery way divide;

Then burning through the air he went
And palaces and temples rent,
  And Cæsar's head at last
  Did, through his laurels, blast.

'T is madness to resist or blame
The face of angry heaven's flame;
  And if we would speak true,
  Much to the man is due,

Who from his private garden, where
He liv'd reserved and austere,
  (as if his highest plot
  To plant the bergamot)

Could by industrious valor climb
To ruin the great work of time.
  And cast the kingdoms old
  Into another mould.

*   *   *   *

What field of all the civil wars,
Where his were not the deepest scars ?
   And Hampton shows what part
   He had of wiser art :

Where twining subtle fears with hope
He wove a net of such a scope,
   That Charles himself might chase
   To Clarisbrook's narrow case ;

That thence the royal actor borne
The tragic scaffold might adorn,
   While round the armed bands
   Did clap their bloody hands.

HE nothing common did, or mean,
Upon that memorable scene,
   But with his keener eye
   The axe's edge did try ;

Nor call'd the gods with vulgar spite
To vindicate his helpless right,
   But bow'd his comely head
   Down, as upon a bed.

The emphatic cadence of this couplet,

   —Bow'd his comely head
   Down, as upon a bed.

is in the best taste of his friend Milton.

Sir William Temple wrote verses with a spirit beyond the fashion of his time, as may be seen by some
translations from Virgil in Nichols's Collection, fresher,
to our taste, than Dryden's. Halifax has got into the
"British Poets." Somers was among the translators
of Garth's "Ovid." Even miserly Pulteney was a
verseman ;—to say nothing of flighty Hanbury Wil-
liams, and crawling Dodington. Bolinbroke, among
other small poems, addressed one of singularly good
advice for a man of his character to a mistress of his,—
probably the same of whom a strange affecting anec-

dote is told in the "Memoirs of the late Bishop of
Norwich," just published.*

Take the melancholy taste of this anecdote of your
mouth, dear reader, with the following effusion from
the pen of the great Lord Peterborough, full of those
animal spirits which he retained at the age of seventy-
seven, and of a love which manifested itself to nearly
as late a period.   It is on the celebrated Mrs. Howard
afterwards Countess of Suffolk, supposed mistress of
George the Second,—famous among her friends for
the union of sweet temper with sincerity.   •

> I said to my heart, between sleeping and waking,
> "Thou wild thing, that always are leaping or aching,
> What black, brown, or fair, in what clime, in what nation,
> By turns has not taught thee a pit-a-patation?"
>
> Thus accused, the wild thing gave this sober reply:—
> "See the heart without motion, though Celia pass by!
> Not the beauty she has not the wit that she borrows,
> Give the eye any joys, or the heart any sorrows.
>
> "When our Sappho appears—she, whose wit so refined
> I am forced to applaud with the rest of mankind—
> Whatever she says is with spirit and fire;
> Ev'ry word I attend, but I only admire.
>
> "Prudentia as vainly would put in her claim,
> Ever gazing on Heaven, though man is her aim;
> 'T is love, not devotion, that turns up her eyes——
> Those stars of this world are too good for the skies.
>
> "But Chloe so lively, so easy, so fair,
> Her wit so genteel, without art, without care;

---

* She came to his house one day, would not be denied by the porter,
and bursting into his room, threw down a purse full of gold, exclaiming
in tears, "There are my wretched earnings—take them—and may God
bless you." Saying which, she departed. There is a mystery in the
story; for what could Bolingbroke want with a purse of gold, and from
such a quarter? But there is possibly a truth of some kind in it, and
evidence that he had a better heart to deal with than his own.

When she comes in my way—the motion, the pain,
The leapings, the achings, return all again."

O wonderful creature ! a woman of reason !
Never grave out of pride, never gay out of season ;
When so easy to guess, who this angel should be,
Would one think Mrs. Howard ne'er dreamt it was she ?

Poetical quotations so soon carry an article to great length, that we are sorry we must cut the present one short ; which we shall do with one of the most interesting as well as latest specimens of our subject, produced in advanced life by a nobleman who possessed and deserved the good opinion of all parties, for he combined the good qualities of all,—the political energy and generous hospitality of the Tories, the liberal opinions of the best of the Whigs, and the universal sympathy of the Radical.   We hardly need add for any one's information, that we mean Lord Holland.   The more than elegant, the cordial *vers de société* of his uncle Charles Fox (we allude particularly to his lines on Mrs. Crewe), the art and festivity of those of Sheridan, and the witty mockery of Canning's, are too well known to warrant repetition ; and, generally speaking, they belong also to the conventionalities of a time gone by, and not likely to return.   But there is a higher and more lasting aspiration in the modest effusion of the Noble Lord ; nor do we know anything more touching in the sophisticated life to which such men must be more or less subject, than this evidence, on the part of a statesman of his years and experience, of his having preserved a young heart and a thoughtful conscience.

SONNET BY LORD HOLLAND, ON READING " PARADISE REGAINED."   1830

Homer and Dryden, nor unfrequently
The playful Ovid or the Italian's song

That held entranced my youthful thoughts so long
With dames and loves and deeds of chivalry,
E'en now delight me.   From the noisy throng
   Thither I fly to sip the sweets that lie
   Enclosed in tenderest folds of poesy
Oft as for ease my weary spirits long.
But when, recoiling from the fouler scene
   Of sordid vice or rank atrocious crime,
My sickening soul pants for the pure serene
   Of loftier regions, quitting tales and rhyme,
I turn to Milton ; *and his heights sublime,*
*By me too long unsought, I strive to climb.**

---

* The present administration is more literary and poetical than any which the nation has seen.   The public are familiar with some distinguished proofs of it; and others of a graceful and interesting nature might easily be adduced.   But though to omit all allusion to the circumstance, at the close of an article like the foregoing, might have been thought strange and invidious, to dwell upon it might subject the writer at this moment to very painful suspicions.

FEMALE SOVEREIGNS OF ENGLAND.

Real character of Lady Jane Grey.—Excuses for "Bloody Mary."—
Elizabeth, when young.—Anne and the Duchess of Marlborough.—
Accession of her present Majesty.

THE accession of a young Queen to the throne, especially under existing circumstances, renders it not uninteresting to glance at the history and characters of her female predecessors. A word also, though it be a word only (for how, without better knowledge of her, can we say more?) cannot but be said of the youthful Monarch herself, whose interest was summed up the other day in an admirable and statesman-like article in the *Morning Chronicle*, as consisting in being to Political Reformation what Elizabeth was to Religious,—its willing and glorious star, not its foolish torch, attempting to frighten it back. If volumes were written on the subject, they could not say more than that single analogy. Our feelings, however, will lead us to add another word or two before we conclude; but we will observe the order of time and look back first.

The females who have reigned in this country previously to her Majesty, are Mary, Elizabeth, and Anne; for though the second Mary, wife of William the Third, was Queen in her own right, circumstances and her disposition left the exercise of power entirely to her husband; and as to poor Lady Jane Grey, to whom Mr. Turner in his valuable history has not improperly devoted a chapter as " Queen Jane," she did but reign long enough (ten or eleven days) to undo the romance of her character and quarrel with her husband. The world, with an honorable credulity, have been in the habit of taking Lady Jane Grey and Lord Guildford Dudley for a pair of mere innocent lovers and victims. Victims they were, but not without a weakness little amiable on one side, if not on both.*

Of the first Mary, long and too deservedly known by the title of " Bloody Mary," (which the truer justice of a right Christian philosophy has latterly been the means of discontinuing), we confess we can never think without commiseration. Unamiable she certainly was, and deplorably bigoted. She sent two hun-

---

* " Mild and modest, and young, as she unquestionably was," says Turner, " the spirit of royalty and power had within twenty-four hours gained such an ascendency in her studious mind, that she heard the intimation of her husband being elevated to the same dignity as herself, with vexation and displeasure. As soon as she was left alone with him, she remonstrated against this measure; and after much dispute, he agreed to wait till she herself should make him king, and by an act of Parliament. But even this concession, to take this dignity as a boon from her, did not satisfy the sudden expansion of her new-born ambition. She soon sent for the Earls of Arundel and Pembroke, and informed them that she was willing to create her husband a duke, but would never consent to make him king. This declaration brought down his mother in great fury to her, with all the force of enraged language and imperious disdain. The violent duchess scolded her young queen, and roused the mortified Dudley to forsake her chamber of repose, and to vow that he would accept no title but the regal honor." *History of England*, as quoted further on, p. 219.— Jane's best claim to the respect of posterity must remain with her taste for literature. She had the good sense to feel, and avow, that there was no comfort like her books in adversity. Her nature seems in other respects to have had a formal insipidity, excitable only by stimulants which did not agree with it.

dred and eighty-four people to the stake during a short
reign of five years and four months ; which, upon an
average, is upwards of four a week ! She was withal
plain, petty of stature, ill-colored, and fierce-eyed, with
a voice almost as deep as a man's ; had a bad blood ;
and ended with having nobody to love her, not even
the bigots in whose cause she lost the love of her people.* But let us recollect whose daughter she was,
and under what circumstances born and bred. She
inherited the tyrannical tendencies of her father Henry
the Eighth, the melancholy and stubbornness of her
mother Katherine ; and she had the misfortune, say
rather the unspeakable misery of being taught to think
it just to commit her fellow-creatures to the flames, for
doing no more than she stubbornly did herself; namely,
vindicate the right of having their own opinion. Recollect, above all, that she was not happy ;—that it was
not in gayety or sheer unfeelingness that she did what
she thus frightfully thought to be her duty. She suffered bitterly herself; and she not only suffered for
herself and her own personal sorrows, but sharply for
her sense of the public welfare, and that of men's very
souls. In sending people to the stake, she fancied

* Michele, the Venetian Ambassador, in the account which he wrote
of her, (see Ellis's Letters, mentioned a little further on,) describes her as
" moderately pretty," according to the translator. But there is reason to
doubt the correctness of a version which in speaking of Elizabeth's complexion, renders " olivastro" by " sallow ;"—at least that is not the usual
acceptation of the meaning of the word " sallow ;" it is also opposed by
the context, as will be seen presently ; and if Michele really meant to say
that Mary was " moderately pretty," and did not use the words as good-
naturedly implying something different, he goes counter to all which is
understood of her face in history, and certainly to the prints of it, which
are those of a melancholy and homely-looking vixen. It is a pity the
rest of the original had not been quoted, as well as a few sentences.

(with the dreadful involuntary blasphemy taught her
by her creed), that it was necessary, in order to save
millions from eternal wretchedness; and if in this perverted sense of duty there was a willing participation
of the harsher parts of her character, she had sensibility enough to die of a broken heart.—Peace and
pardon to her memory. Which of us might not have
done the same, or more, had we been so unhappily
situated ?

Both Mary and her sister Elizabeth passed the earlier portion of their lives in singular vicissitudes of quiet
and agitation,—each unwelcome to their father,—each
at times tranquilly pursuing their studies, and each
persecuted for their very different opinions;—Mary
by her Protestant brother Edward, and Elizabeth by
her Catholic sister Mary. At one time they were
treated like princesses, at another as if they were
aliens in blood, or had been impudently palmed upon
it. Now they were brought before councils, to answer
for opinions that put their lives in jeopardy; now riding
about with splendid retinues, and flattered by courtly
expectants. How different from the retired and apparently beautiful manner in which the present Queen
has been brought up, safe in her pleasant home in Kensington Gardens; and whenever she moves about,
moving in unostentatious comfort, and linked with a
loving mother. Oh! never may she forget, that it was
free and reforming opinions which brought her this
great good; and that if Elizabeth had gone back with
her age, instead of advancing with it, and succumbed
to the anti-popular part of the priesthood and the aris-
tocracy, she, the secure, and tranquil, and popular Vic
toria, might this moment have been dragged before

councils as Elizabeth was, or been forced to struggle
with insurrections and public hatred, like Mary.*

* The following (abridged by Ellis from Hollinshed) is a specimen
of the treatment to which heiresses to the throne were liable in those
days:—"The day after the breaking out of Wyat's rebellion was
known at court, he says, the Queen sent three of her council, Sir Richard Southwell, Sir Edward Hastings, and Sir Thomas Cornwallis, to
Ashbridge, with a strong guard, to escort the Princess Elizabeth, who
lay sick there, to London. When they arrived, at 10 o'clock at night,
the Princess had gone to rest, and refused to see them: they however
entered her chamber rudely, when her Grace, being not a little amazed,
said unto them, ' Is the haste such that it might not have pleased you
to come to-morrow in the morning ?' They made answer, that they
were right sorry to see her in such a case. ' And I,' quoth she, ' am
not glad to see you here at this time of night.' Whereunto they answered that they came from the Queen to do their message and duty ;
that it was the Queen's pleasure that her Grace should be in London on
a given day, and that the orders were to bring her ' quick or dead.'
The Princess complained of the harshness of their commission ; but
Dr. Owen and Dr. Wendie deciding that she might travel without danger of life, her Grace was informed that the Queen had sent her own
litter for her accommodation, and that the next morning she would be
removed. She reached Redburne in a very feeble condition the first
night ; on the second she rested at Sir Ralph Rowlet's house, at St.
Albans ; on the third at Mr. Dod's, at Mimmes, and on the fourth at
Highgate, where she stayed a night and a day. She was thence con-
veyed to the Court, where, remaining a close prisoner for a whole fort-
night, she saw neither king, nor queen, nor lord, nor friend. On the
Friday before Palm Sunday, Gardiner, Bishop of Winchester, with
nineteen others of the council, came from the Queen, and charged her
with being concerned not only in Wyat's conspiracy, but in the rebellion of Sir Peter Carew. They then declared unto her the Queen's
pleasure that she should go to the Tower till the matter could be further traced and examined. Against this she remonstrated, protesting
her innocence, but the lords answered that there was no remedy. Her
own attendants were then dismissed, and those of the Queen placed
about her.   *   *   *   *   *

" Upon the succeeding day, Palm Sunday, an order was issued
throughout London that every one should keep the church and carry
his palm ; during which time the Princess was carried to the Tower.

" The landing at the traitor's gate she at first refused ; but one of the
lords stepped back into the barge to urge her coming out, ' and because

There are not so many records of Mary's youth as of that of her sister. She was brought up in the same accomplishments of music and scholarship, but had not so many; and she underwent similar disadvantages of occasional neglect, but not of such extent.

Elizabeth, to use an old phrase, we can "fetch" almost "from her cradle;" indeed quite so, if we go to Hollinshed, or to Shakspeare, who have recorded her christening. After her mother's downfall, she was very carelessly treated. In Ellis's Letters* is one from her governess, Lady Brian, to Lord Cromwell, asking for instructions concerning her, and complaining that she is "put from her degree," and has neither gown nor

it did then rain,' says Hollinshed, ' he offered to her his cloak, which she (putting it back with her hand with a good dash) refused. Then coming out, with one foot upon the stair, she said, ' Here landeth as true a subject, being prisoner, as ever landed at these stairs; and before thee, O God, I speak it, having none other friends but thee alone.'

" To her prison-chamber, it is stated, she was brought with great reluctance; and the locking and bolting the doors upon her caused dismay. She was, moreover, for some time denied even the liberty of exercise. Early in the following May the Lord Chandos, who was then the Constable of the Tower, was discharged of his office, and Sir Henry Bedingfield appointed in his room. ' He brought with him,' says the historian, ' an hundred soldiers in blue coats, wherewith the Princess was marvellously discomfited, and demanded of such as were about whether the Lady Jane's scaffold were taken away or no—fearing, by reason of their coming, lest she should have played her part.' Warton says she asked this question ' with her usual liveliness;' but there was probably less in it of vivacity than he supposed. Sixty years before, upon the same spot, Sir James Tirell had been suddenly substituted for Sir Robert Brackenbury, preparatory to the disappearance of the Princes of the House of York. Happily for Elizabeth her fears were groundless; Sir Henry Bedingfield accompanied her to a less gloomy prison in the Palace of Woodstock."

* Original Letters, illustrative of English History, &c. With Notes and Illustrations. By Henry Ellis, &c., &c. Second Series. Vol. ii. p. 78.

petticoat, "nor no manner of linnin for smokes." She
was taught to write by the famous Ascham; and her
penmanship was accounted beautiful. From what we
have seen of it, it looks more masculine than beautiful.
Indeed her signature is tall and tremendous enough to
have been that of a giantess.

At the age of fourteen, in her brother Edward's
reign, Elizabeth was under the care of her father's
widow Catherine Parr, who then lived at Chelsea in
one of the royal manor houses, occupying part of the
site of the present Cheyne Row; a spot, that has become curious from the boisterous gallantry that she
seems to have permitted from Catherine's husband, the
Lord Admiral Seymour, brother of the Protector
Somerset,—a couple of ambitious men, who both lost
their heads in those beautiful aristocratic times. Mr.
Turner, agreeably to his very Protestant but doubtless
sincere good opinion of Elizabeth, revolts from the
unceremonious love-making of Seymour, and betwixt
partiality and modesty suppresses the more awkward
details;* Dr. Lingard, the Catholic historian, sternly
brings them forth, and does not disguise his faith in
them.† As we have no claim in this place to the
court-of-law privileges of history, we shall not repeat
these passages; neither do we hold with either of these
respectable writers, in the view they take of Elizabeth's
character in reference to matters of this nature. Times
are to be considered,—manners,—customs,—and a
thousand questions still existing, too important to discuss here, but all very necessary before we arrive at

* History of the Reigns of Edward the Sixth, Mary, and Elizabeth.
By Sharon Turner. Vol. iv. p. 148.
† History of England, &c. By the Rev. John Lingard. Vol. iv.
p. 401.

the candid conclusions of a philosophy which see justice done to all.   If Elizabeth partook of more of the weaknesses common to human nature than her eulogizers are willing to allow, she possessed more virtues than are granted her by her enemies; and whatever may be the pettier details of her history, it is not to be disputed that she was a great Queen, fit to be surrounded with the men whose merit she had the sense to discern.   She perceived the statesman in Cecil, before she came to the throne, and she retained him with her till he died.   She partook of her father's imperiousness, and of her mother's gayer blood; but she inherited also the greater brain of her grandfather Henry the Seventh, to whom she is said to have borne a likeness; and the mixture of all three produced a sovereign, not indeed free from very petty defects (for she was excessively fond of flattery, jealous even of a fine gown, and so fond of dress herself, that she would change it daily for months together), but great in the main, able to understand the true interests of her country, and sovereign mistress even of the favorites who touched her heart, and who could bring tears into her proud eyes.

Elizabeth, when she came to the throne, was not older than five-and-twenty, and what would now be familiarly called "a fine girl."   She is thus described, just before that event, by the Venetian Ambassador:

"My Lady Elizabeth, the daughter of Henry VIII. and Ann Boleyne, was born in the year 1533.   She is a lady of great elegance both of body and mind, although her face may rather be called pleasing than beautiful; she is tall and well made; her complexion fine, though rather sallow;*

* "*Bella carne, ancorche olivastra.*"   But how can a fine complexion be thought "sallow?" and why should not *olivastra* mean "swarthish, olive-colored," as a good old Italian dictionary has it?   We should thus

her eyes, but above all her hands, which she takes care not to conceal, are of superior beauty. In her knowledge of the Greek and Italian languages she surpasses the Queen. Her spirits and understanding are admirable, as she has proved by her conduct in the midst of suspicion and danger, when she concealed her religion, and comported herself like a good Catholic. She is proud and dignified in her manners; for though her mother's condition is well known to her, she is also aware that this mother of hers was united to the King in wedlock, with the sanction of the holy church, and the concurrence of the primate of the realm; and though misled with regard to her religion, she is conscious of having acted with good faith: nor can this latter circumstance reflect upon her birth, since she was born in the same faith with that professed by the Queen. Her father's affection she shared at least in equal measure with her sister, and the King considered them equally in his will, settling on both of them 10,000 scudi per annum Moreover the Queen, though she hates her most sincerely, yet treats her in public with every outward sign of affection and regard, and never converses with her but on pleasing and agreeable subjects. She has also contrived to ingratiate herself with the King of Spain, through whose influence the Queen is prevented from bastardizing her, as she certainly has it in her power to do by means of an act of Parliament, and which would exclude her from the throne. It is believed that, but for this interference of the King, the Queen would, without remorse, chastise her in the severest manner; for whatever plots against the Queen are discovered, my Lady Elizabeth, or some of her people, may always be sure to be mentioned among the persons concerned in them."

It may be added, as a matter not without its interest in the present moment, that Elizabeth and Victoria are the only Queens who have come to the throne young. Mary was thirty-seven years of age, and Anne thirty-eight.

Anne was more the daughter of her mother Anne Hyde, Clarendon's daughter, than of her father James the Second. In the portrait of her sister Queen Mary, the wife of William the Third, you can trace a likeness to the melancholy countenance of James. Anne was the daughter of her mother's joviality, at least as

recognize a clear brown complexion, quite compatible with the epithet "fine."

far as the indulgence of the senses was concerned,—
round and fat, and inclined by enjoyment to be good-
humored and indulgent. She had brown hair and a
fresh complexion: in short, was a regular Hyde, with
the exception of the pride and irritability, and perhaps
the acuteness of that family; and only possessing
enough of her father's stubbornness, to enable her to
turn round against the excess of presumption, and rescue herself from the last consequences of a habit of
acquiescence. Lady Stafford, the wild daughter of a
wild father (Rochester), talked of "orgies" in her palace,—most likely an extravagant misrepresentation;
but whatever the orgies amounted to, they must have
arisen from the weak moments generated too often in
the Queen's latter years by a habit, which it is unpleasant to allude to in connection with a woman, and
which care and temperament, and perhaps her very
easiness of intercourse, conspired to bring upon her.
Drinking of some kind or other is resorted to as a
refuge from care in millions of more instances than the
world is aware of; and perhaps, till things right themselves in society to more final purpose, the wonder is,
that the habit, however dangerous and degrading, is
not still more extensive.

Of Anne's early years some curious accounts have
been left us by the wife of the great Duke of Marlborough,—for a long time her imperious favorite, if two
such words can go properly together. The truth is,
Anne's heaviness and luxuriousness of temperament
made her glad of a dictatress, so long as the jurisdiction only supplied it with what it wanted. It helped
out her slowness of speech, and saved her a world of
trouble and management. The Duchess reigned in
this way so long, that she at length forgot she had a

queen for her slave ; and, in spite of habit, good-nature, and fear, royalty turned round in anger, and got rid of its tyrant by dint of a singular exercise of one of Anne's very defects,—paucity of words. The favorite had unfortunately intimated in one of her angry letters, that she did not want an answer to a remonstrance made by her ; and the Queen, seizing hold of this expression at their final interview, kept repeating it to all which the Duchess alleged :—" *You desired no answer, and you shall have none.*" This doggedness, in James the Second's style, so exasperated the once all-powerful favorite (though it was in reality nothing but a desperate refuge from want of words) that she ventured to threaten her Majesty with the consequences of her " inhumanity ;" and so they parted for ever. This is the whole real amount of the matter, without its being necessary to enter into those would-be political circumstances, which, in almost all such cases, are only the apparent, not real causes of action.

The Duchess in her old age, with the unabated overweeningness of her character, gave the world what she called an " Account of her Conduct ;" purely, as she said, to save her fair fame after death ; but the consequence was, as it always must be when such things are written by such persons (for their character is sure to break through all disguises), that the world were confirmed in the opinion, which they entertained of her vanity and presumption. There is no doubt, however, that all the facts we are about to quote are true, however different were the conclusions they suggested to the world, from what the writer expected. And after being in possession of Anne's general character, we feel that we are here made spectators of it at its earliest and most candid period.

"The beginning of the Princess's kindness for me," says the Duchess, "had a much earlier date than my entrance into her service. My promotion to this honor was wholly owing to impressions she had before received to my advantage; we had used to play together when she was a child, and she even then expressed a particular fondness for me. This inclination increased with our years. I was often at court, and the Princess always distinguished me by the pleasure she took to honor me preferably to others, with her conversation and confidence. In all her parties for amusement, I was sure, by her choice, to be one; and so desirous she became of having me always near her, that, upon her marriage with the Prince of Denmark in 1683, it was, at her own earnest request to her father, I was made one of the ladies of her bed-chamber.

"What conduced to render me the more agreeable to her in this station was, doubtless, the dislike she had conceived to most of the other persons about her; and particularly to her first lady of the bed-chamber, the Countess of Clarendon—a lady whose discourse and manner (though the Princess thought they agreed very well together) could not possibly recommend her to so young a mistress, for she looked like a mad woman and talked like a scholar. Indeed, her Highness's court was throughout so oddly composed, that I think it would be making myself no great compliment if I should say, her choosing to spend more of her time with me than with any of her other servants, did no discredit to her taste. Be that as it will, it is certain she at length distinguished me by so high a place in her favor, as perhaps no person ever arrived at a higher with Queen or Princess. And, if from hence I may draw any glory, it is, that I both obtained and held this place without the assistance of flattery—a charm which, in truth, her inclination for me, together with my unwearied application to serve and amuse her, rendered needless; but which, had it been otherwise, my temper and turn of mind would never have suffered me to employ.

"Young as I was when I first became this high favorite, I laid it down for a maxim, that flattery was falsehood to my trust, and ingratitude to my greatest friend; and that I did not deserve so much favor if I could not venture the loss of it by speaking the truth, and by preferring the real interest of my mistress before the pleasing her fancy or the sacrificing to her passion. From this rule I never swerved. And though my temper and my notions in most things were widely different from those of the Princess, yet, during a long course of years, she was so far from being displeased with me for openly speaking my sentiments, that she sometimes professed a desire, and even added a command, that it should always be continued, promising never to be offended at it, but to love me the better for my frankness.

*   *   *   *   *

"Kings and princes, for the most part, imagine they have a dignity peculiar to their birth and station, which ought to raise them above all connection of friendship with an inferior. Their passion is to be admired and feared, to have subjects awfully obedient and servants blindly obsequious to their pleasure. Friendship is an offensive word: it imports a kind of equality between the parties—it suggests nothing to the mind of crowns or thrones, high titles, or immense revenues, fountains of honor or fountains of riches, prerogatives which the possessors would have always uppermost in the thoughts of those who are permitted to approach them.

"The Princess had a different taste. A friend was what she most coveted; and for the sake of friendship (a relation which she did not disdain to have with me) she was fond even of that *equality* which she thought belonged to it. She grew uneasy to be treated by me with the form and ceremony due to her rank, nor could she bear from me the sound of words which implied in them distance and superiority. It was this turn of mind which made her one day propose to me that, whenever I should happen to be absent from her, we might in all our letters write ourselves by feigned names, such as would import nothing of distinction or rank between us. Morley and Freeman were the names her fancy hit upon, and she left me to choose by which of them I would be called. My frank, open temper naturally led me to pitch upon Freeman, and so the Princess took the other; and from this time Mrs. Morley and Mrs. Freeman began to converse as equals, made so by affection and friendship.

*   *   *   *   *

" During her father's whole reign she kept her court as private as she could, consistent with her station. What were the designs of that unhappy prince everybody knows. They came soon to show themselves undisguised, and attempts were made to draw his daughter into them. The King, indeed, used no harshness with her. He only discovered his wishes by putting into her hands some books and papers, which he hoped might induce her to a change of religion; and had she had any inclination that way, the chaplains about her were such divines as could have said but little in defence of their own religion, or to secure her against the pretences of Popery, recommended to her by a father and a King.

*   *   *   *   *

" Upon the landing of the Prince of Orange, in 1688, the King went down to Salisbury to his army, and the Prince of Denmark with him; but the news quickly came from thence that the Prince of Denmark had left the King, and was gone over to the Prince of Orange, and that the King was coming back to London. This put the Princess into a great fright. She sent for me, told me her distress, and declared, *that rather than see her father she would jump out at window.* This was her very expression.

"A little before a note had been left with me to inform me where I might find the Bishop of London (who in that critical time absconded), if her Royal Highness should have occasion for a friend. The Princess, on this alarm, immediately sent me to the Bishop. I acquainted him with her resolution to leave the court, and to put herself under his care. It was hereupon agreed that, when he had advised with his friends in the city, he should come about midnight in a hackney-coach to the neighborhood of the Cockpit, in order to convey the Princess to some place where she might be private and safe.

"The Princess went to bed at the usual time, to prevent suspicion. I came to her soon after; and by the back-stairs which went down from her closet, her Royal Highness, my Lady Fitzharding, and I, with one servant, walked to the coach, where we found the Bishop and the Earl of Dorset. They conducted us that night to the Bishop's house in the city, and the next day to my Lord Dorset's, at Copt Hall. From thence we went to the Earl of Northampton's, and from thence to Nottingham, where the country gathered about the Princess; nor did she think herself safe till she saw that she was surrounded by the Prince of Orange's friends."

The Duchess of Marlborough's influence over Anne, beginning thus in childhood, lasted perhaps for thirty years, terminating only in the year 1707, which was the forty-third of the Queen's age. Doubtless the course of time, and the shifting interests of policy, conspired to render the Queen more uneasy under her dictation. Royalty naturally loves what inclines most to royalty, when its apprehensions of danger from the Tory principle are gone by; and Anne did not live in times, when to side with the propensity was as perilous as it would be now; nor if it had been, did she possess brain enough to discern it. Accordingly, in proportion as the Whigs and the Duke of Marlborough ceased to be necessary to her, the Duchess's long domination became less endurable, and we have seen how it terminated. But still the main cause lay in the favorite's inability to make those concessions to circumstances, while she exacted of everybody else. Anne's tone of fondness continued almost till the moment of rupture ; nor is it easy to assert, though it is impossible to help concluding, that the fear of discontinuing it was mixed up with its apparent sincerity. The following are specimens of the curious letters written by "Mrs. Morley," from first to last, which the Duchess gave to the world :—

"Dear Mrs. Freeman—farewell. I hope in Christ you will never think more of leaving me, for I would be sacrificed to do you the least service, and nothing but death can ever make me part with you."

* * *

"I really long to know how my dear Mrs. Freeman got home; and now I have this opportunity of writing, she must give me leave to tell her, if she should ever be so cruel as to leave her faithful Mrs. Morley, she will rob her of all the joy and quiet of her life; for if that day should come, I could never enjoy a happy minute, and I swear to you I would shut myself up, and never see a creature."

* * *

The following is an entire letter which appears to have been written in the course of the year in which they separated :—

"Saturday night.

"My dear Mrs. Freeman—I cannot go to bed without renewing a request that I have often made, that you would banish all unkind and unjust thoughts of your poor, unfortunate, faithful Morley, which I saw by the glimpse I had of you yesterday, you were full of. Indeed, I do not deserve them; and if you could see my heart, you would find it as sincere, as tender, and as passionately fond of you as ever, and as truly sensible of your kindness in telling me your mind freely upon all occasions. Nothing shall ever alter me. Though we have the misfortune to differ in some things, I will ever be the same to my dear, dear Mrs. Freeman, who, I do assure you once more, I am more tenderly and sincerely hers than it is possible ever to express."

But Mrs. Freeman had discovered that her Majesty ventured to have some regard for an humble cousin

of hers (Mrs. Masham) as well as for herself, which
she pronounced, on both sides, to be the most ungrateful and amazing enormity ever heard of.   Hence she
fell in a rage, and the rage roused the poor Queen,
and so came the catastrophe.

We have now another Queen on the throne, whom
we have hitherto known in youth, and youth only.
We know her but publicly however ; we cannot be
said to know anything of her real character ; and
probably it is known to very few, if completely even
to those ; so truly feminine is the retirement in which
she has been brought up.   If the report, however, of
her mother's intellectual and moral qualities be well
founded (and the fact of that tranquil education says
much for it in many respects), we may hope that
England will experience the advantage for the first
time, of having a Queen brought up in a mother's
arms, and in a manner at once feminine and wise.   We
may, in that case, look to seeing Womanhood on the
throne in its best character, such as may give life and
advancement to what is best and manliest in the hopes
of the world.   But upon this prospect must rest, for
some time at any rate, the awful doubt arising from
all that is hitherto known of the unhappy chances of
royal spoiling ; which chances, however, should not
prevent us from hoping and thinking the best, as long
as we are prepared for disappointment, and commit
no offences ourselves, either of adulation or the reverse.
Her Majesty's position, at all events, is a very serious
one, both as regards us and herself; and her youth,
her sex, her manifest sensibility (whether for good or
evil), her common nature as a fellow-creature, and all
those circumstances which will make her reign so
blest beyond example, if she turn out well, and so

very piteous and unpopular if otherwise, but of which neither she nor any one else will, or can, have been responsible for the first cause (those lying hidden in the mystery of all things), combine to make every reflecting heart regard her with a mixture of pitying tenderness and hopeful respect, and cordially to pray, that it may be consistent with the good of mankind, and best for it, whatever be their particular opinions meanwhile, to see her fair figure continually hovering over the advancing orb, like the embodied angel of the meaning of her name.

END OF VOL. I.